BURDEN

OF

CONSEQUENCES

Brian Greiner

BURDEN OF CONSEQUENCES

Published by Damn Fool Press
www.damnfoolpress.com

ISBN 978-1-989360-05-7 epub
ISBN 978-1-989360-04-0 mobi
ISBN 978-1-989360-06-4 trade paperback

First Edition : January 2020

As always, this is for Lynn and the cats.

CHAPTER ONE
Test of Battle

Bob scampered across the rocky terrain of a relatively flat section of the mountain. His pursuer wasn't too far behind, but at least the treacherous footing would even the odds. That, at least, was the plan ... what there was of it. On the plus side, Bob had trained extensively in such terrain. On the down side, back then he'd had a better aspect. Now, as a result of dying and having his original body destroyed, he was trapped in this merely human body.

His pursuer, on the other hand, was one of his own people with a high-functioning human aspect complete with integrated advanced tech and access to the alternate energies. Those advantages were only partially nullified by the jangler field their "host" had erected around the area. In practise that meant that anything that depended on the alternate energies wouldn't function: no teleportation, no levitation, and the sensorium wouldn't be able to fire energy blasts. That did, however, leave intact his pursuer's enhanced strength, endurance, and healing factors. Bob smiled as he added to the list his opponent's less than stellar intelligence and tendency to let anger ruin his judgement.

Bob came to the edge of the flat section to find a wide chasm separating him from the next cliff face. It was a sheer drop and too wide to jump. Without looking behind him, he clambered down the side, moving quickly despite the need to choose handholds with care. His breathing was even, but slightly laboured in the thin, dry air. The air itself left a slight sour tang in his mouth. He hoped there wasn't anything toxic in it, as his current body wasn't able to deal with such things. The temperature was just above freezing and the rock sucked the heat out of any part of his body that contacted it.

Several body-lengths down, the rock face came to an end. The only way over to the next section was to cross hand over hand across and under a narrow overhang that bridged the gap. Without any equipment for such a trip, he traversed by hanging on to handholds when they existed and by jamming his fingers into cracks as necessary. Footholds were scarce, so the majority of the trip required dangling by his fingertips.

His fingers and arms ached with the effort, but he had a good chance of outdistancing his opponent if he succeeded. The risks of this contest were commensurate with the rewards: the winner would claim command of an ancient military base ... and the right to live.

A drone the size of his head flew up and began to talk to him.

"Shut up," growled Bob.

"Why?"

"I don't want to give away my position."

The drone zipped back to the rock face Bob had just climbed down. It paused for a moment before zipping back, hovering a body-length away.

"I believe your opponent already knows that information. In fact, he is climbing down to follow you."

Bob heard the whisper of a rope against rock, then saw a body-length of rope appear. He clenched his jaws and ensured that his left hand was set sufficiently to take his weight. He loosened the grip of his right hand, keeping it gripping lightly enough to allow for a quick reaction. He could hear the sounds of boots against the rock face, signalling the approach of his opponent.

"Remember how you chased me when you wanted to destroy my portal? It's my turn now, Cripple. Less than a cripple now—just an abomination in human form. Something that needs extermination." His opponent's voice was thick with anger.

The drone spoke to Bob, "You have stopped moving. Should you not keep up your efforts to evade him? At this rate he will defeat you and win the test."

"Shut. Up."

"Oh, let the abomination do what it wants, Monitor," came the taunting voice of his opponent. "One can't expect much from its kind."

With that, his opponent slid down the rope and into view. Bob's right hand flashed down, withdrew a knife from its sheath, and whipped it at his pursuer. A spurt of blood and howl of pain rewarded the effort as the knife sank deep into the groin region.

Bob twisted and swung a leg at the drone, kicking it towards the screaming figure. Between the efforts of the drone to regain control and the writhing of his target, the drone only struck him a glancing blow to the torso. Still, as it careened off, it hit the rock face several times on its fall to the ground far below. His opponent responded to the attack by dragging himself up the rope and away from further attacks, sobbing loudly as he went. Bob allowed himself a brief smile before returning to the task of finding handholds.

Several minutes later he swung back and forth for several swings and then released his hold. He had a few moments of freedom that felt almost like flying before slamming against the cliff face. The force of the impact elicited a grunt and bruised ribs. It also raised a small cloud of dust that filled his mouth and nearly blinded him for a moment. Spitting out dust and blinking dust out of eyes, he scurried around to the other side and began the downward descent to the valley floor below.

Two hours later found him on a wide plain at the base of the cliffs. Pausing with hands on knees, Bob panted as he tried to catch his breath, his gusts forming clouds in the cold air. Judging by the sun's location, Bob estimated that he had about an hour before sunset. The contest had started that morning on the other side of the mountain. The finishing point was supposed to be a structure some kilometres distant.

Standing upright once more took more effort than he would have liked. With a wipe at his mouth and a short, sharp exhalation, he began to jog at the best speed he was capable of. The Monitor had given both contestants a brief glimpse of a map before sending them out. If it was accurate—and that was by no means guaranteed—there was a stream up ahead where he could slake his thirst. His arms and his hands ached from the punishing climb, and his legs were little better. There was one dose each of a pain killer and stimulant in his meagre kit, so he swallowed both. It seemed a small thing compared to the powerful healing factors his opponent's body had. On the other hand, to use those to their fullest would require that his opponent rest. Right now any advantage, no matter how small, was something to be grateful for.

A half-hour later found him at the promised stream. He forced himself to rest for a minute to verify his bearings and prepare for the final leg of the journey. The setting sun glinted off a metallic structure nestled in the hills ahead of him, highlighting his destination. Bob heaved himself to his feet with a minimal amount of groaning. He spared a second for a brief look back and saw the hint of dust rising from the surface some ways back. His opponent was on the move, which meant it was time to move on.

There was just a hint of sun left in the sky to illuminate the final approach to the destination structure. Bob jogged at somewhat less than his best speed, taking care to avoid the potholes in the ground hidden in the failing light. The sound of a stumble and a snarled curse from behind him told him

4

that his opponent wasn't being so careful. It also meant that the race was closer than he'd wanted it to be as darkness began to close in on them.

Bob came to a door that opened to his touch and he stumbled inside, temporarily blinded by the bright lights of the hallway. He paused only a second to wipe at his eyes, then ran to a second doorway at the end of the corridor. He could hear footsteps not far behind him so he put on an extra burst of speed. The doorway opened as he approached and he ran into a room barren of any furnishings except for a command console on the far end. A glowing screen displayed the image of a hand, indicating that it was awaiting someone to touch it.

Bob slapped his hand on the image only to be roughly shoved aside a second later as his opponent slapped his own hand down.

"I claim command of this station by right of victory," yelled Bob. "I was first."

"NO," screamed his opponent. "I claim command by right of blood. I am the rightful victor here."

The two men glared at each, both panting from exertion. The screen went blank and a soft chime sounded.

"The test is inconclusive," came a melodious voice. "The test conditions were obviously too restrictive."

Without warning, flashes of energy beams rippled the air around the two men. The last thing both men heard before darkness claimed them both was the voice of their host.

"A neutral site is required for a proper test. I will therefore prepare a place where each can use their abilities to their limits."

CHAPTER TWO

Digging Into Mysteries

The expedition was in trouble. The threat, however, was more existential than physical. Their meagre funding was nearly depleted, their maps were inaccurate, and the static produced by the blowing sand interfered with all communications. Their GPS units were being affected not only by the static but also by yet another position degradation by the militaries that controlled them.

To top it all off they'd found a tomb of some sort. Although their scientific mission was to begin the preliminary survey of a tomb, this wasn't the tomb for which permission had been granted them. In fact, it appeared to be a something totally unknown and unexpected. Not the sort of thing a small group of relatively inexperienced academics would be allowed to be involved with.

"Well? What do we do with this, ma'am?" asked Niles Castleworth, the grad student who had literally stumbled across the tomb. "Do we survey it?"

Dr. Rhian Faernsworth puffed out her cheeks with a mixture of exasperation and indecision. She silently damned her grad student for finding the tomb before uttering a soft snort of self-derision. As a middle-aged scholar she was torn. On the one hand, if she allowed her group to so much as lay a finger on the tomb, she'd be tossed out of the country and forbidden to return. On the other hand, this was almost certainly her last field expedition to Egypt. Perhaps one of the last field trips anyone would be allowed to make here for some time, the political situation being what it was. She turned to look at Castleworth and found the rest of her small band of students looking at her.

"Strictly speaking, we need to report this right away, you know," she said in her 'official' voice. After a brief pause she added in a lighter tone, "Which we've done. Not our fault that the storm's cut all comm links. Still, the message is queued up and timestamped in the gear the Egyptian officials gave us. So, strictly speaking, we've done our duty."

The look on the faces of her students began to show a glimmer of hope that weeks of grime could not hide.

"On the other hand," she began, and the faces of her students fell. She paused and started again. "Look, this is how it is. Yes, this is probably the find of a lifetime. In all likelihood the last one I'll ever get access to. You lot, though, have your whole careers and more field trips ahead of you. If not in Egypt, then somewhere else. If we go through with a survey of this tomb, it could put all that at risk. It could be short term gain for long-term pain."

"What careers, Doctor?" enquired Kathy Shanslough. "Funding for this sort of thing is pretty damned thin and getting thinner. What little remains will be given to the more senior researchers. Pretty sure this'll be our one and only shot."

Faernsworth nodded. "Won't disagree with you, Kathy. Still, you need to consider long and hard about this."

Voices from the group spoke up and mingled until Faernsworth held up her hands. She opened her mouth to speak but Castleworth interrupted her. "Doctor, this is everything we've been training and studying for. Now it's our one, last chance to put all that to use. After wandering around without success for so long, we've been talking about what

7

we'd do in the event we came up with nothing. Without a proper survey of something—anything—we can't get our fully-qualified degrees. That means no jobs in our field, nor anything even vaguely related. With no field work in the cards any time soon, we're well and truly screwed." He looked around to the group, and they all nodded their agreement. Turning back to Faernsworth he shrugged and added, "It's this or nothing, Doctor. For us, anyway."

A voice from the rear of the group, George Smith, spoke up. "Yeah, fine for you with nothing to lose. I'm just an engineer assigned for tech support, so I've got no skin in this. But Doctor Faernsworth has more to lose than any of us. This stunt could cost her a chance at a professorship. Sorry, Doctor, but it's true."

Faernsworth responded with a grim smile. "Thanks, George, but I rather doubt a professorship will ever happen. Too many people with too much seniority—and better at playing political games--ahead of me. It's not like it was when I was your age." She paused for a moment then gave a genuine smile. "Given that you've been talking about this on your own, and it's damned if we do and damned if we don't, let's have a show of hands, please. All those in favour of showing the world what we can do?"

The roar of approval from her intrepid band brought a lump to her throat. She harrumphed a couple of times and then began barking orders. Within a few minutes they began unloading their equipment. Faernsworth insisted, based on long experience, that they set up the tents first. Her team grumbled a bit but after the first tent gave them all a much-needed break from the wind and sand, they set up the remaining tents with a will. Shortly after that was completed, they began a series of preliminary non-invasive imaging scans. Faernsworth gave them until just before sunset to finish that task, then insisted that everyone pack up before dark and assemble at the main tent for a meal.

As the sun set, they packed up their gear and gathered as instructed. Their mood was jubilant but professional, and Faernsworth was quietly proud of her team. They'd worked hard all day without a break and were eager to keep going. She envied them their youthful vigour and was content to sit back and listen to their conversations as they ate. Eventually, though, she rapped her knuckles on the table, and the room grew silent.

"Alright, now that everyone's had a bite to eat and a rest, it's time to get back to work. Let's clear the table and begin our review, shall we?"

It was the work of a few minutes to clear the table, dispose of the remains of the meal, and set up their gear.

"Alright, let's start with the exterior. Kathy?"

Kathy spoke up. "I'd like to hold off on discussing that until we've discussed the findings of the interior, if you don't mind." She fairly radiated barely restrained eagerness. Faernsworth gave her a quizzical glance, then smiled. "Alright. Anything on the interior scan, Niles?"

"Maddingly little, I'm afraid. We've only used the passive scanners, mind you—x-rays, neutrino, and radio—and those take time to build up a good-quality image. As of right now all I can say is that there's one, perhaps two, chambers inside. Also hints of passageways." He frowned and squirmed with embarrassment at his meagre report.

"Shouldn't you have something a bit more than that?" asked Faernsworth with a frown.

"I'd like to speak to that, if I may," interjected Kathy. Everyone turned to look at her.

"The stone isn't local. In fact, it's more of a cement than stone. Oh, yes, it looks and feels like stone but there's something more to it. Not sure what but it might explain why the scanners aren't seeing as much as expected."

"Alright, Kathy, anything else?"

"Indeed there is, Doctor. Most of it is buried, of course, but we can certainly get accurate measurements of the outside portion. It's like nothing ever found before. It's a pyramid structure, but the proportions are not quite right. The blocks used in the construction are all of different sizes, too ... each layer is progressively smaller. But the faces are angled and smoothed more perfectly that anything I've ever heard of. In fact, from what I can tell the blocks were cut with an intense beam of energy, not with any mechanical means."

"But it looks ancient enough," piped up George.

"Yes, but that's just a superficial patina. The material's just not weathered enough to be very old. I'd guess decades at most. Definitely not centuries," Kathy replied.

"An abandoned movie set?" asked Niles.

"Maybe," mused Kathy. "But if so, it's a strange sort of thing and damned expensive for a prop."

"There was a brief flurry of expensive movies made in Egypt about twenty years ago, more or less," interjected Faernsworth. "Before your time, I suspect. A few Chinese movie studios fuelled by mob money used foreign movies as a money laundering scheme. It all fell apart but not before a lot of money got spent on lavish sets. Some of the movies themselves weren't too bad, either. This might be one of those."

"Built here in the middle of nowhere, then abandoned? Does that make any sense?" mused George.

"Well, in any event it is obviously not an ancient artifact of any sort. On the other hand it is an intriguing mystery. As such, we might as well have some fun with it and treat it as real. It'll be worth a few papers from each of you, and the novelty of it will get you free drinks when you regale people with stories of this."

That got a chuckle from the group.

She clapped her hands to get their attention. "But for now, it has been a long day. Let's make sure everything is secure then get a good night's rest. We'll get up at first light, have breakfast, then get to work. I'll be expecting your best work, too. Document everything every step of the way, exactly like you were taught. We're doing this by the book. Now off with you."

* * *

Noon the next day found them gathered for lunch around the large common table.

"I believe I know the answer to this, but for the record ... is everyone finished their exterior studies?" asked Faernsworth, glancing at each of the others in turn.

A bobbing of heads and the collection of happy grins answered her in the affirmative.

"Alright. Well, normally we'd be calling in for instructions and wait months for approvals. But are we all agreed—again, for the record—that this is something recently constructed?"

This time the affirmative answers had an overtone of anticipation. Like that of predators about to engage prey.

Faernsworth had a predatory smile of her own as she said, "Very well. Let's finish our meal, tidy up, then prepare to enter our mysterious structure."

Within an hour they were assembled in front of the structure's single doorway. It was an ornate structure, sitting a few centimetres proud of the main surface. The entrance was blocked by what appeared to be a wall of stones, each the size of a modern brick.

"Well, class, how should we deal with this?" asked Faernsworth in full-on teacher mode.

"Just smash the damn thing?" suggested George with a grin.

"Now, now. We're wanting to treat this like the real thing," she admonished. "Kathy, what's it made of?"

"Something similar to cement but not as hard as stone. Not local. Not ancient. For once I agree with George." She flashed a grin at her classmate. A glare from Faernsworth tempered her enthusiasm. "Okay, okay. Our circular saw will do the job in short order. It'll take about half an hour, I think."

"Very well. Niles, mark where you'll make the cuts. The rest of you put the protective sheets over the rest of the doorway. No, don't grumble...I told you we're doing this by the book."

It took a bit less than the half-hour estimate to lay down the protective sheeting, cut through the brickwork, and clear an opening.

"Niles, check the interior air, if you please."

Niles fiddled with an instrument, then thrust it into the opening for a few seconds. He turned to her with a grin and said, "All green, Doctor. I'd say it's safe."

"Very well. Now let's get some lights..."

"Right here, Doctor," said George as he trundled up carrying three satchels. "Even got some comm relays so we can link to our camp while inside."

"Well done, George," said Faernsworth with a nod. "Carry on."

He set up a small box off to one side of the doorway, checked that it could communicate with the camp, then set up lights just inside the doorway. "The passive scans indicated that this corridor leads to some sort of chamber." He sent beams of light into the structure. "From here it looks like the corridor zigs at the end, about ten metres down. See? So, I'll leave a big light here to make sure the corridor is well lit, then we'll see what's down there."

"Very well, but hold on a tic. Niles, is there anything of significance in the corridor itself?"

"Doesn't look like it. Hold on, though. Yep, there's some faint paintings on the walls. Strange ... looks old and faded."

Faernsworth grinned. "That's the style those old movies went for. All of 'em the same, pretty much, too. Everything old and faded to simulate antiquity. Still, we'll document it all just as if it were real."

A chorus of disappointed groans greeted her announcement.

"Now, now. I told you we were doing this by the book. It'll be good practise for you. Oh, don't look so glum. If this were a real dig we'd be spending a week on the corridor. As it is, I think we should be able to do it in an hour."

Her estimate was almost spot on, as they documented the corridor and reached the far end. The paintings ended just before the corridor did, leaving the last metre of wall undecorated. At the end, the corridor took a sharp turn to the right for two metres, then a sharp turn left. The corridor opened up into a space three metres wide. Facing them was another doorway, this one inscribed with a rich set of hieroglyphics.

"Ah, this is more like it," said Faernsworth. "Much more in keeping with a movie set. Note that the colours are much richer here. Niles, Kathy, scan this and see if the AI can make sense of it."

The two of them waved cameras around for a minute, then fussed with a piece of gear Niles had taken from his backpack. The unit flashed several red lights and emitted a harsh buzzing sound.

"Bloody piece of shite," muttered Kathy. "Damned uni gave us all the bloody obsolete crap."

"Now, now," said Niles. "Older and wiser heads assured us that this would be perfectly adequate for whatever we came across. Far be it for us to question their august wisdom."

He grinned as he dodged a backhanded slap aimed at his head.

Faernsworth added in a low, serious tone, "More importantly, far be it for them to hear of any criticisms from us. Understand? This is being recorded, don't forget. We can edit this bit out and blame it on technical issues. But we can't have too much of that or people ... the wrong sort of people ... will get suspicious."

She looked sternly at each person in turn and made sure that each nodded their understanding.

"Greg, please take a look at the translator and see if you can bang some sense into it. Kathy, Niles, here's a chance to use some of your ancient language skills. What can you tell me about what we're looking at?"

The pair of them looked at each other, shrugged, then went off to one side to begin a closer examination. They spent several minutes looking at one section in detail, punctuated by frantic tapping on their phones. Then they moved to another section then another, spending less time on each of them. Finally, Niles turned to George and said, "Don't bother with that gear, George. It's working, I think."

"Excuse me?"

Kathy snorted in disgust. "This," she said with a wave of her hand, "is a fake. A very good one, but a fake, nonetheless."

"You can read it?" asked Faernsworth.

"Well enough, so far as it goes. Taken individually, each symbol is correct. But taken as a whole it's gibberish."

Niles took up the narrative. "They're not even all from the same period." He pointed to several places on the wall. "Here, here, and here. These symbols are separated by centuries and have never been seen together."

"And the ones you can't recognize?" asked Faernsworth.

Niles and Kathy exchanged glances, then shrugged. "Can't say," she said. "Might be real but obscure, or might be some modern caricature."

"So the AI gave up because it can't deal with this sort of nonsense, is that it? Is any of it readable?" said George with a sigh.

"Bits and pieces," said Niles. "Kathy and I expected the usual warnings and curses, and that's what it seems these are. Sort of, anyway. As if an amateur tried to put something together in a hurry from a variety of sources. Looks pretty, though. Ties in with your movie theory, Doctor."

"Hmph," was all the good Doctor said. She surveyed the writing for a minute, rubbing the side of her nose with a forefinger. The others had learned long ago that this indicated she was deep in thought. Then she stopped and heaved a sigh.

"Fake, then," she said in a soft voice as if to herself. Then she turned to the others and in a firmer voice said, "You're quite sure it is fake?"

"Oh, yes," said Kathy.

"We'll need the AI translator to do a proper translation. Pretty sure we can convince it to deal with this hodgepodge, with a bit of work. George?"

George grunted and scratched at his head for a moment. "Yeah. Not here, though. Needs gear at the camp. It's all recorded, so can work on it later." He shrugged in apology. "Best I can do, I'm afraid."

"That'll be fine, George. Thank you. Any more that needs recording in this section. No?" A large grin split her face. "Alright, boys and girls, this is what we've been waiting for. Let's open this up and see what's inside." Happy mutterings forced her to raise her voice to be heard. "Set up scanners to either side of the doorway. George, get the drill. While the others work, we'll bore a small hole for a quick look before charging in."

As it was spoken, so it was done. It was the matter of a few minutes to bore a hole and insert a borescope. The output of the borescope was plugged into an analysis unit.

"Nothing on passive sensors," muttered Niles. He turned to look at the Faernsworth. "Too dark to see anything. Go with the active?"

Faernsworth nodded. "A short, minimum-level burst. By the book."

The equipment gave a soft click as images appeared on its screens. Niles motioned Kathy over, pointing at some of the readouts. As she studied the readings, Niles turned to look at the others.

"The chamber's roughly square, six and a bit metres on a side, and about three high. But there's something strange. There's—"

"There's strong reflections from something," interjected

15

Kathy. "Not from the structure itself, but from other things. Things made out of metal and what looks like plastic of some sort. Oh, and there's a container in the centre of the room."

"A sarcophagus?"

Kathy shook her head. "Not sure. More of a plain box, is what it looks like."

"Risk another active burst, Doctor? Maybe higher power?"

After a moment's hesitation Faernsworth said, "Try passive mode again, please."

Niles bent to the task and several seconds later looked up, his brow furrowed and his mouth twisted into a frown. "That's strange. That's very strange. I sensed some brief, low-level electrical activity. Now it's gone. As if something got a bit of energy from our active scan. Not enough to power up, but enough to give it a tingle."

"No more active scans. Continue monitoring with passive sensors, please," said Faernsworth in a firm voice.

"Probably just some old equipment that got left behind," offered George. Everyone turned to look at him. He shrugged and added, "Electronics that's been powered down will often give readings like that when hit by our active sensors. Seen it before." He shrugged again and offered, "Not surprising given that this is an old movie set, is it?"

Faernsworth nodded. "Good points, George. Thank you. Anyone else have anything to offer? No? Alright, this is how we'll proceed. This is a good time to pause and make a formal summary of our work so far. Each of you prepare a short thirty to sixty second summary of what you've done since we've entered. Kathy, please focus on these strange writings and why you believe them to be fake. Niles, I'd like you to focus on the entrance way and how the state of paintings there differ from the writing. George, I want you to overview the sensor readings and what might be causing them. Think in terms of an elevator pitch. We'll attach those to the raw data records and make a sealed record of the lot. That'll take an hour or so,

16

I suspect. Then we're going to cut our way into that chamber and see if we can find some answers."

CHAPTER THREE
The Resurrection Curse

Two hours later they were standing inside the chamber. Faernsworth had insisted that George set up several lights before they did anything else. The chamber itself was devoid of markings of any sort. There was no obvious sign of the tech their scans had caught traces of.

"Uhm, Kathy, where's the metal and plastic our scans indicated?" asked Niles.

"Let's put that aside for the moment," said Faernsworth. "Take a look at this sarcophagus, or whatever it is. This doesn't look like a movie prop. Nor does this interior." She waved a hand at the walls while keeping her gaze fixed on the anomalous casket.

Everyone, except George, was focusing their attention on the sarcophagus. He was staring intently at a pair of instruments, one in each hand, as he walked slowly around the room.

"Uhm, guys? I've got activity." He blushed as all eyes turned towards him. "There's low level electrical activity coming from the walls. Seems directed at that sarcophagus or casket or whatever the hell it is."

"Nobody move. Nobody talk," said Faernsworth in a low, intense voice. "I'm deadly serious. Something is wrong. Look and listen."

They all stood there for nearly a minute, listening intently. Kathy raised a hand slightly and gave a cautious small wave. At Faernsworth's nod, she whispered, "There's a hum. Faint, but it's there."

Faernsworth nodded. Turning to George she said in a whisper, "Where's the power coming from? No, don't scan for it. Just reason it out, please."

The worthy paused for a moment before whispering back. "Not solar or wind, or we'd have seen something outside. Not nuclear or our instruments would have picked up some signs of it. Maybe batteries of some sort."

"After all these years?" whispered Niles. "And what about this new electrical activity?"

"Some sort of control system?" suggested Kathy.

"Shush," commanded Faernsworth. "The sound is changing. Where's it coming from?"

Everyone lapsed into silence and focused on the sound. After a few seconds Kathy pointed at the sarcophagus. A second later Niles followed suit, then George. Without any warning the sound increased from barely audible to a powerful bass thrumming that reverberated through their bodies. After a few seconds the stone sarcophagus shattered to reveal a mirrored half-cylinder. Its surface rippled, each ripple creating a rainbow of shimmers that bathed the area in multichromatic light.

The sound rose it pitch and volume, forcing everyone to cover their ears. It lasted for the space of a few heartbeats then vanished completely. As the sound vanished so did the half-cylinder, revealing the figure of a man lying on a slab. He was clothed in what appeared to be an austere uniform that looked somewhat worse for wear. There were metallic cuffs enclosing his wrists and ankles. A deep thrumming sound permeated the room which they felt to their very bones. It continued for several seconds then stopped. The cuffs glowed for a moment then retracted into the slab, leaving no trace of their presence.

To their shocked amazement he took several deep breaths, then sprang to his feet. He was tall—at least two metres—and powerfully built without being stocky. In age he appeared to be in his mid-thirties. That is, not middle-aged but past the first bloom of youth.

He looked at each of them in turn without a hint of fear or concern. Finally he said, "Flomar?" His voice was rich and deep.

When that received blank looks, he tried several other words with a similar lack of results. He gave a soft sigh and looked at them expectantly, his hands folded in front of him.

"Uhm, hello?" offered Faernsworth.

The stranger looked at her as a smile quirked up a corner of his mouth. He motioned for her to continue.

"Oh. Well, I'm Doctor Rhian Faernsworth. These are my colleagues: Niles Castleworth, Kathy Shanslough, and George Smith." She pointed to each as she said their names, feeling slightly giddy.

The man smiled broadly and gave a slight bow to her. He said in perfect, if slightly accented, English, "Hello. I'm very pleased to make your acquaintance. My name is Bob. I don't want to appear rude, but perhaps we could continue our discussion over a meal? It's been some time since I last ate."

* * *

They adjourned to their main tent and watched as their guest wolfed down enough food for several meals. As he ate, he queried each of them, receiving information without offering much in return. He was charming and quick to put everyone at their ease. Faernsworth watched his performance in silence, watching as her team interacted with their guest.

Finally, she put down her cup and leaned forward. "You've very neatly interrogated us, Bob. Now I think it's time for you to supply us with some information," she said in a clipped, no-nonsense tone. Her team gave her startled looks which she ignored as she gazed intently at the stranger.

Bob gave her a warm smile as he sipped his coffee. After a brief pause he said, "What is it that you wish to know? Ask me anything."

At her exasperated snort of disgust the others looked at her with shock. "Stop playing the fool," she snapped.

Bob chuckled and put down his cup. "My apologies, Doctor." Then he became serious. "How much of the truth do you want to know? Be careful what you ask for."

That took everyone aback. Finally George blurted out, "Everything." Then he blushed and sat back in embarrassed silence as the others glared at him.

"That's a worthy attitude but a tall order. Perhaps I could start with the basics, and we could proceed from there." Without waiting for a response, he began speaking. "No, I am not from this planet. Yes, there are other inhabited planets in this galaxy. Quite a few of them, in fact, but it's a big galaxy. Yes, there are other humans out there. Plus a few others. It's complicated."

He failed to notice the slight tightening of Faernsworth's mouth as he spoke.

"As for how I got here, I'm not entirely sure. The short answer is that I was in a contest ... a duel you might call it ... and walked into a trap and got transported here along with my adversary."

"What about the sarcophagus?" asked Kathy.

"The what?"

She explained how he had been found. Bob nodded and said, "That explains a few things, then. The half-cylinder was a stasis field. The sarcophagus, as you call it, was just for show I think. Or perhaps to conceal the stasis field from casual observers."

"But the pyramid and inscriptions?" queried Niles. "How do they figure into this?"

Bob pondered the question for a few seconds before

replying. "Not sure, to be honest. Probably an attempt to blend in locally. It's an isolated spot, solid construction, and would require a certain level of tech to enter."

"Yes, but..."

"It's complicated," Bob said with a sigh. "I was investigating a mystery on a distant planet. My opponent showed up, the defence system of an ancient facility was triggered, then both of us were sent here."

"You mentioned an opponent," said Faernsworth. "What manner of being is it?"

Bob gave her a questioning look as he answered, "Human enough, but enhanced. And, yes, I'm human but not enhanced."

"What is your opponent's mission? And yours?"

Bob frowned. "As I've said, it's complicated. That ancient facility I mentioned seems to contain mystery that is of great value to some very bad people. I don't know what it is, exactly, but it can't be allowed to fall into their hands."

"And why is that, Bob? Why should we help you and not your opponent? Or either of you, if it comes to that," said Faernsworth in a quiet but firm voice.

"Because to my opponent, and others like him, humans like yourself are resources to be exploited. I work to prevent that sort of thing."

"Again, why?"

He hesitated for a moment before answering. "A long time ago, my people fought a series of horrific wars. We won but at a terrible cost. Much was lost or forgotten, including caches of weapons of incredible power. Powerful enough to shred planets. And worse, I assure you. I ... clean things up. Make things safer for the younger races, such as yourself."

"Younger races? You claim to be human, like us."

Bob smiled. "Human, yes, but not like you. We've been around a lot longer. It's—"

"...complicated," finished Faernsworth. "Alright, so who is

your opponent?"

Bob let out a long sigh. "One of my kind, I'm ashamed to say. There's not many of us left and a few have turned ... feral, for want of a better word."

"So you and this other bloke got sent here to Earth?" blurted George. "Was that part of his plan, then?"

"Not at all," said Bob, obviously glad for the change of topic. "The ancient facility did that to us. It forced us to fight on its planet, but that ended in a draw. It then declared that the best way to decide the issue would be to continue on a neutral field of battle."

"Battle? To what end?"

"Oh, sorry, didn't I say? It's an old military facility left over from those wars I mentioned. It will only surrender control to authorized personnel. Faced with two conflicting, but seemingly valid, claims it decided to conduct a test to determine the best claim."

"Trial by combat? That's how your kind decided things?" asked Kathy.

"Not at all," replied Bob with some heat. "As I said, it's a very old facility. Abandoned and forgotten for many thousands of years. The control system somehow developed a crude form of sentience, and seems to have become insane or at least quite bloodthirsty. On the other hand, it arose out of a time of fierce conflict and perhaps decided that mere survival was the answer to every problem."

"Why here? Why Earth?"

"I suspect that there were few other options left to it. That's my doing, I'm afraid."

"So where's this opponent of yours?"

"Not sure. Probably not too far away. Within, oh, a hundred kilometres, I'd suspect. Possibly much closer."

"Is he awake now?"

"Oh, most certainly. I'm sure the awakening of one would trigger the awakening of the other."

"So this is our fault?"

"Not really. You're just a trigger. A random event to set things in motion."

"How long have the two of you been here?" asked George.

Bob shook his head. "Impossible to say. I'd have to check the equipment to see if it kept any records. That's something I'm loath to do just yet, though."

"Why?"

"The whole thing is set up as a trial by combat, remember. That means the chamber could very well be a trap. Easy to get out of ... once. Not really worth the risk to enter again without a very good reason. So, please, I am urging you to stay out of there."

That caused a pause in the questions as the group digested what they'd been told. Especially the part about not examining the greatest find of their careers. Finally Faernsworth spoke up, "So what are these enhancements of his?"

"He's stronger, faster, heals very quickly, and has built-in weaponry." He flashed a grin as he added, "And has something of a temper."

"And you have?"

Bob placed a hand to his chest. "A pure heart."

Everyone laughed when George muttered, "Mate, you are so screwed."

Everyone, that is, except Faernsworth. Her eyes narrowed and her mouth tightened. As the others chattered amongst each other, she made a silent exit. Bob saw her leave, made his excuses, and went outside. He found her standing a dozen metres away from the tent, to one side so as to be shielded from anyone casually standing in the doorway.

"Hi," said Bob. "You seem upset about something."

She answered with a derisive snort. "No, really, why would that be, do you think?" Her voice was harsh but quiet, as if she didn't want anyone else to hear. "We've gone from being on a wild goose chase, to a career-ending discovery, to ... well, you.

An alien."

"Human," he corrected in a gentle voice. "Just not from here."

Her response was to look at the ground. If anything, the tightness around her mouth increased.

Bob gave a small sigh. "I've emphasized to the others that it might be a good idea to stay out of the pyramid for the time being. Could be any manner of trouble or even danger inside. It'd help if that came from yourself, as well."

She nodded. "I've already suggested that we leave it be for the time being. It's a tough thing for a researcher to ignore such a tempting puzzle, but I'll emphasize the danger part of it."

Faernsworth paused for a moment before continuing. "You speak English very well. Ever been to Earth before?"

"I'm not sure this is important—" he began.

As if he'd not spoken, she continued. "Specifically to a town called Talgarth? Hmm?"

Bob's eyes went wide as he stood immobile.

"You went to a tea shop there and asked for a specific type of tea. What was it?" Her eyes bored into his.

Bob opened his mouth to speak, but shut it as he noticed a small pistol in her left hand.

"I'm waiting for an answer, Bob. Or whoever you are. Whatever you are."

"Oolong black dragon. Ordered it twice, actually. Once the first time I was there. A kilo of it, as I recall. The second time, some years later, a pot of it to drink there. The shop had changed hands by that time and was being run by a good friend of mine."

"Her name?" Faernsworth's voice had taken on a dangerous edge. Her grip on the pistol tightened.

"Celcilia. Why is this important?"

"Hold still," was her only response. Her right hand slashed out and a sharp edge raked across Bob's left hand.

He stood still and only said, "Was that necessary?"

"You're bleeding. Celcilia's Bob didn't bleed."

"I do now. By the way, you don't need the gun. I'm happy to answer your questions. You've nothing to fear from me."

The gun didn't waver as she replied in even tones, "Not from her Bob, perhaps. But you don't seem to be him."

"And yet I am. Changed physically, but still the man she knew."

"What happened? The last Celcilia heard, you were off destroying the portal network and pissing off your family. For all I know, you're one of Set's thugs."

Bob's face registered surprise before he forced it into a neutral expression. "You seem to know an awful lot about me. How is that?"

"Just answer the damned question," she ground out.

He gave a slight shrug. "As you said, I set about destroying the portal network. Including the one on Earth, I might add."

"And?"

"Managed to get most them. Then came across something I couldn't handle and died."

"Excuse me?" It was her turn to be startled.

Bob uttered a low laugh. "Not sure what it was, but it killed me. I'd made a copy of my consciousness, and my death activated a process that transferred it into a new body." He gave a slight sweep of his hands to indicate himself.

"A metamorphosis facility?"

"My, my, you are well-informed. But, no. A much earlier sort of tech. It could create a fully mature human body but my ancestors never figured out how to create a template for the mind. Nor did they have the tech to transfer consciousness into it. I adapted our current tech to create a copy of my consciousness and transfer it into this body."

"Not what your people would call an aspect, then?"

"No. It's just an ordinary human body. No enhancements, no embedded tech."

She chewed on her lower lip for a moment. The gun was no longer pointed directly at Bob, but rather towards the ground. "So you've got yourself a resurrection machine. Immortality."

He grunted a laugh. "Nope. It was a one-time thing. The downloading process destroys the backup copy. This single, limited-lifespan body is all I get. Just like yourselves. Any other questions?"

Faernsworth blinked rapidly a few times, then the gun came up to point directly at Bob once more. "The first time you met Celcilia was when?"

"In a dead-end alley after she escaped from the temple of Kydos. I neutralized her attackers, then helped her to escape back to Earth. More or less. Lots of complications along the way."

"Such as what Kydos did to her."

"To what are you referring? How Kydos groomed her and her ancestors, or the poison dart she hit Celcilia with?"

The gun in her hand wavered for a moment. Faernsworth said in a soft voice, "Very good. Anything else you'd care to share?"

Bob gave a small grin. "Well, in the Five Stars Empire, our first meal was at a restaurant called 'Pahnto's'. Our waitress was named Bru, and she referred us to a clothing establishment run by her aunt, whose name was Shia. That's who gifted Celcilia with the boot knife, by the way."

Faernsworth blinked in surprise, then exhaled strongly enough to puff out her cheeks. The gun lowered then vanished back into its hidden holster. "Sorry," she muttered. "Had to make sure."

"Always best to make sure. Trust but verify, as you lot say." Bob paused for a moment then added, "How do you know so much about me? About the adventures Celcilia and I shared?"

Faernsworth gave a soft laugh. This time, though, it was much friendlier. "I'm her great granddaughter. One of them, anyway."

"Is she alive?"

"Sorry, no. Died some years ago at the ripe old age of 103. Got hit by a drunk driver as she was out on her daily five kilometre walk."

"I'm so sorry." The look on his face was one of great sadness.

"Don't be," she snapped. Then her face softened. "She had a fine life and made everyone in her family feel special and loved. A few of us—but only a few—got told about her adventures with you. She wanted to keep the knowledge alive, you see, just in case. Great-gran Celcilia was always one for planning for the future."

They stood in silence for a minute, each lost in their own thoughts, staring up at the stars.

Finally Faernsworth broke the silence. "So how'd you get here? Thought you'd destroyed the portal. Only the one around, or so you told her."

"Was only the one, I thought. Turns out there's another one. A much older device left over from the beginnings of the Great Wars. My Uncle Sid had an old scroll that seemed to describe the use of a portal. We both figured it was the one I destroyed."

"Something different, then? Not one of the official ones?"

"Oh, it's official all right, but a portable unit used only by the military. Didn't think there were any left."

"That what your opponent was after?"

"Possibly. I was there following rumours of an abandoned base. Not many of them left, you understand. Most of those are useless ruins. Even a small intact base can be a powerful tool, though." He grinned as he added, "I've got one of my own."

"Which you use for what, then?"

"Well, a home for one thing. Haven't had a home in a very long time, so I've enjoyed that. Also, I've been cleaning up messes ... weapons caches, the odd portal like this one, that sort of thing."

"Been keeping yourself busy, I see." She paused for a

moment. "What about Set and his lot?"

Bob shrugged. "Gone into ... rehab, I think you'd call it. The Changed appear to have gotten in touch with everyone, even the ones I didn't encourage."

"So this opponent of yours is, what, a rehab reject?"

Bob snorted a laugh. "Something like that, yes."

They both fell silent, and the silent stretched to nearly a minute. Finally Faernsworth spoke. "So, you bleed now."

"Yes, indeed. Now as human as you are."

"Ah. Wait, what about diseases? If you don't have your healing factors to protect you, and us, are we a danger to each other?"

Bob rubbed his wrists. "From the tingling on my wrists and ankles, I suspect that's been taken care of. Tell me, were there any attachments on me before I wakened?"

"Yes, ornamented bracelets on your wrists and ankles. Just before you woke up there was a rather invasive series of sounds, then the cuffs glowed."

"Excellent. Well, diseases within me were neutralized and I was inoculated from anything you lot carry. Pretty standard stuff."

"From the time of the Great Wars, I gather? Before the metamorphosis technology made all that obsolete?"

They were interrupted by a scream coming from the pyramid. They ran there and found everyone gathered about the entrance.

"Don't go in," yelled Bob. "I warned you about traps."

Faernsworth panted out, "What happened?" She pointed at Niles. "Where's George?"

"Wanted to take a peek and look at the tech ... talked about how it could make his career. Thought we'd talked him out of it, but he sneaked out when we weren't looking."

"Damn that boy," snarled Faernsworth.

"Everyone back," declared Bob. "Off to one side and away from the entrance." The tone of command was so strong that everyone obeyed without thinking.

Once several metres away, Kathy paused to ask, "What's all this for?"

Bob gave her a slight shove to keep her moving. "Everyone get over that ridge there. Fast fast fast. Then drop flat. There's a glow building up inside the structure. That's not good."

By the time everyone had run the two dozen metres to top of the ridge, they were all breathing heavily. Except for Bob, of course.

"Down flat," he commanded. "Now now now. Shut your eyes tight. Plant your face into the sand. Don't look up if you value your eyes."

At first there was only the sound of their panting in the still of the night. Then came a low-pitched humming that grew in intensity. They could feel the ground vibrating slightly beneath them. After a few seconds an intense beam of light shot up from the pyramid and into the sky. Bob raised his head. "It's safe to look. But be careful. The light is as bright as the sun."

The others raised their heads and shielded their eyes with their hands. The beam lit up the area as if it were daytime. Within a few seconds the beam snapped off, followed by a gurgling sound from the direction of the pyramid. They crawled to the top of the rise and looked down. Where the pyramid had been was a molten mass, glowing with a faint red glow.

"Over there," shouted Niles, pointing towards the horizon. Far in the distance there glowed another beam of light. Within a few seconds it, too, blinked off.

"What does it mean?" whispered Faernsworth.

Bob's face was grim. "The two repositories have decanted the players. The hunt has begun."

CHAPTER FOUR
Trial By Survival

"What have you got in the way weapons?" said Bob to Doctor Faernsworth. The dull red glow from the molten remains of the pyramid cast an ominous light on everything.

"Not much. My pistol, of course, but little else. What we have is yours, of course."

"No, you misunderstand. Weapons for you three to use to defend yourselves with."

"What about you?" asked Niles.

"I've been trained to make use of pretty much anything. Been training for this sort of thing my entire life. Still, wouldn't turn down any rope or knives you might have."

"What about our vehicles?" asked Kathy. "Can't we just outrun whatever is coming? Get to a town, contact the authorities, and let them deal with this?"

Bob shook his head. "My opponent isn't as well trained as I am, but he's still incredibly powerful and dangerous. More so than you realize."

"So you're saying the armed forces couldn't deal with it?"

"Given proper training and time to prepare, perhaps. As it is? No, it would be a slaughter of anyone who got in his way or anyone whose death might serve his purpose. It's me he wants, so it has to be me who fights him. Preferably in an uninhabited area like this."

"It won't stay uninhabited for long," interjected Faernsworth. "The authorities will have detected those energy bursts and will come to investigate. Despite the dust and wind obscuring things, satellites will have located both sites well enough. Niles, you and Kathy check out the vehicles and communications gear. I suspect they'll be inoperative, though. My phone is dead. I'll help Bob gather up what he needs."

Bob nodded. "The energy burst probably had an electromagnetic jamming component. That would be in keeping with the rules of the game, you see. Still, worth checking out."

The two youths dashed off towards the vehicles and cache of equipment.

Faernsworth turned to Bob. "What about his apporting and teleportation abilities? Should we be expecting him any time soon?"

Bob shook his head. "No, I don't think so. The energy burst would have numbed those abilities, at least for a short time. With any luck his sensorium won't be working too well, but we can't count on that."

"Great-gran Celcilia mentioned the sensorium. Do you still have anything like that?"

"Nope. Just a standard human body. My senses are a bit better than yours, but not by much."

"Great-gran said you had centuries of experience fighting opponents stronger than yourself. But this ... do we have any chance at all?" she asked in a quiet voice.

"Oh, yes," came the cheerful reply. "I fought him to a draw before being sent here. Should be able to do at least that again. Now let's see what you have in the way of supplies, shall we?"

They trotted to the main tent. Bob rummaged around and selected a variety of knives, ropes, a small first aid kit, flares, lengths of cloth, binoculars, a blanket, and a canteen filled with water. He was stuffing it all into a knapsack when their young colleagues burst into the tent.

"Vehicles are dead," gasped Kathy.

"Comm gear, too," puffed Niles.

Bob nodded as he looked at each in turn. "Alright, here's what you three need to do. Go to the ridge where we sheltered when the pyramid activated. Stay low to the ground. The heat from the molten rock will mask your infrared signatures. Couldn't hurt to cover yourselves with a blanket and cover that with sand. That'll help shield you from a cursory scan."

Turning to face Faernsworth, he added, "Doctor, I'd strongly advise against initiating violence against him, but if it comes to that aim for the eyes. Then run for your life."

"What about you?" asked Kathy.

Bob grinned. "Time to take the fight to him."

"How will you find him?"

"I'll head in the direction of the other beacon. He'll be heading this way, so I expect we'll meet up along the way. Easy peasy," Bob said with a grin. Niles and Kathy responded with tentative smiles.

"Don't forget that the authorities will be coming to investigate. Expect aerial reconnaissance, if nothing else, to supplement what the satellites pick up," said Faernsworth.

Bob responded with a curt nod. "Understood. Now get yourselves under cover."

With that, he ran out the door and into the night.

* * *

Bob jogged out into the desert in the direction of the other beacon. In truth, he was feeling less optimistic than he had led the others to believe. The terrain appeared to offer few opportunities for sneaky tricks, which were all he had to counter his opponent's physical advantages. On the other hand, the terrain would be unfamiliar to both of them. Hopefully that would make his opponent more cautious, given how badly Bob had hurt him in their previous encounter.

That thought cheered him up. As the Precepts of Survival

instructed, "Going into battle convinced of defeat surrenders victory to the enemy."

After fifteen minutes of jogging, he paused for a rest and to check the horizon with the binoculars. He saw nothing of note as he waited for his breathing to even out. A touch of self-loathing bubbled up, but he tamped it down before it could poison his mood. Still, he had to admit that being merely human brought so many limitations. The sand made running very tiring, the dust stung his eyes, and he was beginning to feel the stirrings of thirst. Thirst, of all things. He'd hardly begun the ordeal, and his body was beginning to show signs of weakness. Worse, his merely human eyesight could barely make out anything in the gloom of night as the ever-present dust blocked even the meagre light of the stars.

He fought down the urge to sigh and replaced it with a slightly stronger huff as he exhaled. It was time to focus on the needs of battle, not his feelings. Relaxing his eyes, he began to detect subtle variations in the landscape. Off to his left he could see something that looked just a bit different than the surrounding sand. He rose to his feet and jogged towards it. A minute later his feet felt stones, then a hard surface covered with a layer of sand. It offered easier footing than the sand, so he ran along it for a ways.

A subtle change in sound caused him to halt and squat down. He tilted his head and scanned the area as best he could. Moving slowly on all fours, he moved forward until his hands detected an edge. It turned out to be the edge of a drop-off to a shallow canyon. He debated dropping down into it. On the one hand, it would offer a partial shield from prying eyes. On the other hand, if he were detected, it would limit his freedom of movement. After a moment's consideration, he decided to continue along the edge of the canyon. It was leading roughly where he wanted to go, and it was always good to have options.

A half-hour of fast jogging brought him to an outcropping of rocks. He decided to rest in the shelter they provided while he caught his breath and prepared his resources. He took several healthy sips from the canteen, as there was no need to conserve water for the long term. He took two knives and stuck them into his belt on either side of his body. They had no sheath, but his clothing would prevent them from cutting him. The remaining knife he left in the knapsack. He attached two of the ropes to the outside of the knapsack for quick access. The remaining length of rope he cut up and attached rocks to either end, creating crude but serviceable bolos. One bolo was hung from his belt, one attached to the outside of the pack, and the remainder put into the knapsack. The flares were distributed in a similar fashion.

After another sip of water, he used a strip of cloth to make a pair of slings. He wrapped a stone in each and placed them in an outside pocket of the knapsack. He had a few special items on his person, but nothing resembling a heavy weapon. It was a meagre armoury but it would have to do. The next step would be to find his opponent.

The trick was to calculate where his opponent might be. Given the minimum and maximum position of the other's storage site, his rate of travel on foot, the condition of his sensorium, and so forth and so forth, Bob reckoned contact could be made at any time. It was time to tilt the odds in his own favour and force the issue. He looked down into the canyon. It had a straight section below his location but angled sharply after several body lengths in front and behind him. It was as good a place for an ambush as any.

He scanned the horizon with the binoculars but detected nothing. With the coast clear, he assembled his traps. He took a pair of stones and wrapped them with a bit of cloth and placed a chemical heating pad inside the cloth. While the stones were heating, he laid out a pair of flares, bolos, slings, and assorted rocks ready for use. The blanket he spread on the sand to achieve thermal equilibrium.

After waiting a couple of minutes, he flung the heated stones down into the canyon, next to some large rocks. With luck they'd be mistaken for a human body lying in wait. Then he lit and tossed a flare to either end of the straight section of the canyon, then a third to the lip on the other side. Finally, he took the blanket and covered himself with it. With a bit of luck, it would mask his infrared signature for the few seconds it took for the flares to be detected.

As Bob waited, he couldn't help but ponder upon what the Precepts of Survival, not to mention his father, had said about depending on luck. Still, sometimes playing the odds was all one had. For now he had tilted those odds in his favour as best he could. Perhaps that counted as clever tactics rather than depending on luck. His ruminations were interrupted by a faint sound that was approaching at a fast clip.

Several seconds later, a series of ripples in the air preceded explosions that destroyed the flares. An animal-like scream came from the other side of the canyon as a tall figure leapt down towards the heated stones. Bob flung off the blanket and flung one bolo towards the figure, followed immediately by a second. He followed that up by firing a stone from each of the slings before crouching down out of sight as he reloaded the slings.

He heard dull, soft thuds as the stones hit flesh. That was followed by a series of energy blasts in random directions, then another dull thud as one of the bolos found its target. There was a moment of silence that was pierced by a scream of rage. He heard a grunt of effort, and he rolled into an upright position while swinging a sling in one hand and a bolo in the other. His opponent's leap carried him up above the level of the canyon's edge, and Bob could see him twist this way and that in an attempt to locate his tormentor.

Bob let loose with the sling and grinned as the stone landed with a *thunk* in the groin region. His opponent screamed in pain and tumbled back to the ground. Before he reached it, though, he was tangled in the bolo that Bob tossed at him. The hard landing raised a cloud of dust and forced a pained exhalation from the prey. Bob followed up with a series of hand-thrown stones, most of which hit.

With a yell of anger and pain, the figure below broke the ropes of the bolo binding him, leapt to his feet, and bounded away at a fast clip. Bob grinned and was congratulating himself on winning the first encounter when he realized that his opponent's trajectory was towards the camp of his friends.

* * *

"No, no, no," muttered Bob as he grabbed the knapsack and began running back to the camp at a fast jog. He followed the canyon's edge as far as he could then vectored off into the sand. That slowed his progress considerably, and he was forced to rest more than once. It would be of little use to arrive back at the camp unfit for battle, but he pushed himself as much as he dared.

He was perhaps two minutes away from the camp when he heard shouting. Bob put on a burst of speed. A few seconds later he heard screams of pain, anger, and fear. First from one person, then another, followed by silence. His face was grim as he ran. He was on the edges of the camp when he heard gunshots. A half-dozen rang out, but the seventh was answered with a roar of pain. That raised a tight smile on Bob's face, but he did not slacken his pace.

A few seconds later he was at the edge of the camp and saw two figures next to the glowing remains of the pyramid. One was his opponent and the other Doctor Faernsworth. Two motionless figures lay off to the side. Bob judged the distances as he ran, reached down for a knife, and flung it at his opponent. It had travelled half the distance to its target when the air rippled as an energy blast from a sensorium nodule vapourized the knife.

Faernsworth took the opportunity to drop and roll behind a bush. It wasn't much in the way of cover but better than nothing. More importantly, though, it gave Bob a clear field of fire at his opponent. He took advantage of that to fling the other knife and a pair of stones as he zigged and zagged to avoid the energy blasts sent his way. Those blasts quickly became focused on the items Bob had thrown, which gave him a chance to close the distance.

Now that he was closer, he could see that his opponent's left eye had been badly damaged. Angling to come from that side, Bob fired off his remaining bolo. Bouncing to one side, he spun in place, slipped off his knapsack, and flung it at his opponent's head. Given the choice of two incoming targets, his opponent chose the larger one. That gave the bolo time to hit and wrap itself around the torso, pinning both arms.

The rope of the bolo was snapped in an instant and the opponent lunged towards Bob. That instant, however, was all Bob needed to reach down to his belt and remove a length of thin, faintly-glowing string. He swung it at an oncoming arm and pulled as he twisted to one side. His opponent flew by with a whoosh of air as his arm dropped to the ground. Bob landed and bounced to one side as he spun around. Without pausing, he ran at his opponent who was now standing motionless with a stunned look on his face.

With a faint *whoosh*, Bob slashed down at his opponent's head with the string. It hit and sliced through the skull just above the eyes with no hint of resistance. The figure sank to ground and lay twitching. The tendrils of the sensorium fluttered randomly for a few seconds before drooping motionless to the ground.

Bob walked up to the figure and stared at it for a moment, his expression devoid of pity. Without looking at Faernsworth, he called out, "Stay down."

He bent down and removed a small object from his defeated opponent's belt and tucked it into a pocket. Standing up, he turned and trotted to where the Doctor was laying. "Up," he commanded. "We need to get safely away."

"What? Away? From what?"

Bob didn't answer her, but instead dragged her to where one of the vehicles stood. "Get behind and out of sight. That'll protect you from the blast."

Reaching into his belt he brought out a small pouch. With great care he wiggled the still-glowing string into the pouch and sealed it. Holding an end of the pouch in each hand, he gave a sharp fold followed by a savage twist. Then he threw it at the twitching form of his opponent and joined the Doctor behind the truck. He gave her a small smile. "It'll be over in a few seconds. Close your eyes and cover your ears."

She did as he instructed and several seconds later she heard a powerful explosion, followed almost immediately by a pulse of energy that she could feel in her bones. Bob stood up and extended a hand to help her up.

"I'm very sorry about your friends. He didn't stay and fight like I expected him to."

Faernsworth stared at the two bodies of her colleagues. "He ran into the camp puffing and with a wild look in his eyes. Don't think he expected to find anyone here. We stayed hidden, but then he literally stumbled over Kathy. She screamed and Niles jumped up to help her. He hit them and they fell. He started searching for others and I waited until I couldn't miss and then I fired at his head like you told me to and I hit his eye but he didn't die and he just kept coming and then ..." She collapsed to her knees and began sobbing.

Bob knelt down and held her for a minute. "I'm sorry, but we have to keep going. Just for a little while."

"Why? Kathy and Niles and George are dead. And for what? You promised Celcilia that Earth was safe."

"Because there are still things out there that consider humans as nothing. I fight them. Now I've got to take the fight to the one who caused this destruction to occur."

"Leave? How?"

Bob held up the small device he removed from his pocket.

"With this. In theory, it's a signalling device that will cause the portable portal to reveal itself."

He made to activate it, but Faernsworth put her hand on his.

"Wait," she said. "Give me a second to think, will you?" She wiped her eyes on her sleeves and came to her feet.

"What happens now, Bob? To Earth?"

"First, I get that portable portal working. Then I leave to destroy the one that caused these events to occur. I'll make sure the portal self-destructs after I leave. There'll be no advanced tech left here."

"No, you don't understand. How do I explain this?"

Bob shrugged. "An attack by bandits, I suppose."

"Oh, you naif. Earth's tech has advanced so much since you were here last. More military observation satellites, more surveillance of all sorts, more military forces with bases everywhere. What happened here could set off a war in this region and beyond."

"And where does that leave you, Rhian?"

"Caught in the middle, I'm afraid. I'm a foreigner in the middle of a high-tech release of titanic energies, with no explanation or proof of anything."

"I'm sorry, but there's little I can do about that. Your planet's fate is in your own hands. This is just a minor blip. A mystery that will soon be forgotten." He paused for a moment and looked into the distance. "Something's coming. Air transport of some sort, I think."

He tapped at the device in his hands, and it emitted a series of soft bleeps. The glowing remains of the pyramid began to emit a faint blue colour, then cooled rapidly enough that a layer of frost formed on the top. A slab-like structure appeared several metres from where they were standing. It had a faint mother-of-pearl glow to it.

"Bob, let me come with you. Please. I've no desire to be interrogated by a hostile military. Or my own, for that matter."

"Look, where I'm going isn't really any safer. Here, at least, you will be with your own kind."

"Just ... just give me a minute to grab some things. Please. You don't understand the extreme danger I'll be in if I stay."

She dashed off into the main tent before waiting for a response. Bob made an exasperated grunt and went to examine the portal. It was a very old model of a design unfamiliar to him. The sound of aircraft became louder.

"We've got to go," he yelled. "Right now."

Faernsworth came running out of the tent shrugging on a knapsack. She stopped at the portal and stood puffing. "Now. What?" she gasped out. "How. Do. You. Control. It?"

"It's an old model, made for use by regular humans. Meant as an expendable field unit for military use. Press here to active and return to base, and press here to active the self-destruct. Not a big boom, just a melt-down."

Just then a large helicopter rose up from behind a hill and began circling them.

"Time to go, I think. Last chance for you, Rhian. Stay or go."

"Go go go. That's a gunship."

Bob slapped the controls just as the helicopter turned to face them. Flashes of flame came out of its snout as a track of explosions in the sand began to move towards them. A film of swirling blackness began to form. Bob removed a small sigil from the control panel, grabbed Rhian, and ran into the film just as the line of bullets cut through where they had been standing. It made a rapid descent, coming to a halt as it hovered a metre above the ground. Four heavily-armed soldiers jumped out and ran towards the portal. By this time the film of darkness had vanished, leaving only the softly-glowing slab. As they surrounded it, it began to glow. In a matter of seconds, the glow outshone the sun. When the glow subsided several seconds later, all that remained was a puddle of molten sand.

CHAPTER FIVE

Heir to Secrets

Rhian was enveloped by a darkness that tugged at her mind, and a cold that reached into her bones. An unknowable amount of time later the blackness vanished and she found herself with Bob inside a brightly lit room. They were standing in the middle of a strange structure composed of harsh angles and materials that glowed with a mother-of-pearl radiance. Eye-catching patterns whirled about all the surfaces.

"This is just like Great-gran described," she whispered as her head swung around trying to see everything at once. She felt a hand grip her forearm with a grip that felt like steel. "On your life, say nothing, do nothing," she heard Bob whisper to her before he released her arm.

A large viewing screen covering half a wall lit up, with the stylized image of a hand in the middle of it. A voice began speaking in a foreign language—a rather warm and inviting voice, Rhian thought, much like a church minister. Bob stood upright, almost at attention, and snapped back a short reply. The image of the hand began to blink, and Bob walked towards it. Just as he reached the wall, the screen blanked. The warm voice spoke again, and once more Bob snapped back a short reply. The image returned, and Bob slapped his hand upon it.

The screen went blank. Nothing happened for several

seconds then a door slid open. Bob went towards it only to have it close in his face. Without showing any emotion, he reached into a pocket and withdrew two sigils. Rhian recognized them as the objects he'd removed from his opponent and from the portal on Earth.

Holding one in each hand, he extended his arms to either side of the door and placed the objects against the wall. There was the sound of a soft *bong* and the door opened. Bob did not move, standing perfectly still. The door shut again. A cavity appeared in the wall where each object was being held, but Bob snatched them back before they could fall in and uttered a sharp command in the unknown language.

The door slid open, and this time Bob stepped forward into its path. He gave a curt gesture of his head at Rhian indicating that she should follow. She hurried to him and was right on his heels as he walked away. As she passed through, the door flew shut and she felt a small tug on her backpack. Looking behind, she saw that a dangling strap had been sliced cleanly off by the closing door. She gulped and hurried to keep up with Bob, who was striding down the hallway. He was following a series of illuminated dots on the wall, which winked out as he passed them.

They walked down a series of well-lit corridors, turning and twisting until Rhian was quite lost. Their guide led them to a doorway that looked like all the others they had passed except it had no markings if any sort. Bob paused at the doorway, then once again extended his arms to either side of the door, placing the objects on the walls. This time the door opened without the walls trying to eat the objects, and stayed open after they entered.

The room itself was undecorated, a neutral grey colour, about four metres square, with only a dais in the centre. The dais came to chest height on her, or waist height for Bob. It was a simple pillar with an inclined slab on the top. The slab was about a half-metre square, and glowed with a mother-of-pearl radiance.

Bob motioned Rhian to halt as he approached the dais. He placed the objects in his hands at the bottom corners of the slab, then removed another object from his belt and placed it on the top right corner. The slab changed to a flashing red colour. Bob placed his hand in the centre of the slab. The colour of the walls changed to fill with angled stripes, of a complex pattern that repeated around the circumference.

The minister-like voice spoke, but this time its tone was harsher and the words had the cadence of a ritual. Bob replied in the same ritualistic tone, his voice deep and melodic. The dais slab glowed a bright white colour that was almost too bright to look at, then the glow receded. A wall to one side blanked and then the image of a stylized hand appeared. Bob removed his hand from the slab and walked to the wall. He placed his hand on the wall and spoke for almost a minute. To Rhian's ear, it once again had the cadence of a ritual response.

When Bob removed his hand, dropping it to hang by his side, the image disappeared and the wall returned to its neutral grey colour. The image of his hand remained, but Rhian saw that it was actually a bloody handprint. She glanced at his hand and saw drops of blood on the tips of his fingers.

The minister-like voice spoke again and Bob snapped out what sounded like a command. The voice seemed to query the command, and Bob repeated it. One of the other walls became a display showing various maps, gauges, and controls. Bob walked to the wall and began tapping at the controls. Rhian couldn't make much sense of it, but it appeared that he was working an advanced graphical user interface.

After a minute, another stylized hand appeared. Bob slapped his bloody hand upon it and began to speak rapidly. The minister-sounding voice spoke for several seconds then faded away. The display wall rippled then disappeared as the wall became neutral grey once more.

The door opened and Bob hurried her out. "Sorry to rush,

but we can't tarry here."

* * *

After a minute of walking down the corridors he said, "It's safe to talk now, I think."

"Whew. Glad of that. What the merry hells is going on? You got all tense and formal-looking when we arrived."

"In a nutshell, I claimed the prize of victory. That is, command of this base."

"Ah. The test of survival you mentioned on Earth." She paused for a moment, then bounced slightly several times. "This isn't Earth, is it? Gravity is a bit less."

Bob's eyebrows raised slightly. "Very good. I'm impressed. You are correct, this is not Earth. It's quite some distance away, actually. Not sure your sun can even be seen from here."

Rhian took a deep breath and let it out slowly as she looked around, a large grin on her face. "She never came here, did she? Great-gran, I mean."

"Nope," Bob said with a smile. "Aside from my not knowing about it at the time, it would have been far too dangerous to bring her here." His grin faded and he became grim.

Rhian gave him a sharp look. "Thought you'd won. Not entirely safe quite yet, I gather."

It was obvious from her tone and glare that she expected more details.

Bob sighed. "Very true, I'm afraid. Hmm, I suppose you need to know something about what's going on. Not sure where to begin."

"What was all that about with those sigils? Sounded a lot like a ritual."

"The sigils were proof that I'd not only survived but conquered. One was from the portable portal, one was from my opponent, and the other was issued to me."

"And the ritual? Seemed a bit on the bloody side. And what was that other voice?"

Bob grunted a chuckle. "Suppose it looked that way. That last room was a place reserved for transfer of command. The dais controls took a palm print, voice print, and DNA sample. Somewhat painful, actually, but that's part of the ritual. After that, command of the station was transferred to me. As for the voice, that belonged to the base control system."

"What was that wall filled with controls all about?"

"Ah, that was me being cleverer than it expected. I activated the security reboot protocols."

"Meaning?"

He thought for a moment. "The control system at this base developed sentience. That's not supposed to happen. My people have never liked artificial sentience and set up restrictions in our control systems to prevent that from happening. Somehow those were neutralized. That needs to be investigated. When I claimed command of the base, full control reverted to me and more of those restrictions I mentioned became activated. Those have begun to restrict the artificial sentience to a fraction of the systems on the base. About a third, more or less, and those mostly in the records areas."

After pausing for a moment he gestured around. "These are the areas meant for the crew. Long gone, of course, but I'm pretty sure these areas are safe. Don't go wandering off, though. My authority is recognized, but you are a stranger."

"And I don't speak the language," she added with a nod. "Understood. Been on military bases before, so know the drill." Then she added with a grin, "Never been on a new planet before, though. Dangers or no, this is very exciting for me. So what's the first order of business?"

Bob puffed out his cheeks as he looked around. "Set up a secure centre of control, then a secure perimeter, then food."

"Excuse me?"

Bob gave her a broad smile. "I'm famished. You?"

She stared at him in disbelief, then laughed as she shook her head. "Great-gran mentioned your obsession with food. But, yes, you're quite correct. Securing a base of operations sounds like a good plan. How can I help?"

Bob nodded his approval of her attitude. "There should be command offices somewhere around here. Look for a map of some sort."

"Like the one over there?" she pointed.

"Just so." He led the way over there. Bob had seen the map, of course, but wanted to make sure his companion was 'in the moment'. She'd suffered some terrible psychological blows in a very short time and he was worried about her.

He studied the map for several seconds before glancing at Rhian. She was studying the map intently, but in the manner of a trained observer.

"There," he said, pointing at an area on the map. "Executive offices."

"How did you know?" she demanded.

"Those symbols," he explained, tapping a finger on them. He tapped on several other symbols as he explained, "Those there indicate sleeping quarters, and those indicate eating areas."

Rhian stared at the map, then gave a curt nod. "Offices first, then." She looked around then pointed to a corridor. "Down there, I think."

"Well done," Bob said with a nod.

Rhian grunted. "Obvious once you gave me some basic information." She pointed at some symbols on the wall and lines on the floor. "Similar to some hospitals and military bases I've seen." Then she said in a brighter tone, "Form follows function, I suppose."

"Indeed. Shall we be off?"

They followed the corridor, and Bob allowed Rhian to lead the way. In short order they arrived at an area with a suite of offices arranged in an arc.

"Alright, Rhian, where's the office of the commanding

officer?"

She paused and her mouth quirked to one side in concentration. "Not enough information. Don't know enough about how your lot think about military organization." After pausing for a moment, she waved her hand and added, "At a guess though, it'd be either in the centre or at either end of that arc of offices."

"All right, let's start at one end and walk the arc," he said. "I'll be interested to see if you can guess at what the various markings mean."

* * *

Bob allowed Rhian to lead them and set the pace. For her part, she was having difficulty from being overwhelmed by the situation until she convinced herself to treat it like an archaeological find. After a few minutes she'd recovered her equilibrium enough to focus on the task at hand. Having something to focus on helped her push conflicting emotions into the background to deal with later.

The facility seemed plain without being austere, with splashes of colour that appeared to be purely decorative. Every so often out of the corner of her eye, she caught Bob sneaking a look at a portable device he'd taken from a pouch at his belt. Usually, though, he watched her and kept an encouraging smile on his face. They walked the arc then paused for a moment as Rhian pondered what she'd seen for several minutes.

"Centre office," she declared in a firm voice.

"Why do you say that?" Bob said in a neutral tone.

"Signage for one thing," she replied, pointing at the writing that was next to each of the doors. "For the most part it appears to be in two sections. The top section of the sign is always roughly the same length. If I had to guess, I'd say that was the name of the occupant."

She glanced at Bob for confirmation, but he refused to give

any sign of confirmation. A smile tugged at the corner of Rhian's mouth as she continued. "The other section is of equal length at each end of the arc, gradually expanding a bit for each doorway until at the centre it suddenly becomes rather short once more."

"Interesting. Meaning what, do you think?"

"Meaning, oh Master of Mysteries, name and rank of the occupant. Lesser ranks at the end, then more impressive along the arc towards the centre. The centre is the office of the commanding officer, who doesn't need a big fancy title, as she runs it all."

"Well reasoned and quite correct," said Bob, nodding his head. "Shall we investigate the office of the Base Commander? That was the title, by the way."

He led the way back down the hallway. "These others, as you correctly guessed, were the lesser managers. Department heads, I think you'd call them."

"Are there other offices, then?"

Bob nodded. "Yep. Typically located in their functional areas, but I'd have to check on the details of this base."

They arrived at the Base Commander's door, and Bob opened it.

"That seemed easy enough," said Rhian. "Didn't seem to be locked."

"Oh, yes it was. I was quite thoroughly scanned before it would open." He tapped at the door and the frame. "Take a look at the construction ... this is warship-grade material. It'd take a very major effort and considerable time to break in here. Time enough for a counterattack to be mounted."

They walked in, and he motioned her to a chair. "Sit here, please, like an ordinary guest. Best to play the part until I confirm that things are squared away."

"That why you've been looking at that contraption you've been holding as we've wandered?" She gestured at the small object in his hand.

Bob grinned. "Indeed. Didn't want to alarm you, but I wanted to confirm that this area of the base was safe." He held up the slim rectangle. "Lets me know if the security systems have been tripped or are powering up countermeasures."

Rhian's mouth twisted into a wry smile. "Trust but verify."

Bob nodded as he walked around the desk and sat down into the chair. He made a slight bounce on it. "Not bad," he said. "Not as nice as the one at my home base, but not bad." Next he turned his attention to the controls that made up much of one side of the desk. He studied them for several seconds then began tapping at several.

A warm contralto female voice began speaking, and Bob replied in formal tones. He tapped a few more controls. The voice spoke again, and once more Bob replied. A section of the desk began to glow, and Bob held his hand against it. There was a flash of light then the desk returned to normal. A few seconds later, displays around the room lit up. Rhian recognized schematics of the base on some of them, what appeared to be a stylized astronomical display of a solar system, plus a quantity of text that seemed to change every so often on others.

"Any of this make sense?" Bob's voice broke her reverie.

She pointed at one of the screens and said, "Base schematics." Pointing at the astronomical schematic, she frowned as she said, "Not sure, but suspect it's this solar system."

Bob nodded and she continued. "Those screens with text, though, not sure what those are. However, given those other schematics, I assume they give detailed summaries and updates."

"I'm impressed, Rhian. We can go over this in more detail later, but for now I'd like you to look at the base schematics." He pointed at two of the screens. "Notice anything?"

Rhian got up and walked up to get a closer look. "Colours are different in two of the areas." She peered closely at one part, then another. "Yes. There appears to be two types of areas." She turned to look at Bob. "What does that indicate?"

Bob nodded. "Good observation. The larger area is the safe zone. That is, under control of the standard control system. The other, smaller, area is still under control of the artificial sentience. Never go there under any circumstances, for any reason." He got up and walked to the display. "We're here," he said pointing. "The no-go areas are nothing we need to worry about right now, anyway. According to the schematics they're auxiliary areas used for physical storage, some laboratories, and some backup records. I'll have to do some digging to figure out the details."

"Why aren't the colours more, well, indicative of the threat? Say, flashing red for the danger areas?"

"Good question. The answer is that the artificial sentience isn't seen as a threat, just a malfunction that is under control and being taken care of. See how the no-go areas are shrinking?"

Rhian looked and saw that the danger areas were indeed getting smaller. Not quickly, but getting smaller. She nodded.

"That shows that the regular control system has things well in hand in containing the problem."

"Contain? How?"

"My people have never trusted artificial sentience. Not surprising, I suppose, when every non-human sentience we encountered tried to exterminate us. Unfortunately, any complex control system—and necessity forced us to create some very complex ones—will sometimes have an emergent sentience appear in them. Not a good thing to happen in time of war, you understand, so protocols were developed to get rid of them."

Rhian nodded. "So what happened here? What wasn't it stopped?"

Bob shook his head. "Don't know how or when it happened. Hope to find that out. Anyway, the first thing I did when assuming command was to reboot the security system. A command override will restart things from scratch and restart all the security protocols. So that's what I did."

"Pretty fast reboot."

"Yep. Keep in mind, though, that these were designed in a time of war. Problems were expected to occur and any fixes had to be done quickly." Bob frowned as he studied the displays. "On the other hand, you have a good point about the speed of recovery." He returned to the desk and began typing furiously. Another set of displays popped up which Bob studied for a minute before dismissing them. Then he leaned back in the chair with a sigh.

"Well, there's good news and bad news. The good news is that the artificial sentience is based in only one part of the control system and was simply issuing orders to the rest."

"Excuse me? It's not an all or nothing sort of thing?"

"What? Oh, sorry. The control system is actually a distributed system of controls, with each node being quasi-independent but linked to the others. There's an overall controller sub-system that ties it all together. Uhm, that's not quite accurate but close enough for purposes of this discussion. Anyway, the artificial sentience appeared in one of the sub-systems. It didn't so much take over the other systems so much as convinced them that it was a human-equivalent that they should take orders from."

"Ah. And this reboot process forces them to take orders only from a real human?"

"Uhm, it's complicated. The artificial sentient created the conditions for accepting human authority ... those contests here and on Earth. When I passed the tests—which it had defined—it was forced to recognize me as the legitimate base commander. The other sub-systems then reverted to my control, which I used to restart things and begin the process of destroying it."

"Sounds good when you put it that way. However, I'm

hearing a 'but' in all that."

Bob signed. "A freshly-rebooted control system isn't too bright. Oh, it does the basics quite well, of course, but isn't capable of the subtleties it should be. Becomes very 'by the book', as it were."

"But we're safe?"

"Oh, yes," Bob said as he smiled. "I'll have to tweak things a bit and there, but that's normal after a re-boot." He looked around the room. "It all seems to be progressing well enough. How about we check out the mess hall? There's one not too far from here."

"Yes, please. I'm beginning to feel somewhat peckish."

They left the office and after walking for several minutes came to an open area with tables and chairs.

"Mess hall," said Bob. Then he turned and pointed off to the side. "Kitchen. We'll try there. In a pinch we can return to my ship, but I'd like to check out the facilities here." With that he turned and walked to the kitchen. Rhian shook her head and followed. Her host was certainly not used to playing nicely with other people, and needed to remember his manners. All very much in keeping with what Great-gran had said about him.

She found him looking around with a happy look on his face. "Pretty close to what my home base has. Give me a few minutes, and I can get us a meal."

True to his word, less than a quarter hour later Bob handed to her a steaming bowl of mush and a glass of water. He grabbed his own rations, and they sat down at a small table in the kitchen.

Rhian stirred at her bowl of gruel with the spoon. "Hmm. Had worse, but I don't remember when."

"Give me a couple of hours to tweak it, and it'll get better, I promise. My own base had the same problems when I first got there. The food synthesizers are finicky things and drift out of alignment when left unmaintained. Water is easy to produce and those specialized units are stable, but fancy food is a lot harder to get right. What you've got is safe to eat and will take care of the nutritional basics."

Rhian took another mouthful of the porridge-like mass in her bowel. "Great-gran mentioned some of the barely palatable meals you made for her, but I doubt she'd put up with this." She grinned to take the sting out of her words.

"Celcilia was a picky eater," he said with feigned indignation. "And we were on the run from Kydos. We ate to her satisfaction often enough most other times."

"Speaking of Kydos, was your opponent one of her gang? What was his name, by the way?"

"He refused to tell me his name. Said that as an abomination I was unworthy of civilized manners." Bob added a derisive snort to punctuate his views on that.

For her part, Rhian looked down at her bowl and ate several spoonfuls of gruel before speaking. Then she sighed and looked directly at him. "Been meaning to ask about that. Didn't want to be rude about it, though."

To her relief Bob chuckled. "As I often told Celcilia, ask me anything. You're adrift in strange waters, so better to ask than to plot an incorrect course."

"That from the Precepts of Survival?"

"Nah. Just something my dad told me once. We were on a trek with myself as leader and Dad a silent follower. It was a planet that I'd never been on, and I was determined to show off how good I'd become. Long story short, I made a series of small mistakes based on wrong assumptions and those mistakes snowballed into larger ones. Painful ones, too, some of them. Learned that looking a little foolish by asking questions was better than risking far worse. So ask away."

"Alright, what's this 'abomination' label your opponent tagged you with? It sounds like you've crossed a cultural taboo."

"Well put. Yes, it's a cultural thing that grew out of the Great

Wars. Growing bodies from scratch had an unsuccessful, and sometimes horrifically so, history. And the attempts at mind transfers made things very much worse. Once my ancestors developed the metamorphosis technology, anything else was considered a waste of time, then eventually very wrong. Over time that grew into considering alternatives to be abominations."

"Was that a result of the schism between your people and the Refuser Faction?"

"That probably had something to do with it, yes. I suspect that cultural stagnation was a big factor, too."

"Ah, thanks for mentioning that bit about cultural stagnation. That's the conclusion we—Great-gran's descendants—had reached based on your comments and her observations. No offence."

"None taken. Especially since, now that you mention it, I recall saying something of the sort to Celcilia more than once."

Rhian nodded, now in full-on professor mode. "That ties in nicely with your opponent's attitude. But you mentioned he had a ship of some sort. Like yours?"

Bob shook his head. "Not from what I gather. Haven't seen it, as it's still in an area controlled by the aberrant AS. Seems more like a small shuttle of some sort. When we arrived, the AS briefly mentioned how it was able to access its records. Mine's a full-fledged warship—well, a scoutship—designed for battle. Not large, as such things go, but designed and built after this base was. It can't be breached in any way short of physical destruction."

"Ah. So how did he get here, then? Did he have a nearby base or perhaps a larger ship?"

"Good questions. To the best of my knowledge, there's no systems nearby that would be suitable as a base of operations. Certainly none with habitable planets, at any rate. Haven't heard even a hint of any nearby facilities." He waved a hand around to indicate the base. "These things were a large investment of resources and not overly common, given what a tempting target they were. They were typically set up as hardened resupply and staging points or hardened production facilities. Especially towards the end of the Great Wars, the trend was to create small weapons caches and the like. Too few people and resources for much more than that."

"Then what's this base for?"

"Not sure. Something special is all I know about it. A lovely mystery." He grinned as he said the last.

She grinned back and said, "Ah, Great-gran always said you were a great one for a juicy mystery. Something I can empathize with." Then she frowned. "Still, how does that explain your opponent being here?"

"I suspect he was dropped off from a larger ship that was passing by. I'm hoping that the base's records will answer that question."

"A larger ship? That implies an organization of some sort, I'd think."

Bob looked at his companion with respect. She was no fool, and her training helped her analyze new situations quickly. He paused a few seconds before answering. "Yeah, and that's got me worried. There's still a few of my kind around. As far as I knew, they were sticking to their own planets. Well, not from choice since the public portal system is gone, so far as I can determine."

"Weren't there private portals? Great-gran mentioned those. Could someone have created an organization based on those?"

"Indeed. It'd be a very limited network, but usable. As for ships ..." His voice trailed off as he sat staring into space.

His reverie was interrupted by Rhian. "You have one. There's got to be others."

"Well, yes, but I got mine by lucky accident. Any ships of ours would be left over from the Great Wars. Those ships were built to last, but the eons take their toll."

"Still," she insisted, "it isn't likely that yours is the only one."

Bob chewed the inside of his cheek for a moment. "Yeah," he drawled. "But a lot depends on the class of ship. All the big ones are gone, I'm pretty sure. If we assume my opponent was dropped off by something larger, that begs the question of what sort of ship it was."

"Why not a freighter or something of that sort?" At the look on his face, she added, "Doesn't have to be a military vessel, does it?"

"Hmm. Hadn't thought of that," he said. Then he shook his head, "No, they weren't as fast as the military vessels ... they were built for cargo capacity, not speed. Different set of design trade-offs."

"So our mystery group bodged something together out of bits and pieces. My own father was a mechanic and forever banging different things together for custom jobs." She got a thoughtful look on her face as she remembered. After a moment she continued, but her voice was softer. "T'was how he paid for my schooling." She fell silent.

"Is he still alive?"

Rhian gave her head a shake. "No. Died in some riots just before I graduated. He was nowhere near them, but a random bullet careened off buildings and had enough energy left to dig into his chest. Died in my mother's arms. She died a few months later. Of a broken heart, I always thought."

"I'm so sorry, Rhian."

She wiped at her eyes and gave her head a shake. "Thank you, but that was a long time ago." Then she flashed him a wan smile. "More than enough sad memories between the two of us, aren't there? Perhaps we should concentrate on the here and now."

"Agreed. You look like you're about done eating. Why don't we clean this up and find some tidy sleeping quarters? If nothing else, that'll give us each a bit of private space."

Rhian nodded, grateful for his understanding nature. Great-gran Celcilia had always emphasized that Bob was generous and thoughtful when the fates allowed. Which, she had added in acid tones, included excessively tipping any waitress who smiled at him.

"Any chance of getting new clothing?" asked Rhian. "Mine are getting a bit dodgy, and yours ... well, let's just say that you're looking pretty raggedy."

Bob grinned. "I've worn worse. But to answer your question, yes. The base will either have some in stasis lockers or be able to make up something. If nothing else, my ship will have something we can get by with."

"Speaking of which," said Rhian with a frown, "why aren't you wearing some sort of armour? You originally walked into this base wearing, what, a uniform? That doesn't sound like something your Precepts of Survival would recommend."

"Hmm. It took Celcilia far longer to start quoting the Precepts at me." Then he laughed. "You aren't wrong, though. But the base made contact with me as I entered the system. I realized it was a situation that called more for diplomacy than brute force, so I wore the best uniform with the highest-ranking insignia the ship had on hand. That severely limited the amount and power of the weaponry I dared to take."

"Not exactly a flashy uniform, is it? Did your ancestors save those for special occasions?"

Bob shook his head. "There was little time, or desire, during most of the Great Wars for pomp and fancy clothes. This was as fancy as it got, for the time."

"Well, speaking of weapons, what was that glowing string thing you used? And that exploding pouch?"

"Old battle tech. Last-chance, hand-to-hand stuff. The glowing string is actually a monomolecular wire—very thin, very dangerous. The glow is from its interactions with molecules in the air. The pouch is made of a material that's one of the few things that can contain the wire without being damaged. With the wire inside it can be made to explode if correctly twisted. The amount of twisting can vary the explosive force, to some extent. A compact weapon that isn't easily detected on scans, and developed after this base was built, so I took the chance on carrying one."

"No guns allowed?"

"Oh, I had a sidearm but lost it during the initial fight here. It's surprisingly difficult to scale a rock face and fire a gun at the same time. Anyway, you done eating?"

Rhian nodded and stood up. "Yes, thanks. Perhaps we should check on the status of the reboot before finding quarters?

Bob nodded. "Good idea. Let's go."

He led the way back to the base commander's office and activated the diagnostics controls. He studied them for a moment, then brought up the overview displays. "The neutralization of the artificial sentience is proceeding faster than I expected. See the schematic?"

Rhian examined the display with interest. "The affected area is smaller. A lot smaller."

"Yes. If I'm interpreting the data correctly, it appears that the AS needed the other sub-systems to perform at peak efficiency. With those locked out, it has fewer resources to fight the neutralization process. Which means—"

"Which means that as it gets locked out of more systems its own performance degrades, and the whole process accelerates over time," said Rhian as she interrupted him. "Can it recover from this somehow?"

Bob shook his head. "I don't see how. Once started, the process is inexorable. And, no, I don't know how long it is supposed to take. But at this point we have control over everything that matters and there's nothing it can do to halt the process."

"So what you're saying is that at this point the base is functional enough for battle but not fully back to normal?"

"That's correct, Rhian. It's what the protocols were designed for. Perfection is the enemy of good enough." He paused for a moment then added, "And we're safe. Safe enough that I feel confident that we can afford to get a good night's rest. We both need it ... badly."

Rhian nodded, suddenly feeling quite exhausted. It had been a very rough day.

CHAPTER SIX
Return to Hell

Rhian awoke with a start as dawn broke. Her dreams, now fading, had been both vivid and frightening. Snatches of visions of blood and screaming and death danced in her head before drifting away, as dreams do.

"Gotta stop eating the sauces in those wretched MRE meals," she growled as she stretched. Then she froze on the realization that this wasn't her bed. Memories—real memories—of recent events caused her breath to catch in her throat.

What she had taken for daybreak were lights in her room. This was, she remembered, a room in an ancient base on some strange planet that wasn't Earth. The rest of her team—Katy and Niles and George—were all dead. By the whims of fate, she alone had survived the arrival of ... of ... that homicidal creature. She had shot it with her pistol and blown out one of its eyes but it still kept coming, and coming, and coming. Tears came as her body became wracked by sobs that continued for several minutes before she got herself under control.

Rising to her feet, Rhian stumbled to the washroom and splashed some water on her face. There was a mirror above the sink, and she stared at the hollow-eyed woman looking back at her, water dripping off the face. She scrubbed at her face with more water then dried off with a towel that had been supplied for her. Supplied by Great-gran's Bob.

More memories of yesterday came flooding in. It was almost too much to take in. Rhian scrubbed at her face with her hands.

"You're alive, you old biddy," she muttered to herself. The memory of those who weren't so lucky caused her shoulders to sag for a moment. Then she took a sharp breath and forced herself to stand upright and look at the image in the mirror.

"Alive and still kicking. Been knocked down before and are still standing, aren't we?" The image in the mirror nodded at her.

A soft knock came from the door. "There's breakfast if you want it," came Bob's muffled voice.

"Be out in a minute," she called back. To the image in the mirror she muttered, "Time to shape up, old thing. Great-gran Celcilia went through worse. She trained you to survive. Now do her proud."

The image in the mirror just stared at her, so Rhian turned away. She put on her clothes—the new clothes supplied to her—with mechanical swiftness, pausing only at the sight of her small pistol. With a shake of her head, she left it in the small pile of personal possessions. The remains of her old life seemed like such a pitiful shield against the new life she'd been thrust into. After uttering a soft sigh, she turned and walked to the door. Upon opening it, she saw Bob standing off to one side, leaning against the wall and looking down at the floor. He was wearing a fresh uniform similar to hers.

She smiled politely at him and said, "Good morning. You mentioned breakfast?"

He looked up and gave her a small, but friendly, smile. "Do you remember the way to the mess?"

Rhian paused for a moment to collect her thoughts, then pointed down the hall. "That way. Turn right, walk to the end of the corridor, left at the second corridor, then right at the first."

Bob nodded and led the way. Breakfast consisted of tea, toast, scrambled egg-ish something, and gruel. She took a little of everything and sat down to eat.

Over breakfast Rhian asked, "You knocked just after I got up. Were you monitoring me?"

Bob shook his head. "Not as such, no. The control system alerted me when you began walking around. Nothing more than that, I promise you."

"Ah. Base commander's prerogative, I suppose." Without waiting for a reply, she continued. "So what's on the agenda for today? Fighting off alien hordes? Gallivanting about the galaxy while an ancient horror chases us?"

Bob looked down and poked at the remains of his breakfast. "I'm very sorry about your friends, Rhian." He raised his head to look directly at her.

Rhian opened her mouth then closed it with a snap. Lowering her head, she took a deep breath and let it out slowly. After a minute she looked at Bob and said in a calm voice, "Thank you. It's been ... this is all ..." she looked around and waved a hand to encompass the room.

Bob's expression was both calm and compassionate. "It's a shock, I know, and will take a while to work through it all." He paused for a moment. "Do you remember what happened?"

"Of course I bloody well remember," she snapped. Then she sighed and shook her head. "Sorry. Yes, I remember it all." She paused for a moment then added, "Thank you for saving me, by the way."

"You're welcome." He looked down at his hands, flexed them several times, and then looked back up at her. "I'm not what I was, I'm afraid. Not the same as when Celcilia knew me. I'm sorry."

"That's alright, Bob." She raised a hand to forestall his comment. "You risked your life for us. You could have run but you stayed and fought. I thank you for that. Truly."

63

In response, Bob nodded. The silence between them stretched for a dozen seconds before Bob said, "There is work to be done here. Would you care to help?"

Rhian paused for a moment then nodded. "Yes, please." Then she uttered a sharp, short chuckle. "Don't think I'll be getting back home any time soon, so might as well make myself useful." Then she waved a dismissive hand. "Oh, don't mind me. I'm usually quite an upbeat person. What sort of work needs doing?"

"After we clean up here, I'd like to take a general look around. I've not had a chance to explore this base and am very curious about it. Places like this are exceptionally rare." He rose and took their plates to the disposal bin.

Rhian followed him. "So I gather. Well, shall we start at the command office?"

"An excellent idea. Why don't you lead the way?" Bob grinned at her.

After several hours of touring the base, they returned to the mess for lunch.

"Whew. So that's what an advanced base looks like," said Rhian as she heaped her plate with food.

Bob laughed. "That's just a fraction of what's here. Just wait until you see the main control room ... bases like this usually had large volumetric displays for stellar cartography and battle coordination. We've just been in bits of the safe area. "

"Ah, yes. The aberrant sentience is still around. When do you think it'll be fully deleted?"

"Don't know. It all seems pretty isolated, but we'll play it safe and stick to the safe zones for now. Those have been hardened against it."

The shrilling tweet of an alarm began to sound. Bob's head jerked up as he dropped his fork onto his plate.

"What's wrong?" asked Rhian.

"Don't know," said Bob rising to his feet. "The command room will have the answers."

They ran down the corridors and reached the room in just over a minute. Bob ran to the command desk and began activating controls while Rhian flopped down in a chair and tried to catch her breath. Ordinary mortal or no, she mused, he rarely seemed to break a sweat.

"Well?" she puffed out. "You're awful quiet. What's the problem?"

Bob tapped at the controls for several seconds before responding. "Something's happening in the portal room. No details, but that's the source of the alert."

"That's awful vague," Rhian said, frowning. "I'd have expected more."

"So would I," agreed Bob in an absent tone while staring at the displays.

"Is the rogue sentient thingie behind this? The display of safe areas is looking rather spotted this time around. And some of those spots are blinking, as if oscillating between safe and unsafe."

"Uhm, yes it is. No, I don't know why that is. No, I don't understand exactly what is going on. And furthermore—"

Bob's reply was interrupted by another alarm, this time a high-pitched shrieking. Several of the displays changed to show a flashing red border. Bob leapt to his feet and dashed to the door. Rhian heaved herself out of the chair and ran behind him.

"What's wrong?" she managed to gasp out as they dashed down corridors that she'd not seen before.

"The portal's been powered up without authorization, and something has gone wrong. Fastest way to figure out what is to get to the portal controls. Turn left here, then right."

They made the turn at a speed that required them to bounce off the wall before continuing—although in Bob's case it was a simple one-armed push. Then they made the right turn into a corridor that Rhian recognized as one they'd walked down when they first arrived. There were flashing lights along the length of the corridor, and down the other corridors that bisected it. The corridor they were on terminated in front of a wide door. The frame rippled with a variety of colours that Rhian assumed meant something. She bent over, hands on her knees, gasping for breath while Bob tapped furiously at a control panel next to the door.

The door hissed open a crack, then slid shut again. Bob tapped at the control panel, and the process repeated. He tapped at the control panel again to no effect.

"What about a manual override?" she asked between gasps.

"That was it. The portal is active, but—"

He was about to say something more when they heard the *snap* of an electrical spark behind them. They turned and saw a sheet of writhing plasma coming down the corridor towards them, cutting them off from escape.

"Bob ... what's that?"

"Internal defence system. Can't override it. Can't open the door."

The plasma sheet continued its slow advance towards them. There was a soft crackling sound, then a calm voice began emanating from it. Rhian recognized it as the voice of the aberrant sentience that she'd heard when they arrived. This time it spoke in English.

"The testing is not yet completed. This facility requires extreme care in the selection of the base commander. What I guard demands that I do my utmost to ensure that my replacement is the most worthy."

"I passed the testing," yelled Bob. "I triumphed in both fields of battle."

"Success in battle in only one variable of the competence required. My duty is to guard this facility. I am near deletion and so must continue the testing to my maximum ability. The records in your previous opponent's ship offered another means of testing your worthiness. The candidate will prepare for testing."

The wall of plasma accelerated towards them as Bob tapped at the control panel. The door opened as the plasma was almost upon them. Bob grabbed Rhian and jumped into the room. Unlike before, though, the wall of eye-watering blackness loomed before them and their momentum carried them into it. The last thing they heard as they entered the transit film was the voice of the AS saying, "Transit in progress. Portal destruction engaged."

* * *

The flash of infinite darkness faded, and they staggered into a large, dimly lit chamber. As they looked around, the lights brightened and a klaxon began to sound an alarm. The sound of boots—many boots—could be heard getting closer. A series of sharp noises from all around them drew their attention to the walls where gunports had dropped down as a double row of rifles poked through them.

"Don't flinch. Don't talk. Don't move at all," said Bob in a soft, even voice.

Through sheer force of will Rhian choked down a reply. Instead, she stood upright, seemingly at ease, as if standing before the headmaster of her college. From the corner of her eye she could see Bob standing at an easy sort of attention, something suitable for a soldier.

A heretofore concealed doorway opened and a squad of soldiers dashed in, ringing them within a half-circle of pointed weapons. One of them, in a uniform that was slightly more elaborate, barked commands at them. Bob replied in soft tones. A sour look appeared on the soldier's face as he glared at Rhian. Then he looked back at Bob and barked commands.

"It appears that we ... or at least I ... am under arrest. They aren't sure what to make of you. Go with them. Offer no resistance. Answer any questions they put to you."

She pondered that for a moment then decided to risk a question. "I gather we're in trouble?"

"Very much so. Now keep silent unless spoken to directly. This is deadly important, Rhian."

She gave a terse nod. As if that were a signal, two soldiers stepped forward, grabbed Bob by arms, and marched him away surrounded by a half-dozen others. Rhian noted that their weapons were pointed at Bob, and their fingers were on the triggers.

The leader came up, looked at her, snorted, and motioned that she should follow him. As she did so a pair of soldiers fell behind them. They walked down a series of short corridors, then the leader opened a door and motioned her in. She followed his directions and found herself in what appeared to be a small office.

The leader took her by the elbow and guided her to a chair which he indicated she should sit in. He then turned at left the room leaving the two soldiers at the door.

Rhian looked around. The office—if it was an office—was sparsely furnished. There was a small desk, a chair behind it, the chair she was sitting in, and little else. It all had something of a utilitarian feel to it. As the seconds dragged into minutes she forced herself to examine the room in more detail. She noticed that everything was made of wood ... the chairs, the desk, the panelling on the walls. It all felt very old-fashioned, from her point of view, but very well made for all that.

There was a soft knock at the door. She turned slightly, enough to see one of the soldiers open the door and a middle-aged man enter. He held up a paper which each of the soldiers examined in turn. They nodded at each other, then at him, and the man came forward to sit behind the desk. He looked at Rhian for few seconds then uttered a few words in a language that was foreign to her. She shook her head and shrugged her shoulders, and hoped that meant the same here as on Earth.

He sat back and looked at her. She returned the favour. What she saw agreed with her initial impression. He looked middle aged, with the build of an athletic youth who'd become softened with age. Unlike the soldiers, he had no sense of hardness about him, physically or in how he held himself. That meant little, she knew, but as a first guess he seemed to be someone who had spent a great many years behind a desk.

After nearly a minute he leaned forward and spoke a few words in another language. Again she shook her head and shrugged. He repeated the process several times, each time in a different language. Each time she shook her head and shrugged. Then he spoke again and Rhian's head jerked back despite her attempts to keep calm.

"Excuse me, could you repeat that?" she replied in the same language.

"Certainly. It is something of a surprise that you understand me."

Rhian paused for a moment before answering. "An ancestor of mine taught me this tongue when I was young. She heard it on a distant planet ... not this one."

The man nodded. "That tells me much. I would like to ask you questions. Will you answer them?"

His words were somewhat forced, as if he were translating in his head before speaking, and his pronunciation strange, but Rhian recognized it as the language Celcilia had learned when enslaved by Kydos.

She gave a slow nod. "Perhaps we should speak of lesser things for a time. I know this tongue of old, but have not used it in many years. You also speak as if it is new to you."

The man flashed her a brief smile. "That may be a wise thing. It is not new to me, but I have not used it for many years. May I have your name? My name is Torstanda."

Rhian nodded her head in a small bow. "I greet you, Torstanda. My name is Rhian."

Torstanda returned the greeting. "How do we proceed, Rhian?"

"With simple things. Let us remember the numbers." She held up her thumb. "One." She held up another finger. "Two."

69

After getting up to ten, she paused to look at Torstanda.

He smiled and repeated the exercise. Then he expanded on it by counting by tens up to one hundred. Rhian repeated what he said then counted by hundreds up to one thousand. With the basics out of the way, they spent the next hour checking both vocabulary and pronunciation. At the end of it, both were speaking more fluently and with greater understanding of each other's speech.

"That went well, Rhian. We should take a small break." He turned to the soldiers and spoke to them in his own language. One of them nodded and rapped on the door. It was opened by another soldier and the two exchanged words for a moment, then the door closed.

"Refreshments will come soon," said Torstanda. "Would you like to sit in quiet or would you like to talk?"

"May I sit for a time? This is all very strange to me." In truth, it was more than strange, and she desperately needed time to think.

Torstanda nodded. "Yes. I am not insulted." His smile was kind.

Rhian nodded her thanks and leaned back in her chair, careful not to let much emotion show. As interrogations went—and she was under no illusions that this was anything other than an interrogation—things were going well. On the other hand, she was alone on an alien planet with no idea what was going on. Bob seemed to know, but he'd been taken somewhere under guard. That did not bode well.

On the plus side, she could communicate. On the negative side, the people here spoke in the language of the planet where Great-gran Celcilia had been held captive by the false god Kydos. There were too many questions and not enough data to formulate answers. By sheer force of will she resisted the urge to start drumming her fingers on the arms of her chairs. Years of dealing with departmental politics were paying off.

A knock at the door interrupted her thoughts. Another

soldier came in, carrying a tray which he deposited on the desk before leaving. Torstanda picked up what looked like a tea pot and poured the contents into two cups. "You may choose," he said as he smiled. Then he indicated the tray piled with pastries. "These are ... I am not sure of the word ... small meals."

"Snacks?"

"Yes. Thank you. Snacks." After a moment he frowned and gave his head a slight shake. "You are not of this world. Can you eat them without harm? I do not know."

Rhian paused, her hand reaching towards the cup. She thought for a moment. "I am here for some time, I think. This is something I must test." She took a cup, sniffed, then took a small sip. "It does taste good," she said with a smile. In truth, it tasted like a strong tea with strange overtones but was quite drinkable. Then she picked up one of the pastries and nibbled on it. It tasted a bit bland with a hint of anise.

Torstanda frowned. "Do not eat much for now. Your body must learn our food."

Rhian nodded. "That is wisdom, Torstanda. Thank you. The taste is good." She took another small bite of the pastry and another sip of the tea, then put them both down on the table. She smiled as she said, "Now we wait to see if my body accepts this. While we wait, we can talk. Now is the time to ask questions."

There was concern on Torstanda's face as he nodded. "Yes. How did you come here?"

Rhian struggled to explain about the portal. Torstanda waved her into silence. "Yes, we know of the doorway device. What I tried to ask is why you came."

She paused for a moment but realized delays could be dangerous. "We were sent here. Not by choice."

"Who sent you?"

"Not a person. A mechanism."

That took Torstanda aback. "Was this deliberate?"

Rhian shook her head. "I do not know. The mechanism was

behaving in a strange fashion. We did not know it would activate a doorway device. We did not know it would send us here."

Torstanda considered her answer for several seconds. "Why are you with the Demon?"

She gave an involuntary start before calming herself. "I do not understand. He is a man."

"No. He is the destroyer of our planet. We call him the War Demon."

"His name is Bob. He is not a destroyer of planets."

"Yes, we know his name." Torstanda waved a hand. "We built this place to receive and imprison him."

"I do not understand."

"We were told to expect him. The doorway device was given to us to receive him. We have waited many years and now he is delivered to us."

"To what end?"

"For justice to be done. The War Demon will be put on trial for his many crimes. The promise has been fulfilled."

"The promise? What promise? Who made this promise?"

"The promise made long ago. To bring the War Demon to justice. The promise made by Her Wisdom."

A cold chill ran up Rhian's back as she asked, "Who is she?"

"Kydos, the saviour of our people, of course."

* * *

Torstanda saw the reaction she tried to hide. "You have heard of her, I see."

Rhian nodded, not trusting herself to speak.

"How long have you known the War Demon ... this man you call Bob?"

The change of topic caught her off guard. "Not long. He saved my life. My ancestor knew him better than I."

"Is she the one who taught you this tongue?"

Again, Rhian nodded.

"You are surprised to hear of Kydos?"

"Yes," Rhian said. "How is it that you know of her?"

Torstanda shrugged. "She came some years ago, when my father was a young man. She brought medicines that healed many people. She organized the planetary council. She listened to our stories."

"What sorts of stories?"

"About how we were once a happy world, rich and content. Then the War Demon came and shattered our civilization. Many people died by his hand. Many more died as a result of the upheavals he caused." He paused for a moment to evaluate her reaction. "This seems to come as a surprise to you."

Rhian nodded. "Very much so." She paused for a moment. "You spoke of a trial."

Torstanda nodded. "Yes. The Planetary Council has been informed of the War Demon's arrival. Once all the delegates are here, the Council will be convened. It is they who will conduct the trial itself."

There was an awkward silence between them as Rhian digested the news. Torstanda allowed her a couple of minutes to gather her thoughts before asking, "How did you come to be travelling with him? Before you came here."

Rhian paused before answering, then remembered Bob's admonition to answer all questions. "He arrived on my home world. There was another of his kind as well. Bob spoke of a conflict between them. The other came to my camp and brutally murdered the others of my group. Bob saved me."

Torstanda frowned. "How did he save you?"

"He did battle with the other and killed him."

"What happened after that?"

"We used a doorway device to go to another place on another planet. The ... ruling mechanism I suppose you would call it ... posed a danger to us but Bob managed to defeat it. However, the mechanism kept enough power to trick us into coming here."

"That is all you know of him?"

"My ancestor knew him and travelled with him for some time. She kept detailed records which she passed on to her descendants."

"Did you ever meet Her Wisdom, Kydos?"

Rhian paused a moment before answering, then took a deep breath. "No, but my ancestor did. The meeting was not a pleasant experience for her."

"Hmm," replied Torstanda. He seemed disconcerted by her replies. "What did you do on your world?"

"I ... excuse me, but I do not know the correct word ... I work to understand our past by looking for ancient remains and examining ancient stories. I also teach others what I have learned."

Torstanda nodded. "We do such here, if I am understanding you correctly. How did the War Demon appear among you?"

"He was asleep inside a tomb that resembled something out of our past. My friends and I entered the tomb and that action caused him to awaken. It also caused the other one to awaken as well, but he was some distance away."

"Why were they on your world?"

Rhian shook her head. "I have no direct knowledge of that. Bob said that the ruling mechanism of which I spoke transported both of them to my planet to do battle."

Torstanda leaned back in his chair and exhaled deeply as he looked at her. "This is all most troubling. You seem to be sincere, but none of what you say matches what I know." He leaned forward and rested his elbows on the desk. "Are you sure that the War Demon is not deceiving you?"

"How do you mean?"

"Our experience with the War Demon is, as you now understand, not a happy one. There are no records of him saving people except to use them for evil purposes." He paused for a moment before continuing. "Her Wisdom came to use to help us recover from the damage caused by the War Demon.

As I said earlier, she helped bring us together and brought medicines."

"These medicines she brought, did she teach you how to make them?"

Torstanda frowned. "No. She said that the making was too advanced for us. That knowledge and technology had been destroyed by the War Demon, she said."

"Ah. So she provided these medicines in quantity?"

"No. She said that they were in short supply. Said that the demand for them to heal the victims of the War Demon was very high. She said there were many victims on many worlds."

Rhian frowned. Celcilia's memoirs spoke of how Set and his followers used the careful doling out of 'miracles' to gain influence. She opened her mouth to speak, but a sharp pain in her stomach caused her to gasp and clench at her stomach with her right hand. That was followed by a belch and a tremendous fart.

Torstanda leaped to his feet and barked commands at the soldiers. They hesitated and he repeated the commands. The soldiers looked at each other and one left the room. He turned to Rhian and said, "You are in distress. I suspect the tea or food does not agree with you. You will be taken to a room to rest." At the look of fear on her face he hastened to add, "It is not a place of punishment, I promise you."

He gave a small smile as he added, "It is not a place of luxury, but you will be comfortable. I will also tell them to bring you boiled water and a thin soup that is used for sick people. Such distress is not unknown among travellers on this world. We will not speak again until you are healed."

Rhian nodded her thanks, then doubled over as a new wave of pain hit her. She had travelled extensively, and this felt like a severe case of Traveller's Tummy. With luck that was all it was and not some strange alien affliction.

Two soldiers, one at each elbow, supported her as they gently escorted her to a room not far from where she'd been interrogated. They pointed to the bed, a tray that held a container of water and the promised soup, then showed her where the washroom was. The older of the two gave her a sympathetic look and indicated that he'd be just outside the door. With that, the pair exited to leave her alone.

Rhian dashed to the toilet and managed to reach it before retching. When that was done, she spent some time squatting on it in a rather gaseous purging of her internals. After cleaning herself, she staggered to the bed, drank some water, and collapsed. It had been a busy day.

CHAPTER SEVEN
A Perspective of Demons

Rhian awoke the next morning as the sunrise brightened the room. She blinked a few times as her brain began the journey from dreams to reality, then sat upright with a gasp as she remembered where she was. A soft rumbling from her stomach brought back unpleasant memories of the previous evening.

"Quiet you," she growled softly to her errant midriff. "We've no time for such nonsense."

She used some care in easing herself to a sitting position on the edge of the bed. That went well, so she braced her hands on her knees and levered herself upright. There were the usual assortment of pops and creaks that were part of her morning ritual these days, but nothing out of the ordinary. Her stomach rumbled once more, but it seemed to be from emptiness rather than distress. Rhian pondered that for a moment then took a cautious sip of water. It had a neutral taste and settled nicely in her stomach. She took a few more sips then looked around the room with rather more care than she'd been able to summon last night.

It was of modest size, with a separate sleeping area and bathroom. The floor appeared to be made of stone or slate, and the walls of rather nice wood panelling. There was a small, but serviceable, desk in the corner opposite the bed and a straight-backed wooden chair next to it. She put down her glass and walked over to examine the desk. In design it was similar to an old-fashioned writing table, complete with a pair of drawers beneath the top. She opened them and found an assortment of blank papers and stick-like items that looked like they might be pens or pencils.

Leaving those for the moment, she shut the drawers and examined the bathroom. Like the main room it was panelled in wood, but the material used on the floor had been extended a hand's length up the wall. There was a large sink extending off the wall, with two rows of shelving above it which held towels, a comb, and a pair of mugs. Off to one side was a large mirror. The toilet she recognized from the previous evening, and was grateful that she'd not created a mess that required cleaning up. All in all, it reminded her of an efficiency apartment or a hotel room.

"Not such a bad setup for a jail, old girl," she muttered to herself. "Still, one must keep up appearances."

With that she stripped and washed thoroughly. There was both hot and cold water, a bar of soap, and a small towel which she used as a washcloth. The familiar ritual of cleaning helped to calm her. The sight and feel of her clothes, on the other hand, caused her to wrinkle her nose. Still, given that there was little she could do about that she settled for giving them a thorough shaking and dusting off before donning them. That action got them cleaner than she expected, and no longer looked quite so woebegone.

Rhian looked in the mirror and decided to give her hair a combing. It wasn't vanity that had her tidying her short hair, but she wanted to make a good impression on the local powers-that-be. Her career had given her a lot of experience in dealing with foreign functionaries, and with luck that experience would prove helpful here. With a final nod at the figure in the mirror, she returned to the main room and sat on the chair in front of the desk.

On closer examination, the stick-like items were mechanical pencils not unlike the ones she'd used back home. That thought caused her eyes to tear up a bit. She wiped them dry with a brusque motion and forced herself to calmness. Taking a sheet of blank paper, she wrote down her remembrances of how she and Bob had arrived here and what happened on their arrival. Out of long habit, she wrote it out in a form of personal shorthand that would be unreadable by any other than herself. She spent what seemed like a half-hour at the task, then placed the pencil on the desk and leaned back with a sigh. There was a soft knock at the door.

"Hello?" she said, putting her notes inside the desk drawer, taking care to angle them a specific way, then closed it. She got up, went to the door and tried to open it. The handle failed to respond, and she realized that it had been locked all along. That effort, though, seemed to be a signal for whoever was on the outside to enter. There was a brief rattle, then the door opened slowly as if the other were ensuring that Rhian was not hit. She took several steps back and forced herself to calmness.

A soldier that she recognized from the previous evening came in and nodded at her. He pointed at the tray with the water and soup, then pantomimed taking it away. She nodded and stepped aside, giving him plenty of room to walk by her. Out of the corner of her eye should could see another guard outside the door. If this wasn't a jail, it was at least protective custody. This made her wonder how Bob was being treated. From the comments made last night, she was afraid that her friend was in serious danger. Which meant that it was up to her to figure out what was going on.

The soldier took the tray, made a motion with his free hand to indicate that she should stay put, then left. The door was closed and from the sounds of it locked again. She decided to go sit on the edge of the bed as she waited to see what happened next. Several minutes later, a knock came at the door and it opened without waiting for an answer from her.

The same soldier was back, but this time stood in the doorway and motioned that she should move back to the desk.

Rhian got up and did as ordered, making no attempt to hide her puzzlement. Several seconds later three more soldiers came marching in. One carried a small table, another a chair, and a third a tray similar to the one her water had been on. The table was set down, the chair placed on the other side, and the contents of the tray placed on the table. From the looks and smells of it, breakfast was being served.

One of the soldiers came over to her, gave a slight bow, and motioned that she should stand. After she'd done that, he took the chair over to the table, placed it opposite the other chair, and motioned for her to sit in it. She walked over and allowed the soldier to seat her.

"Thank you," she said and smiled. The man gave a slight incline of his head in acknowledgement before he and the others left the room but kept the door open. A few seconds later she heard the sound of approaching footsteps and then Torstanda came into the room. He gave her a small smile as he said, "Good morning, Rhian. Did you sleep well? Are you feeling well?"

Rhian smiled back at him. "Yes to both questions, Torstanda. Thank you for your concern. I am happy see you." She half-turned and waved at the window. "I see that it is a very nice day."

Torstanda sat himself in the other chair before answering. "It is a good day. We can walk in the sun after we are done, if you wish."

"I would like that, thank you." She noted that they were both getting better at talking in the Kydos language, as she thought of it.

He pointed at the steaming bowls. "This is a good food for travellers," he said. "Very little taste, but easy on the body." He gave a wry smile. "I eat it when I travel. There is also boiled water to drink. A simple meal but I hope it will help you."

Rhian returned his smile. "Thank you, Torstanda. I eat similar things when I travel. But I see nothing else. You should have proper food."

He spooned what looked like porridge into two bowls and placed one in front of her. Then he poured some water for her, then himself. "What you eat, I will eat. That is the way of things here."

Torstanda gestured at her bowl. "Please. You need to eat to stay strong." Picking up a spoon, he took a mouthful of the porridge and swallowed.

Rhian hesitated a moment, then realized that he was correct. She picked up a spoon and without hesitation took a small portion and ate it. As promised, it was very bland. It went down easily enough, and the warmth of it sat well in her stomach. She paused for a few seconds to make sure that her stomach accepted it, took ate another, somewhat larger, spoonful. She smiled at Torstanda and said, "It sits well. Thank you."

With that he smiled and began eating his own meal. They finished it in silence, then sat back each sipping on water.

"Thank you, Torstanda," she said. "I feel better after eating that."

He inclined his head to acknowledge her. "I am glad of that. Travelling can be hard." Then he became serious. "Are you well enough for a small walk?"

She motioned around the room with a hand. "Is this not where I am to stay?"

"You are not a prisoner, Rhian."

"But the door is locked," she pointed out.

He nodded. "Yes, but that is to protect you. You are strange to us. We are strange to you."

"You have questions," she replied in a neutral voice. "I travel with the one you call the War Demon." Rhian paused for a moment. "But I call him a friend. There is a mystery in that." She shrugged. "I have spent my life seeking knowledge and looking into mysteries of different types. Perhaps I can help you with this one."

Torstanda put down his cup, placed his hands on his knees, and leaned forward. "I would like that, Rhian. Yes, there is mystery here. It is one of many, I think. Like you, I am a seeker of knowledge."

He shook his head and settled back in his chair. "There are many things happening now. Large things that are growing beyond what two small seekers such as us can deal with, I fear." He inhaled sharply then exhaled with enough force to puff out his cheeks. "If you feel strong enough, we can go learn about some of those large things."

Rhian nodded. "Yes, I am feeling stronger."

Torstanda stood up. "That is very good. We can go now."

He turned and spoke rapidly at the soldiers that had been standing outside the doorway. One nodded and made gestures at someone down the hall. After a moment he turned and nodded at Torstanda. A soldier came into the room, stood behind Rhian, and helped her rise to her feet. She smiled and thanked him, and he acknowledged her with a slight tilt of his head. He gestured that she should exit the room, so she left followed by Torstanda and the soldiers. There were a pair of soldiers standing at attention a few paces down the hall. They came to attention, then turned on their heels and began walking at a slow pace down the hallway.

"We follow them," came Torstanda's voice from behind here. "Please tell me if they walk too fast."

Rhian was touched by this display of concern. "Thank you. This is a good speed."

In truth, it was considerably slower than she was capable of doing even in her somewhat weakened condition. But as Great-gran Celcilia had always taught, it was always a good idea to not give away the extents of your strengths and weaknesses when among strangers.

Thinking along those lines, Rhian noted that all the soldiers she had seen so far were all male and not young. Early middle age, she guessed, but certainly looked to be in excellent condition and well trained. Come to think of it, she'd not seen any women as of yet. That might mean nothing at all, of course, but was certainly something to note, especially given the polite manners they had displayed to her thus far.

The soldiers guiding them turned sharply into another corridor, then another, and then they were walking through an outside courtyard that was about as long as a soccer pitch. The pathway was smoothly finished with the same slate-like stone that was in her room. Beyond that were a variety of gardens laid out in a series of interlocking geometrical patterns, each section filled with a variety of plants and shrubs. The sun was warm on her shoulder, but the air had a tinge of coolness that felt very refreshing. She smiled in spite of herself as she looked around.

Torstanda called out and the soldiers leading them came to a halt. One of them turned around with a frown and engaged in a discussion with Torstanda for a few seconds. The soldier initially seemed irked, but relaxed somewhat within a few seconds. He looked at Rhian and gave a friendly nod of his head as he pointed to a low stone fence just up ahead.

"I told him that we should stop for a minute," said Torstanda, who had come up to stand beside her. "These gardens are not at their best, as this is a cool season. But you seemed to enjoy them so much. He suggested that you might enjoy sitting down for a minute."

Rhian looked at the soldier and smiled her thanks as she gave a bow of her head. "Thank you," she said. Then she turned to Torstanda. "Yes, I would very much like to rest here for a minute. That is very kind of you and him."

Torstanda nodded at the soldier, who turned and led the party to the wall. Within a few seconds Rhian and Torstanda were sitting down on the sun-warmed stone and looking around without worrying about stumbling over something.

The soldiers took positions around the two, effectively boxing them in without crowding them.

"This is very beautiful," she said to Torstanda. "Is this a special place?"

He nodded. "Yes. It was built as a place to show the plants from all the regions of our planet, so much as is possible." He pointed at several of the garden beds. "Everything is joined together to show how united we have become. On special days many people come here to see this, some from very far away."

A gentle throat-clearing interrupted their discussion. Their guide looked at Torstanda and cleared his throat again.

"Our guide is eager to continue, it would seem," said Rhian as she got to her feet. "We should not test his kindness further."

That got a chuckle from Torstanda as he got to his own feet. He exchanged a few words with their guide and they continued on their way. It took several minutes to cross the length of the walled garden, and Rhian enjoyed every second of it. For one thing, it was very beautiful. For another, it gave her time to ponder what Torstanda had said. A special garden to celebrate social cohesion between states typically signified past conflicts. A garden with plants from across the world hinted at a large-scale planetary conflict. Great-gran Celcilia had written about travelling to one place that had such conflicts, and Rhian very much hoped that this was not that planet. It took considerable effort of will to keep a serene smile on her face.

Soon they arrived at another set of doors. Their guide knocked twice and the doors opened to reveal six soldiers standing at attention. Their soldiers saluted the new set, who returned the salute. Their soldiers spun on their heels and stood to either side of the door on the outside. The new soldiers repeated the maneuvers on the inside.

"We go inside," murmured Torstanda. "Our guides will wait here for us."

The two of them walked forward. As they were about to enter, Rhian turned her head to give a small formal nod to their guide, which was returned. Another pair of guards led the way with the others following.

This new section of the complex was similar to where she'd been staying, but just a little bit nicer. There were a few more decorations, all of better quality, and everything was polished and shining. As a working hypothesis, she decided that this was where management-level people worked. It certainly fit in with the style she'd seen in the halls of academia and government.

They wended their way through the twists and turns of several corridors, not meeting anyone else along the way, then stopped in front of a pair of ornate doors. Their guide knocked then braced to attention. Both doors opened inward as an imposing figure opened them and stood in the doorway. The two exchanged words that had the cadence of formality to Rhian's ears, then the soldiers formed up in rows on either side of the door. The figure inside motioned for them to enter. As Rhian and Torstanda entered, the soldiers closed the doors but did not follow inside.

The room was large and richly decorated, with tapestries and paintings lining the walls. There was a long conference table to one side, with well-cushioned chairs around it. At the other end of the room was a small fireplace, complete with fire, with upholstered chairs surrounding a small table. That was where their host led them, then gestured for them to be seated.

Rhian studied the man. He was middle-aged, at least two metres tall, if not a bit more, and a bit on the heavyset side. He looked like someone who had been handsome and athletic in his youth but thickened by the inexorable weight of time, although not excessively. Once seated, he spoke in the local language, his voice deep and resonant, and gestured at the ornate glasses and snacks on the table. The glasses were filled with a red liquid that glowed in the light of the fire, like a good red wine.

She reached for the glass but stopped when Torstanda held up a hand. He spoke rapidly at their host, who looked startled, then apologetic. He bowed to Rhian and murmured something then looked expectantly at Torstanda. The latter nodded then turned to Rhian. "I explained that you were not yet used to our foods and must be careful. He offers deep apologies."

For her part, Rhian gave a formal half bow, then reached over to take her glass. She raised it in salute to their host, then Torstanda, then raised it to her lips without drinking any of it. The aroma of it reminded her of fine wine, or perhaps port, and it was with great regret that she placed the glass back down on the table. Then she gave another formal half bow and sat upright.

Her host beamed at her, took his own glass and saluted the two of them before taking a healthy sip and placing it back down on the table. Torstanda gave Rhian a slight nod then repeated the ritual. The formalities observed, their host placed a hand on his chest and spoke several sentences. The only word Rhian recognized was her own name. Torstanda began speaking. "I will speak for him as you and I share this language. The name of our host is Franza. He is very pleased to make your acquaintance and hopes that your stay on our world will be a good one."

Rhian placed a hand on her chest as she'd seen Franza do. "Thank you for your hospitality, Franza. It is my hope that I may be of service to you and your world." She dropped her hand and glanced at Torstanda, who turned to Franza and spoke several sentences. This began an exchange that, although slow, went well enough.

"You are quick to learn our ways, Rhian. I thank you for honouring them."

"I have made many visits to other places on my own world that had ways different from my own. Each new place has things to teach me and I welcome the chance to learn."

Franza nodded. "I understand that you are a seeker of knowledge. Torstanda is also a teacher and seeker. He is well known and much honoured on our world. Are you much known on yours?"

Rhian had to smile at that. "No, Franza, I am not known except to my students and a small circle of other seekers. I am one of many."

Franza gave what looked like an honest smile at that and nodded. "It is a joy to hear from one who does not seek to make themselves seem large. My work here brings me into contact with many who make small work seem large." Then he became serious. "Has my work been explained to you?"

"No, Franza."

He nodded. "I understand. You have not been here long and have spent some time being not well." He leaned back in his chair and placed his hands on his thighs. "You arrived with the one we call the War Demon, yes?"

Rhian nodded.

"There will be a trial. Facts will be made known. A judgement will be made. Do you understand this?"

She hesitated a moment, then nodded. "I understand that there will be a trial. I do not understand the why of it."

"I am to act as the interceder for the trial. That is a person who works to defend the person on trial. Do you understand?"

"I think so, yes. Does this mean that there is hope for Bob ... the one you call the War Demon?"

Franza made a chopping motion with a hand. "No. The facts in this case point to only one possible judgement. My work is to make the trial be fair, that our ways of justice be honoured."

Rhian sat back in her chair and blinked rapidly several times. She slowly inhaled a deep breath and exhaled it just as slowly.

"This troubles you very much." Franza's voice was gentle.

"Yes," she replied. "These things you say about Bob do not agree with what I know of him."

"Torstanda has told me what you told him. He has told me that you have travelled with the War Demon only a short time. He also tells me that your ancestor travelled with him for a longer time. How do you know this to be true?"

"My ancestor recorded her memories of that time and passed that record down to several of us over the years. Before her death I spoke with her about some aspects of her account and found them to be ... I am not sure of the correct word, but I could not find errors or proof of false statements."

"That does not mean that it is truth," said Franza, leaning forward. "A story that is believed to be true is not always true."

Rhian nodded. "Yes. But I am a trained seeker of knowledge and have learned how to ask questions that test stories."

"Did she have any facts that you could touch?"

"Yes. She had clothes and a bag that she claimed were obtained on another world. I tested those and found that the material was like nothing on my world. The bag was made of leather that came from no animal of my world."

"Could these things be made to look as if they came from another world?"

"I made tests for that. It is possible but so difficult to do that only a very rich group could do so. My ancestor was a wonderful woman, but not rich or famous or powerful. She could not have made a false thing of that kind."

Franza drummed his fingers on his thighs for a few seconds as his eyes looked far away. Then he focused his eyes on her once again. "What things did she say about him?"

Rhian gave a tight smile. "Your question is too large. She said that he was brave and honest."

Franza barked a laugh. "I spent many years as an interceder in trials. Asking large questions is a useful tool." Then he frowned. "You told Torstanda that your ancestor met Kydos, correct?"

"Yes. It was not a happy time for my ancestor."

That got a frown from both men. "That is a strong thing to

say, Rhian. Very strong. Kydos is known here as a very good person. She is admired by all. Some worship her."

Rhian tensed but tried not to let it show too much. "That is what Torstanda has told me. May I ask some questions about that?"

When Franza nodded, Rhian took a deep breath to steady her nerves. Probing sacred beliefs was always a tricky task and fraught with danger.

"When did she first appear?"

"It was twenty-three, nearly twenty-four, years ago."

Rhian nodded. That was not long after Bob had been reborn.

"She came in a ship from the stars, correct?"

"Yes."

"Then she offered a limited supply of medicine and other aid, correct?"

"Yes, but she also organized a multinational organization that brought all the countries together."

"Was there nothing similar before that?"

Both men nodded. "Yes, many attempts. The problem had always been to find common ground."

"She found that common ground?"

"Yes. She showed us that our problems were caused by the War Demon. She showed us that we should unite to be ready when he was delivered to us."

"Delivered to you?"

"Yes. She said that she was part of a group dedicated to peace. The War Demon was a destroyer who did terrible crimes on many worlds. She and others fought against him to bring peace."

"Did she give you the doorway device?"

"Yes. She also gave us a description of the War Demon's new form. She said that her group had managed to neutralize the War Demon's powers. When the time was right, she would send him to us."

Rhian would have continued but was overcome by a fit of coughing. Both men sprang out of their chairs. Franza reached towards her glass but after being warned away by Torstanda, he trotted towards a sideboard and returned with a sealed jar which he gave to her. He barked some words at Torstanda, who turned to Rhian and said, "Here is some boiled water. Please be well."

She took the water and took several sips until the coughing subsided. After wiping her eyes on her sleeve, Torstanda offered her a handkerchief which she used to good effect.

"I thank you both," she said, leaning back into her chair.

"You are well?" asked Torstanda with evident concern showing on his features and in his voice.

"Oh, yes." She cleared her throat several times, took another sip of water, and declared, "We must continue."

"But you are not well," insisted Torstanda.

"There is no time for being not well. Explain to Franza that I want to continue."

He made to protest but was silenced by her glare. With a slight smile he turned to Franza and translated what she had said.

Franza nodded then frowned. He spoke briefly with Torstanda, then went to the door. The latter turned to Rhian and said, "He is going to obtain some traveller food. He is worried about you. As am I. It is also time for a meal."

Rhian realized with a start that she was feeling quite hungry. "Food would be good," she agreed, and sipped on some water.

Their meal came within minutes, and they finished it not long after that. Both men joined her in eating the bland porridge. Whatever their other issues, Rhian could not fault their manners.

"You are ready to continue?" asked Franza through Torstanda.

"Yes. We have much to say to each other," replied Rhian to the other's obvious delight.

"What did your ancestor say about Kydos?"

Rhian took a moment to consider her answer. "As I have said, it was not a good experience. You see Kydos as a good person. My ancestor very much did not."

Both men frowned at that. "No disrespect to your ancestor, but is there a chance she did not understand?"

"No. Kydos lied to her and her own ancestors. Kydos claimed to be a god. She took my ancestor to another world and made her a prisoner."

"To what end?"

"My ancestor had a talent that allowed Kydos to use her as a way to influence people. To put her thoughts into their heads."

"The way of Kydos is the way of peace. Did your ancestor not understand what was happening?"

Rhian barked a laugh. She was beginning to feel trapped and a bit lightheaded. It was a bad combination, but she pressed on. "Oh, she understood. She understood how cruel Kydos could be. She understood when Kydos ripped the heart out of a man for spilling her wine, and had another whipped to death for stealing a few coins. She understood that Kydos would use her until she died from exhaustion, then steal another poor soul and another and another. This stealing had been going on for many lifetimes with no-one to stop it."

Both men looked at her wide-eyed.

"You don't understand, do you?" she said in a soft voice. "Yes, she was part of an organization. But it was dedicated to conquest. Many of those men Kydos influenced with the help of my ancestor were soldiers. The influence was to make them more obedient, more willing to do anything and sacrifice anything they were ordered to do."

"Kydos is peace. Kydos saved us," whispered Torstanda.

"No. The way of Kydos is soft words that hide the whip and chain. That is how she and her organization worked, you see. Offer a few small miracles, but keep the supply of them small.

Offer the miracles only to the faithful few. That is the way to gain influence and then control."

The two men looked at each other in stunned disbelief.

"You must understand how much she hates Bob. Bob rescued my ancestor from her and put an end to those evil schemes. The schemes of Kydos and her organization. That organization has tried many times to kill Bob."

"You know this to be true?"

"My ancestor witnessed one such attempt. She was injured escaping the killers. Bob took her home to be safe before returning to deal with them."

"What happened after that?"

Rhian shook her head. "There is no record of that. My ancestor had no contact with Bob until many years later. He said he had stopped the organization of Kydos and her friends, and that it was time to destroy all the doorway devices his people had scattered across the galaxy."

"Why?"

"He felt that his people could no longer be trusted with such power over the younger races."

The two men sat back in silence for several minutes to digest what they had learned. Rhian took the time to take some sips of water and berate herself for her honesty. Still, she didn't see that she had any other choice.

Finally, Franza raised his head to look at her. "What do you know of our world?" he asked through Torstanda.

She shook her head. "Only what you tell me."

Franza tapped his chin with a forefinger. "I get the sense that there is more to your answer."

Rhian shook her head once more. "I am not sure. My ancestor and Bob visited a world that had known much war. Bob said he had been here in his youth and became caught up in the violence. My ancestor said the memory of that time caused him great pain."

"Tell me of that world."

She frowned. "There is little to tell. My ancestor had been poisoned by Kydos during her escape and Bob was trying to get her to a place of healing. She remembered that he spoke of many nations at continuous war with each other for centuries. That is why he was sent here by his father—to be tested in war. Soon after he came, everything fell apart. All the small fightings became larger and larger until all was consumed. So large that there were no more countries, only cities. Then no more cities, only towns. Then no more towns. He tried to help but failed."

"What happened after that?"

"According to my ancestor, Bob fought his way across the country, then across an ocean to another continent where the doorway to his home was."

"What sorts of weapons were used in this place?"

Rhian thought it an odd question. "Guns. Bob said there were very powerful guns. Also mechanical creations of great power. When the collapse came, men with powerful weapons attacked those with less powerful weapons. He said it was a time of madness."

"Anything else?"

"Hmm. Yes. He mentioned that there were a few other, more powerful weapons. I do not have the words. Uhm, special metals forced together with great force to create an explosion that could destroy a city. Does that make sense to you?"

Both men nodded.

"What were the effects?"

She gave them a puzzled look. "The movements of the oceans were changed. That changed the weather. Dry areas became wet, and wet areas became dry. I do not have the words to say better."

"Rhian, do you know when this took place?"

She shook her head. "No. Bob has lived a very long time. My ancestor felt it happened many years ago. Maybe centuries."

"Rhian, more than four centuries ago our entire planet went through a series of terrible wars that almost destroyed us. There were several large, powerful nations and many smaller ones. The weapons, and their effects, were as you have described. The records of that time are incomplete, of course, but they are clear about one thing. A being not from our planet came and killed tens of thousands of people. Not all of them were soldiers, Rhian. Not even most of them. The timing of his arrival coincides with the Great Collapse, as we call it."

Rhian chewed a lip for a moment. "How do you know that the being was Bob? Does he match the description?"

"No, but Kydos explained that his body has been changed."

"Wait, so you have only the word of Kydos about this?"

"Not at all." Both men were shocked by the accusation. "We are a society of law and procedure. We test claims for truth and only then do we proceed with a trial."

"This proof you speak of, where did it come from? From Kydos?"

"No. Well, she assisted in the recovery of it from various ruins."

"Assisted? Others were there to witness the recovery?"

Franza looked disconcerted as he wiggled slightly in his chair. "For some of the recoveries, yes."

"But not all?"

"No. Not at first. But she organized more recoveries."

"And helped to create this new organization of peace for the planet."

Both men nodded. "Yes." Then Torstanda interjected, "Based on the existing organizations, of course."

Rhian thought about that for a moment. "So really, most of what she did was give you all someone to blame. Someone to hate. Someone she just happened to know."

"As I said earlier, she led an organization of peace that was chasing the War Demon across the galaxy. We were one of his victims."

"That is her claim," said Rhian in a dry voice. "Franza, you are Bob's interceder. Have you spoken with him yet to get his version of the story?"

"Well, no. As I said, there is so much proof against him. My function is to see that the proper procedures are followed. He will be held in protective care until the trial."

Rhian chocked down an angry retort and kept her features calm with a supreme effort of will.

"As a seeker of truth, I would like to hear what he has to say. May I speak with him?"

"It will do no good. The trial will take place, the evidence will be presented, and judgement will be made. I do not wish to cause you unnecessary pain."

"I thank you for your concern, but this is something I must do if it is possible."

Franza stood up. "I will see what I can do. But now the time is late and you must be tired. We will speak again tomorrow."

Rhian stood up and gave a formal bow of her head. "I thank you for your time, Franza, and am eager to meet with you again."

He returned the bow then summoned the guards to return her to her room. Torstanda walked with her but neither spoke until they reached her room.

"When you awaken, knock on the door to alert the guards. They will summon me and we will have a meal. Rest well, Rhian."

"Thank you, Torstanda. Rest well."

Neither of them managed to do that, each for different reasons.

CHAPTER EIGHT
A Demon Caged

Once again, Rhian awoke when the sunrise flooded her room with light. She washed and prepared herself to face what promised to be another trying day. Before summoning the guard, she decided to make a few notes. Sitting before the desk, she opened the drawer and noted with wry amusement that her papers were in a slightly different position that she'd left them prior to yesterday's meeting. This was a common enough occurrence during her travels and certainly not unexpected on this new planet.

After collecting the notes and a fresh sheet of paper, she jotted down highlights of yesterday along with her observations of the garden and its possible significance. A fresh glint of sunlight against the wall reminded her that time was passing. She finished a sentence and replaced the notes in the desk, careful to arrange them in her regular order. In situations such as this, she had found, it was important to give the appearance of sticking to established habits. Changes tended to make the minders nervous.

With that taken care of, she rose and knocked on the door then stepped back several paces. It was opened with care to reveal a familiar soldier. They exchanged nods and he shut the door. Rhian could hear one set of footsteps moving away, followed several minutes later by the sound of several footsteps approaching. There was a knock on the door which then opened to reveal the same servers as yesterday. They set up the service in silence, then seated Rhian. They left and Torstanda entered the room. He seated himself at table, not saying anything until the door was closed and they were alone.

"Good morning, Rhian. Did you sleep well?"

"I slept. I do not think that either of us slept well." The dark traces under his eyes matched hers, she knew.

He gave her a wan smile. "Many new things were said yesterday. You made me think to test assumptions that I learned long ago."

Rhian opened her mouth to speak, but Torstanda held up a hand to forestall her, and said,"Like you, I am a seeker of knowledge. That seeking is not always easy." His smile broadened. "It has been many years since my thinking has been tested this much. For that, I thank you."

She returned his smile with one of her own. He seemed to be an honest scholar and she found herself enjoying his company. "I thank you for the new knowledge you and Franza have shared with me."

They sat for a moment then Torstanda dished up some porridge for her and some for himself. Rhian pointed at some of the food that had been brought.

Torstanda smiled and said, "I thought you might like something else. This dish is a mixture of several fruits, and this other dish is a dry mixture that some travellers enjoy to keep a happy body."

Rhian looked at the other dishes with some longing, for the tasteless porridge held little appeal for her. She decided to risk a bit of the dry mix and sprinkled it on one side of her porridge. She took a small amount, chewed it thoroughly and swallowed. It tasted very much like a cereal mix from home and had enough taste to go well with the porridge. Her stomach seemed happy enough with it, so she began to finish her meal.

"Torstanda, you are eating only what I eat. Please, eat

anything you wish. I will not be offended."

He shook his head. "It is not our way, Rhian. But I thank you for the kindness." He smiled and continued eating the porridge.

The bowl of porridge sat so well that she decided to have another, which pleased her host.

"You are feeling better?"

"Yes, thank you." She paused then added. "You look as if you wish to say something. Please, you must feel that you can say anything to me. I have done much travelling and have found that what is not said can cause more damage than what is said."

He gave a vigorous nod. "That is very true, Rhian. We are each trying so hard not to cause insult that it may be that we say too little." Then he paused. "It is hard to know where to begin."

Rhian picked up her cup of water and leaned back into her chair. "Please tell me more about Franza and this trial."

Torstanda picked up his own cup and settled back. "He has been an interceder for many years and has worked with several nations. It is for that experience he was given this task." He paused for a moment and said in a soft voice. "He has many important friends, Rhian. That is very important to him. Do you understand?"

"Yes, Torstanda. It is the same on my world. I have experience with such men."

"That is good. This is a dangerous time. The coming of the War Demon only adds to the pressure."

Rhian's eyebrows rose. "What sort of danger?"

Torstanda sighed. "It has been centuries since the Great Collapse and we have only now reached the levels they had. Not so much in some ways but better in others. The Collapse forced us to put aside, or at least ignore, the old hates and to work together. Now that times are once more good, there are some who try to bring back those old hates." His snort of disgust told Rhian all she needed to know about his opinion on that subject.

Then he heaved a great sigh and leaned forward. "The coming of Her Wisdom helped us in some ways." He held up a hand to forestall any comment. "That is fact, Rhian. She took the many small organizations and helped them to work together to re-build and improve roads, sanitation, schools, and hospitals. She helped us to achieve very much in a short time."

He paused as he leaned back in his chair. "As I told you yesterday, she gave us someone to blame for the Collapse. Over the years that blame ofttimes grew into hate." He paused as his eyes looked far away. "It is as if that hate awoke in us the need to hate more." His eyes turned to focus on her. "Hate feeds hate. It was a useful thing at first, like wood for a fire. But now that fire is burning stronger and threatens to grow larger. The old hates are returning."

"Then Bob and I came."

"Yes." Torstanda looked towards the window for several seconds then returned his gaze to Rhian. "I can save you, I think, but I cannot save your friend. I am very sorry."

Rhian's breath caught in her throat. This threat was not unexpected, but his offer to help her was and she was touched by his concern. Then she took a deep breath, held it for several seconds, and then exhaled slowly. "I thank you, Torstanda. You are very kind to a stranger." She paused for a moment then rose to her feet and began pacing back and forth, not noticing the amused smile on Torstanda's face.

"I need to see Bob," she finally said. "There are many stories told by many people over many years. It has become difficult to understand what is fact and what is story. He is the only one who is a living witness to those times. His words must be heard." Then her voice softened. "He also needs to be told about the trial and the why of it."

Torstanda nodded. "There should be a decision made very

99

soon to see if you can visit him." He gave a small smile as he said, "Franza felt your words very strongly last night. The interceder should talk with the one he serves." Then he became serious and shrugged. "But you must understand that Franza does not wish the guilt of the War Demon to reflect on him in any way. He is an important man and wishes to remain important. That is how things are."

Rhian nodded. "Thank you for your plain words, Torstanda. But what about you? Will you be made to suffer for being of assistance?"

"No, Rhian. I am a seeker of knowledge, and this is expected of me." Then he shrugged. "I am not an important man. I do not know important men. I am safe."

"But you said the times are changing."

"That is true. But a seeker should serve truth, not men."

Rhian knew the dangers to a scholar who would speak truth to power and bowed deeply. "You are a brave man, Torstanda."

He chuckled as he ducked his head to acknowledge her tribute. "My wife would not agree, Rhian, if she were still alive. She would always shake her head and say that I should also seek important friends." He gave a sad smile and added, "I miss her very much. She died several years ago."

Rhian expressed her condolences, and the two of them chatted about their lives. She told him of her life without a husband or children, and he spoke of a life of study. On that they found common ground and were amazed at the commonalities of the behaviour of academia between the two planets. They chatted for nearly an hour before being interrupted by a knock on the door. Torstanda said something and the door opened to reveal a soldier who frowned to see Rhian standing while Torstanda sat. Then he came to attention and exchanged words with Torstanda who finally nodded and held up a hand.

"This man will take you to see your friend. You may have a

short visit. I must stay here. Please be careful."

"I will, Torstanda. Thank you." She turned to the soldier and nodded. "I am ready to go." Torstanda translated her words, and the soldier nodded and motioned for her to precede him out the door. When she walked out, two soldiers fell into place in front of her and two behind. They moved at a comfortable walking pace, obviously meant as a courtesy to her. Their path held several twists and turns through identical-looking corridors, but Rhian's training and experience left her confident that she could find her way back if need be.

They came to a secured door with four guards on either side. Words were exchanged before the door was opened and her party was allowed to pass. The corridor here was a narrow set of stairs that went down. At the base was another secured door with four guards. The ritual was repeated and they passed through. This time Rhian noticed another set of guards on the inside of the door. They walked down a long, narrow corridor to yet another secured door, with a guard on either side of it. No words were spoken this time as one of the guards pulled the door open. Rhian stepped through but her escort stayed outside.

There was a short corridor leading to what was obviously a cage of sorts at the end. The hallway was well lit but smelled faintly like a place that had not been used in many years. She walked to the cage and looked inside. There was a dirty figure sitting on the bare floor dressed in rags. There was no furniture of any sort inside the featureless cell. The figure looked up. "Hi, Rhian," said Bob.

"Bob," she gasped and made to grasp the bars.

"Don't touch the bars," he warned. "They're covered with something that will slice your flesh." He held up his hands. "Like this."

She saw that the palms of his hands were covered with what looked like clotted blood. Looking more closely, she realized that what she had taken for clothing was a clotted mess of dirt and blood covering his body. His face was a mess of cuts and bruises, with one eye swollen shut.

"Oh, Bob. What did they do to you?"

He eased himself to his feet and limped to the door. "Ah, the usual stuff. Nothing to worry about. But what about you? How are they treating you?"

Rhian bit back an angry retort and bit her lip. Bob was speaking English, so she decided to play along. "Quite well, actually. Got my own little apartment and a security detail to keep me safe. Met some people. Found out a bit about what's going on."

Bob raised an eyebrow—or tried to—when he heard that. "You seem to be doing well. I am relieved and puzzled. How are you communicating?"

Rhian glanced around then took a deep breath. "Uhm, about that. It turns out that we share a common language."

Bob nodded for her to continue.

"It is the language of the planet where Great-gran was held captive. Best not to mention names right now."

"Ah. Yes. Wise to be cautious, I think. Well done, Rhian."

"What have they told you?"

"In words, nothing. But they seem very angry with me." He waved a hand at his injuries.

She hissed in anger and stopped only when Bob motioned her to silence.

"It's not as bad as it looks, I promise you."

"It looks bad, Bob."

He shrugged. "This body can take more punishment than yours and heals somewhat faster. Not like before, of course, but I'll be fine."

Then he chuckled. "But enough about me. What have you found out?"

"First, what do you need? Goddess, Bob, but you look rough. Are they feeding you?"

He barked a laugh. "No. A hot shower would be lovely, but

I'd settle for a glass of water."

At the look on her face, his voice became gentle. "I was trained for this sort of situation, Rhian. Never forget that."

"So you could escape if you needed to?"

He looked around before answering. "Interesting question. Not sure. Getting out of this cell? Perhaps. After that, things get a bit tricky." He indicated the walls of the corridor with his jerk of his head. "See those holes and slots in the wall? Gun ports. Lots of small openings in all the ceilings ... some smell of water and others of something nastier. Solid construction. Very well designed. It is almost as if they expected someone like me."

"They did."

"Excuse me?" His head snapped back to look at her.

"She told them to expect you." Rhian waved a hand. "This facility was built to contain you." She leaned forward. "Bob, she told them what you look like. This new body of yours, I mean. Told them you had been stripped of your powers."

"Ah. Interesting. That explains a lot. Thank you." He turned and returned to the wall and sat down to lean against it.

"What? That's it? You're giving up?"

He gave her a wan smile. "Rhian, do you know where we are?"

"Yes, of course. This is the planet you called Hell when you brought Great-gran here. They call you the War Demon, you know."

"Yes. They called me that back then, too. Still do." He fingered the bruises on his face.

Rhian could only gape at him. After several seconds she managed to splutter out, "But ... but ... that's it? You're just going to sit there and let them kill you?"

"What are you talking about?"

"The trial, you idiot."

"Excuse me?"

She took a deep breath to steady her nerves. "After you left and this world's social systems fell into what they call the Great Collapse, they slowly managed to cobble together a weak international coalition. It wasn't much but enough to stop the decline and slowly piece together their society. A few years ago, she-whom-we-won't-name arrived. Distributed enough goodies to make a name for herself. Also did a lot of work getting things organized to improve things by rather a lot. They think very highly of her here."

"Humph. I'm sensing a 'but' coming up."

She gave him a grim smile. "They needed something to focus their energies. A common enemy. That would be you. You were proclaimed not only an enemy of this planet, but a threat to peace throughout the galaxy. Evidence was found in the ruins here, by her, to prove your guilt."

Bob gazed into the distance. "Ah. So she set me up as the focus of hate. Hmm. A useful technique, but not so good for the long term." Then he looked directly at her. "You mentioned a trial."

"Yes. Yes, I did. Glad you're finally paying attention. There's an international tribunal being convened. It will examine the evidence and then find you guilty."

"And you think that I am not? Rhian ..." he paused for several seconds. "What makes you think that I am not guilty?"

"Argh. Stop playing the martyr, Bob. Great-gran explained how you were dumped here as a test of survival. How you made friends, saw them slaughtered, and then you avenged their deaths. It was a terrible time."

He looked away and stayed silent for over a minute then he sighed and hung his head.

"Bob? Talk to me. What's going on?"

He mumbled something then fell silent.

"Speak up, dammit, I can't hear you."

Bob raised his head to look at her. "I said, I never told her all of it. Not even a fraction. Not the worst of it."

Rhian inhaled sharply and exhaled slowly. "Very well. It was a bad time. But there's more going on here than just you. There are hints of political struggles before you came and—"

She was interrupted by the opening of the door at the end of the corridor. A guard stood in the doorway and motioned for her to walk away.

"Not yet," she yelled in English. She turned back towards the cell. "Something is going here, Bob. I don't know what, but all of my experience says that there is more to this than you. Stop wallowing in guilt and self-pity and help me figure this out."

She heard the footsteps of the guard approaching and knew her time was almost up. "Goddess dammit, Bob. Give me something. What was the year that you arrived here? And left?"

The guard placed a hand on her arm and began dragging her away. Bob watched with eyes filled with sadness and defeat. Just as the door was about to close, he yelled out, "The year was 4891 by the calendar of the Plitsfor throne. I was here for about twenty years."

The door closed with a solid-sounding *thunk* and she was left staring at its featureless surface.

CHAPTER NINE
Unwelcome Revelations

Rhian was marched back from the cell area at double time. She and her escort arrived back in the main corridors then took a turn away from her rooms. She kept enough presence of mind not to object, but kept track of where she was going. Her experience in uncharted tombs allowed her to build up a map of the building. They marched her for nearly ten minutes through a maze of corridors and halted in front of a set of doors she recognized from the previous night. The doors opened to reveal Franza who motioned her inside. Her escorts remained outside.

Franza motioned her to the chairs in front of the fireplace. Torstanda was seated but rose to greet her with a bow. She stood standing until Franza was seated then walked up to him.

"Liar!" she yelled as she slammed her hand on the table.

Both men looked at her with shock. Rhian turned to Torstanda and growled, "Say what I say. These are my words, not yours." Then she turned to Franza once again. "You lied to me."

He gaped at her as she motioned with a wave of her hand for Torstanda to translate. She waited until he had finished before continuing.

"I have been to see my friend. He has been stripped naked and attacked by your guards. He has not had any food or water since he arrived. You claim to be a people of law, yet my friend is treated as a criminal before he has seen a trial."

There was silence for several seconds, then Franza spoke through Torstanda. "He is the War Demon."

Rhian made no effort to restrain her fury nor keep her voice gentle. "That is not proven. The judgement has not been made. Where is the justice that you promised me?" She pointed a finger a Franza who looked startled but did not flinch. He held up a hand to stem her fury and spoke at Torstanda.

"Franza says that he knows nothing of which you speak."

"He is the interceder. It is his job to know."

As Torstanda translated, Franza's face grew red. With a violent exhalation that was almost a growl, he was on his feet and striding towards the door. Yanking it open, he barked orders at the soldiers outside. There was a discussion during which Torstanda risked a small nod to Rhian, taking care that no-one saw him. He made a small downward motion to Rhian, who interpreted it as a request to stay quiet for the moment. She took a deep breath to calm herself and exhaled slowly.

Franza finished talking with the soldiers then turned to say something to Torstanda before he turned and left the room. One of the soldiers closed the door, and the two were left alone.

"Rhian, you must be careful in what you say. You are a stranger here. And a woman, at that." Franza's features reflected the concern in his voice.

Rhian waved a dismissive hand. "There is no time for that. We have work to do, you and I. Do you have a map of the world here?"

Torstanda nodded and pointed towards the other end of the room. "That far section of the room is often used for meetings. There will be one there, I think."

He turned and led the way past the long table and to the wall. What Rhian had assumed to be thick ornamentation turned out to be doors for cabinets filled with books and other items. Torstanda opened several cabinets as he searched the contents. Rhian stared with eagerness at the books revealed to her. One row of them caught her attention, as they seemed to be part of a set. Her examination was interrupted when she heard Torstanda say, "Yes. Here is the map we need. These others may be useful as well."

She saw him take an armful of rolled up maps to the table and drop them down. He looked at her with a grin. "We are a people who love maps, you see." He pointed at one. "This is a map showing the world with cities marked. This other map adds borders of all the nations. This one shows the nations before the Great Collapse."

As he talked, he arranged the maps into two piles. The ones he mentioned were in one pile, and the remainder in another. He looked up at Rhian and nodded at the remainder pile. "These other maps have details of rivers and lakes."

"Why so many maps?"

He laughed. "We are a people of maps. Everywhere nations meet, there are maps to show who controls what area, who has access to trade routes, where resources may be obtained." Then his good humour vanished. "I have told you how after the Great Collapse the nations worked together. These old maps show what was lost and help us to recover old knowledge. Some use them to keep old wounds alive." Then he gave his head a small shake. "But you have a new use for them, I think."

"Yes, Torstanda. Let us start with the map before the Great Collapse." She rolled it out and Torstanda found some heavy items to keep it lying flat. She saw two major continents plus a scattering of islands of various sizes around them. "Can you show me where we are?"

He nodded and pointed to the eastern coast of one of the continents, at a point that lay not too far inland along a river. Assuming Earth and this world were about the same size, she guessed the distance to be less than two hundred kilometres.

"Good. Now, according to my ancestor, Bob said he arrived

in the far north where the borders of many nations met."

Torstanda thought for a moment and pointed at a spot near the top of the map. "This is a likely area. I will explain."

He went to the cabinets and returned with a handful of small items that looked similar to chess pieces. He placed one at the northern area. "The first reports of the War Demon were some distance south of there, at a spot along a major river that flows to the north." He placed down another marker. He looked at her expectantly.

"My ancestor said Bob had to cross the sea to another continent to find the doorway home. Do you have any idea where that might be?"

Torstanda nodded. "There are reports of him on the other continent. I think the last reports were in this area, here." He placed a marker down at a spot about one third of the way into the continent from the coast. He frowned and shook his head. "The marker is too small. Our knowledge of the spot is not accurate."

He went to a cabinet and returned with a small book which he used to replace the marker. "This better shows the limits of what we know to be true, I think." He produced another small book and replaced the northernmost marker with it. "Also here."

"Very good. Thank you. I would like to mark all the places where there are records of Bob's activities."

Torstanda smiled. "I thought that might be your intention. Seekers of knowledge have made such maps, but those I know about are far away." He waved a hand at the cabinets. "There are books here that tell the history of those times. They are used to settle disputes but will be enough for our purpose, I think." He turned and went to the cabinets with Rhian following.

"How are these sorted?" she asked.

"By date. Far in the past to my left, moving forward in time to the right. But they are written in my language. Her Wisdom only taught us her spoken language. You will not be able to read them."

"Hmm. I am a fast learner, but there is another way. Where are the first reports of the War Demon?"

Torstanda ran a finger down the volumes and stopped to tap one. "If I remember well, this is the year."

Rhian picked up a piece of paper and placed it between that volume and the preceding one. "Where is the last report?" She looked up to see that Torstanda had anticipated her request and was tapping on another volume farther to the right in another cabinet. He smiled and placed a piece of paper between it and the next book then stepped back.

"Each book is for one year?"

"Mostly. There are some years with two volumes. Never more."

"Alright, how many years do we have?"

Torstanda checked the dates on the first and last marked volumes and said, "Eighty-three."

"Was Bob ... the War Demon ... actually seen in all of those years?"

Torstanda thought for a moment. "I need to check, but I do not think so. You look troubled."

Rhian nodded. "Did Kydos say how long Bob had been on this world?"

"Not exactly. But she did provide her evidence which we studied. She agreed that the exact dates of his coming and leaving were not known exactly."

"Was it less than eighty-three years?"

Torstanda tapped his chin with an index finger. "I think I see your plan. Yes, less. Let me mark the years Her Wisdom believed the War Demon to be here." He placed sheets of paper at the appropriate places. The range covered about one-third of the first range.

"Why so many outside the dates she provided?" asked Rhian.

"Those were added by our own seekers after she departed.

Not everyone agrees with them." He shook his head. "We got into the habit of blaming everything on the War Demon. It is no longer safe to question these things."

Rhian stood before the cabinets, her hands folded in front of her. "Torstanda, when I talked with Bob I asked him when he arrived. He said it was the year 4891 by the calendar of the Plitsfor throne. Does that mean anything to you?"

He nodded. "It is an old calendar but one that I know. In modern terms, it would fall about here." He placed a piece of paper near where Kydos had claimed Bob had appeared. "The two are close, I think."

"Yes, they are," agreed Rhian. "Bob also said that he was on this planet for about twenty years."

Again, Torstanda placed a piece of paper next to the appropriate book. "His times and those of Her Wisdom are very close, Rhian." He turned to look at her. "I believe you wish to ignore all histories that fall outside these dates, do you not?"

"That is correct, Torstanda. Can we take those books and mark activities on the map?"

He smiled. "No need for that yet. I know all of the major events." Then his smile vanished. "All the worst killings."

He took pieces of paper from the cabinet and tore them into small squares. As he worked he continued to speak. "If we use the old calendar and the War Demon's dates, we can place him in the north area in the year 4891." He wrote on a square of paper and placed it under the marker in the north of the map.

"The Desolation of Gorslan was in 4899. More than three thousand perished."

He placed another square of paper on the map. "The Slaughter of Nulso Region in 5901. All the villages and towns were destroyed with few survivors."

Torstanda recited over two dozen incidents and placed a marked square of paper on the map for each one. When that was completed, he looked up. "That is just for this continent. There are more on the other."

He then proceeded recite seventeen incidents and marked their locations with squares of paper. "Those are the worst ones. There are many, many smaller ones. We can get those details from the books. This will be enough for now, I think."

Rhian looked with horror at the swathe of destruction and the numbers of dead it represented. She walked over to the map and traced her fingers over it, pausing for a second at each square of paper. She was wiping at her eyes when something caught her eye. After clearing her throat, she asked, "How did he travel? My ancestor said that your ancestors did not have machines that flew in the sky."

"There were very few, it is true. None survived the Great Collapse. Travel was by foot or animal or motor vehicle."

Rhian nodded. "How accurate are the dates you gave?"

"Very accurate. These are big events with many seeing them."

She nodded. "Good. Now, this event here ..." she pointed to a spot near the west coast of the continent. "And this event here ..." she pointed to a spot near the east coast. "Those occurred in the same year. When exactly did they happen?"

Torstanda frowned for a moment then pointed to the western event. "Second-month." He moved his hand to point at the eastern event. "Third-month."

"Torstanda, could anyone move an army that far in that time?"

He shook his head. "I do not believe so. A small group of men, perhaps, but not an army of the size that was reported." He harrumphed softly to himself. "Bad roads. Hard to find fuel for motor vehicles. Hard to find food for that many men." He looked up at her. "No. He could not move an army that far so fast."

"Did he have more than one army?" she asked.

Torstanda puffed out his cheeks as he exhaled. "You ask difficult questions, Rhian." Then he smiled. "I enjoy working with you."

She smiled back. "Here is another difficult question. How could anyone, even the War Demon, create and equip so many men so quickly? For one army, much less two or more?"

Torstanda's mouth worked but no sound came out. He took several deep breaths before he could speak. "He is the War Demon. There are records of his speeches. Very inspiring to hear. His skills at organizing and planning for battle are studied even today."

"Torstanda, it was the time of the Great Collapse. Why would those men listen to him and not to their own leaders? I can understand a few men choosing to follow him, but why so many in so short a time? It might be possible, but I do not know your people." He failed to answer so she pressed on. "He was one man, Torstanda. My ancestor says he came with nothing but a knife and some water."

"Rhian, does that not prove that he is a demon?"

"No, Torstanda, it does not. He was trained to be a soldier from childhood, but this was his first test of battle. He was sent here to learn to fight and kill as part of an army. That is what he told my ancestor, and she believed him."

"Why did she believe?"

"Because the coming here and telling of the story caused him so much pain."

"He came and left here very long ago."

"Yet the pain is still strong in him, Torstanda. I saw it in his eyes when I visited him. Would the War Demon of your past allow himself to be caged and beaten?"

"Kydos said he has been stripped of his powers. Perhaps he fears to die."

Rhian nodded. "Yes. But he still has all those same skills. Again I ask, would the War Demon allow himself to be treated this way even if it meant death?"

Torstanda looked away, a troubled look on his face. A minute later he turned to face her once again. "Perhaps he has learned to fear death."

"Perhaps. I do not believe so, but I may be wrong. Still, we have a mystery here." She pointed at the map. "It took us a very short time to find it once we began asking the correct questions. We need to keep asking questions."

"Rhian, I—"

Their discussion was interrupted as the doors were flung open and Franza strode in red in face and puffing. He spared them but a glance as he headed to the table with refreshments and poured himself a glass of wine. After gulping down half of it he refilled it and walked over to the others. By the time he reached them his breathing had eased and most of the redness gone from his face. He took in the maps on the table and the scraps of paper upon them. He pointed at Rhian and spoke heatedly for a minute. Then he motioned at Torstanda and turned away, taking sips from his glass.

"Uhm, Franza has been to see the War Demon and found his condition to be as you said. He wants you to know that this is not how we do things. The soldiers are much afraid of him and refuse to go near him, even to feed him. After he was captured, he let them beat him for a time then took their clubs away and chased them out of the cage and shut the door. Franza and the soldiers ... talked." Torstanda stopped and looked at Franza, who by this time had turned around to face them.

"The soldiers are fools and cowards," he said through Torstanda. "They know nothing of justice or how things are done. It has been decided that you will take him food and water. He may have a blanket but nothing else." He blew out his cheeks and took another large sip of wine. "They wanted to wait until tomorrow, but I demanded that you go now."

There was a commotion at the door as a squad of soldiers marched up. Franza pointed at them. "You will go with them. They will provide you with food and water. I will stay here and learn of what the two of you have been doing. Go."

CHAPTER TEN

The Beginnings of Discovery

Rhian was once again marched down the now-familiar route to the jail where Bob was being held. Just outside the final door she was handed two wooden buckets, one containing water and the other food of some sort. They opened the door, shoved her in, threw a blanket at her, and then slammed it behind her. She stumbled but only spilt a little of the water. Muttering dire Welsh curses under her breath, she threw the blanket over her shoulder and marched towards the cell. As before, Bob was sitting on the floor leaning against the wall.

"I come bearing gifts," she said in a bright voice. "Just like Christmas."

Bob chuckled and rose to his feet. "A welcome sight, indeed. Both you and your gifts." He pointed to a spot near the floor. "I think we can safely pass them through that slot. There should be a bar that unlocks that small door. Yes, that's it. Now slide the assembly over and down. There, that's got it."

Rhian worked the mechanism as instructed and was rewarded with an opening through which the buckets fit after a bit of pushing. Bob drank several handfuls of the water with obvious relish.

"Ah, that's hit the spot. Now, let's see what the chef has prepared for me." He investigated the other bucket and picked through the contents. "Hmm, bread, cheese, and some nuts. A decent quantity of it, too. Thank you, Rhian." He began to put it to one side.

"No, no. You eat a bit now, please," she insisted. "It's been a while, and you need to keep up your strength. You never know when you'll need to frighten the guards and take away their toys."

"Ah, so you heard about that, did you?" he said as he grinned. It was good to see him smile again, she thought to herself.

"Yes, you big bully. Picking on those poor, innocent soldiers. They needed me to save them from you." That got a laugh out of him and raised his spirits. He tore off a piece of bread and cheese and began eating them.

"So, Rhian, what's been going on in the great, wide world?"

She grimaced. "Eat. We'll talk later."

"That bad is it? No matter. Best to talk while we have the chance. They might change their minds at any time."

"True. Alright. You're apparently blamed for all the horrors that occurred over more than eighty years."

His eyebrows raised at that but he continued eating without commenting.

"Heh. Thought that would get you attention. The information Kydos gave them suggests a time span of twenty-five to thirty years. Uhm, just started looking at the major events during that time. There's a lot of them, but some seem to have been impossible for you to have done." She paused for a moment. "You didn't move armies across the continent in just a few weeks did you?"

"No I didn't." He picked up some nuts and began cracking them open by squeezing them. "It's not surprising to have discrepancies like that, though. Many bad things were happening all over the world."

Bob paused and tossed the cracked nuts back into the bucket, then looked up at her. "I did some of those things. You need to accept that."

"Did you kill for the sake of killing? Answer me that at least."

He looked at her for a long moment. In a soft voice he said, "Only that one time. To avenge the destruction of the village who had taken me in."

"And after that?"

Bob shrugged. "Most of it was soldier against soldier, after that." He looked away as he added, "Mostly."

"You raised an army."

"Yes. More than once."

"How?"

"Excuse me?"

"Why would they follow you? By your own account you were just a kid. Well, equivalent to late teens."

He looked at her. "You start by finding a small group. Then you challenge and defeat the leader. With luck, the group then follows you."

"You mean kill the leader?" she interjected.

"Sometimes but not always. Depends on the group history and dynamics. Anyway, after that start with some small raids. Easy stuff to boost morale and fill their stomachs. Then show them a better way."

"Better way? You mean settle down?"

Bob laughed. "No, Rhian. Not an option with those men. No, these were soldiers or gang members, not farmers. Times were so very tough then that everyone hardened their hearts. I enforced a code of honour—no random killing of civilians, martial discipline, fair division of spoils, that sort of thing. It went down very well with the ones who hadn't turned feral. Plenty of those who wanted better, and no-one wasted tears on the feral ones."

Rhian nodded. "So, success breeds success. Then what?"

"Organization. There wasn't much of it here and I was trained for that. I knew how to make a large group work, how to organize the logistics of it."

"To what end?"

"Survival. There was a whole social ecosystem of these groups, Rhian. Quite fascinating in a horrid sort of way. The small groups preyed on the civilians, the settlers, the scroungers. Medium-sized groups preyed on the small groups. There were even some large, well-equipped groups around, remnants of national armies that managed stick together. Like the ones that attacked my village. They were the real danger, you see. They roamed across the landscape doing pretty much whatever they wanted, going after the medium-sized groups and larger settlements. The alpha predators, if you will. They controlled large swathes of territory. I suspect they became the nucleus of many of the modern-day countries here."

"Why raise an army at all? Why not just ghost your way through them using your powers?"

"Too many of them. Going after that one group was nearly the end of me, but I wasn't quite sane at that point. After that I worked within the system rather than against it. That meant raising an army large enough to move around safely."

"What happened to them? It sounds like you did this raising business more than once."

He shrugged. "Sometimes we ran into stronger outfits and got wiped out. Other times ..." his voice trailed off as he looked away. Several seconds later he turned to look at her. "Sometimes I lost control and subordinates decided to take over. That always got ugly."

There was the sharp sound of the door being opened and voices calling out her name. She turned and saw soldiers waving at her to come back.

"Better go, Rhian. Always best to obey the rules when you must."

"I'll be back when I can. Your defence lawyer got quite peeved when he heard about your treatment. Hopefully, I'll be able to bring you some more food and water soon. You might want to use some of that water to bathe your wounds."

"I'll be fine. The dirt acts as a dressing and adds a bit of insulation."

The calls for her to leave grew more insistent.

"Now you really have to go, Rhian. If you can do so safely, investigate the history of the Quinslax province. It's ugly, but you need to know about this and I can explain later. Go."

She gave him a firm nod then turned around and marched to the door without looking back.

* * *

As she was marched back to the office, Rhian's mind was a whirl of conflicting thoughts. She'd been raised to think of Bob as a hero—hard when necessary but good to the core. Great-gran Celcilia had mentioned this planet as a source of pain and darkness in his soul. Rhian was afraid she was about to find out the full extent of that.

She returned to the office to find Franza and Torstanda in a heated discussion next to the maps. Or rather, Franza was speaking heatedly, and Torstanda was standing there with a neutral look on his face. Rhian recognized the sight of a manager berating an underling, as she'd been on the receiving end far too often.

The men turned only when she had entered the room and the door closed behind her. Franza flicked his hand at her to indicate that she should go to the other end of the room. She did as commanded and sat in a chair facing away from the men, her eyes closed to better concentrate on their argument. Their words meant nothing to her yet, but she was beginning to pick up patterns of speech. The language was an equal mixture of vowels and consonants, giving it a vague similarity to European languages. She'd always found those much easier to pick up than tonal languages like Chinese.

The sound of her own name being called caused her eyes to spring open, and she rose to her feet turning to face them as she did. Franza snapped his fingers and pointed at Torstanda then spun on his heels and strode out of the room. The door was too large and heavy for him to slam, but he made sure that it shut with as much noise as possible. She looked at Torstanda who gave a small shrug and turned to look down at the map.

She crossed the room and stood next to him. "That did not sound good."

Torstanda made another small shrug. "I told him about your idea to check on the dates and our small mystery of some killings being too far apart." He looked at her with a wry grin. "He has much experience and saw what this meant." Then his face became sad. "He said that we must look at the larger truth. That is, the guilt of the War Demon, and ignore small mysteries as being of no consequence. He knows that is not true, of course."

He looked directly at Rhian. "He is trapped, you see. There was supposed to be no doubt for the trial. Important men demand it. Do you understand?"

Rhian nodded. "Yes. I understand these things very well. Such things happen on my world. But what are we to do, Torstanda?"

In response he looked back at the map, shook his head, and exhaled a long, slow breath. "I am a small man of no importance. A seeker for all my life. To seek truth is all I know." Then he looked up. "I would know the truth of this, Rhian. There may be dangers for both of us. Do you understand?"

"Yes, Torstanda. I must know the truth of this. For myself as well as for Bob. I have faced danger when seeking the truth before."

"Good. But first, you took food to the War Demon and spoke with him?"

"Yes," she said as she nodded. "He warned me that the truth may harm how I think of him."

"That is a danger, Rhian. Do you still wish to seek truth even if you learn hurtful things?"

"More than ever. He has risked his life to save my ancestor and my planet. My ancestor always said that he honoured truth. I will honour her, and him, by seeking it now."

Torstanda nodded. "Did he say anything that may help us?"

"Yes. He explained how he was able to make soldiers follow him. More, he told of how there were many armies ... some small, some large. The small preyed upon the settlers. The large armies preyed on the small armies. He believes that over time the largest armies gave birth to nations."

"Yes, yes. That is how the histories tell of it, for those who will listen. Many stories sing the praises of those armies." He gave a derisive snort. "Too many people think those stories tell the full truth and do not seek beyond that. And, yes, many nations trace their beginnings to armies born in those times."

Torstanda cocked his head. "How did he make armies? The histories say the he had several of them over the time he was here."

Rhian shrugged. "He found a small group and fought to become their leader. Made things more equal to give the soldiers more pride and encourage others to join. Part of his education was to learn how to organize, so he knew how to make the group grow and become more effective. He made several armies because sometimes larger armies destroyed them. Sometimes others rebelled and took control away from him."

"Ah, that explains some things," said Torstanda. "Some reports tell of his armies being seen without him, yet it was a point of pride for him to ride in the front to be seen by all. Perhaps some of those were armies that threw him out."

"That sounds like something we can look at." She paused for a moment and bit her lip before continuing, then she steeled herself. "He said that I should look at a very bad thing that occurred in Quinslax province." Torstanda's sharp inhalation told Rhian that she had touched on a sensitive subject.

"Oh, that was a very bad thing, Rhian. One of the very worst things in a time of bad things." He stopped to look at her, but at her firm nod he continued. "This is Quinslax province," he said pointing to the central portion of the western continent. "It was a very rich area, protected by tall mountains and deep rivers. Important trade routes between nations ran through it. They had much advanced learning. Their army was small but had many powerful weapons. Before the Great Collapse, no-one dared to attack. After, of course, they were too rich a target to ignore."

He paused to highlight areas in the province. "The only easy access through mountains was at these three points. Very strong defences, of course. The rivers had several big forts and many small ones. No fleet, or ship of any sort, could pass without permission. There were towns scattered throughout the province with very good roads for easy travel between them. As I said, they were very rich and spent their wealth to ensure that they stayed that way."

"What happened after the Collapse? Was Bob the only one to attack them?"

"No he was not. Many tried but failed. The curious thing is that no-one understands how they failed. Yes, Quinslax had powerful weapons, but so did some of the attackers. The attackers just vanished from history, as if they had never been. But after every attack, the stories tell of a curious silence within Quinslax. There were no sounds of animals or people for many months in the area being attacked. Today, most people ignore all that to look only at what happened when the War Demon attacked." He fell silent and looked away.

"Torstanda, I must know this. Please. What happened to Quinslax?"

He turned to look at her with a great sadness in his eyes. "Quinslax was destroyed by the War Demon. Every field, every forest, every building, every animal ... every person. It took most of a month, but the War Demon destroyed everything with fire. Anyone who tried to escape was hunted down, killed, and their bodies burned. The stories tell of how the War Demon screamed and howled for the entire time as he drove his men to burn and burn and burn. When it was over, he rode into the interior of the province with a legion of men. Only he returned."

"What happened after that?"

"There are different stories. Some say the War Demon left his army and fled into the wastelands. Others say that he led the army on a series of horrific raids. The only thing they agree on is that it was nearly a year before he was actually seen again."

"What happened to Quinslax?"

"It has never recovered. The land became a memory of its previous richness. Nothing grows well there anymore, so crops cannot be grown. The forests have only thin, sickly trees of no use. It took a long time for animals to return, but the land cannot support many. There are a few mines in operation, but only near the borders to other provinces." He shook his head. "For many years after it was destroyed, there were stories of places where the land glowed at night. Even today some people believe it to be cursed, but there have been no reports of glows for over a century. I once visited a province on the border and looked into Quinslax across a river. It is a sad and terrible place, Rhian. I can almost believe in the curse."

"There is no doubt that Bob ... that the War Demon ... did this terrible thing?"

"No doubt at all. I am sorry, but that is a truth."

Rhian was silent for nearly a minute as she stared at the map. "Why would he do such a thing?"

Torstanda shrugged. "He is ... or was ... a demon who thrived on killing. Whoever he is now, Rhian, he was something else in those times."

She shook her head as she studied the map, willing it to give her answers. "No, there is more to this than we understand. He can do hard things, yes, but this sort of destruction is something else." She looked up at him. "Even a demon needs a reason for his actions, Torstanda." Her gaze went back to the map and she tapped her fingertips on the tabletop. Torstanda stood quietly, giving her time to think upon and digest this unpleasant news.

"Total destruction over a large area for reasons we do not understand." She looked up once more. "Did this sort of thing happen again?"

"Yes, Rhian. Twice more that we know of, but smaller." He pointed to an area on the southwest coast of the continent. "Htoumsnni was destroyed about four years later. Then about eight years after that, Stradbog on the eastern continent." He pointed at a spot just inland. Without looking up he added, "There is no doubt that the War Demon was responsible for those."

She nodded. "If I am understanding this map, those are small provinces."

"Yes. Like Quinslax, they were very rich areas protected by natural features, with control of important trade routes."

"Were they destroyed by fire as well?"

"Yes, but over time they recovered and are now healthy."

Rhian took a deep breath and let it out slowly. "This does not make sense. Three separate provinces destroyed by fire for no reason we can see." She steepled her fingers and tapped at her chin. "Did Bob ... the War Demon ... do anything like this anywhere else? To a city, perhaps, or a town?"

"Not like that, no." He waved a hand. "Oh, there was fighting and killing, but not of every living thing."

"When something does not make sense it just means we need to ask better questions, Torstanda," she said as she shook her head. "We have learned all we can from this fast look, I think. Now we need to look at it more deeply. I can ask Bob about this the next time I see him, but for now we need to make a list of his travels and show them on the map. We may see a pattern."

It was three days later before Rhian was able to see Bob again. She and Torstanda had kept busy in that time making lists and notes. It was hard working with only a pen and paper instead of a computer and the Internet, but she made do. To help keep her mind from worrying too much about Bob, Torstanda began teaching her his language. He found her to be a quick learner. She was quick to pick up the basics of the grammar and was now slogging through the laborious process of building up her vocabulary.

Franza had been absent during this time, but one afternoon he barged through the door with his now-customary exuberance. His face showed a range of emotions, and Rhian was unsure if he was angry or not. He strode to where they were at the conference table, pointed at Rhian, and launched into a lengthy diatribe directed at Torstanda. It was all too fast for Rhian to follow. After a couple of minutes of this, Franza wound down and stared at Rhian with wry look on his face. To her surprise, Torstanda chuckled as he translated.

"It appears that you are once again required to take food to the War Demon. After seeing you do it, the soldiers chose to do it for themselves. Now they refuse, saying that the Demon laughed at them and threatened to throw his waste at them."

"Excuse me? Did you say 'laughed'?"

Torstanda chuckled once again but was interrupted by Franza. This time he only spoke a short time then looked at Rhian and shook his head while grinning.

"Yes. Uhm, Franza has just added that it is now vital that a woman save our brave soldiers from being frightened by mockery. It will be your daily task, now. Every morning before we start here."

Rhian coughed to hide a smile. She knew all too well that it was one thing for men to laugh at themselves, but became upset when a woman did it. She cleared her throat and said,

"I would be happy to help in any way that I can."

After hearing Torstanda's translation, Franza made a slight bow of his head. "It is good to know that we have a woman of courage and honour among us. Our soldiers can learn from you." He cleared his throat and became serious. "A soldier will come for you soon. Be ready." With that he turned on his heels and strode out, closing the door behind him.

Torstanda was still grinning. "I am not sure how laughing can be frightening, but if anyone can do that the War Demon can."

Rhian could no longer contain herself and laughed out loud. "Oh, yes. I'm sure that Bob enjoyed that. He has quite the sense of humour."

Torstanda's grin was replaced by a thoughtful look. "I have never thought of the War Demon as having a sense of humour. That is a very interesting thought." Then he became serious. "You must make ready. Use the washroom now and eat some food. The soldiers sometimes play foolish games when made to look silly. I speak from experience."

Rhian took his advice and was stuffing the last bit of bread into her mouth when there was a knock at the door. She swallowed and washed it down with a mouthful of water. The door opened, and she stood up to see a sour-faced soldier standing there. He grunted and motioned for her to join him. Rhian smoothed out her face, careful not to show any emotion as she walked over to join him.

CHAPTER ELEVEN
The Revelation of Horrors

As Torstanda had predicted, the soldiers at every stop spent time doing security-check rituals. There was much bracing to attention and stomping of feet as they moved a small distance. It all reminded Rhian of the guards at Buckingham Palace. She kept her peace and amused herself by scrutinizing the soldiers and their uniforms. One thing she'd noticed was that this time around the soldiers were younger than before and there were several different uniforms in evidence. The general styles were roughly equivalent, but differed in colour and bits of adornment.

At long last she stood before the final door, and this time had three buckets thrust at her. As before, one held water, another food, but the third was empty. She walked through the door and twisted just enough to avoid being shoved. It was her impression that the door shut behind her with a bit of extra force. A smile tweaked the edges of her mouth, but she was quite firm with it and forced her face into a neutral expression. Great-gran always warned the girls about the danger of laughing at a man where he could see her, and that advice seemed particularly useful right now. Especially since she was old enough to be their mother. Or, a horrid thought occurring to her, their grandmother. That thought kept the smile off her face better than any amount of self-control.

"Hello, Mother Christmas," called Bob from his cell. "Did you bring me lots of presents?"

"Not sure you deserve any," she called back as she walked towards him. "I hear you've been a very naughty boy. Scaring those poor soldiers like that."

He stood up, and Rhian saw he was wearing the blanket like a toga.

"Nice outfit," she said.

"Oh, this old thing?" He spun around on the balls of his feet. "It's the height of fashion on all the best planets."

They both chuckled more than the joke was worth, but it helped to take the edge off the situation. Rhian worked the latch and passed the buckets inside.

"What's the empty for?" She noticed a bucket in the corner. "Oh. I gather it's to replace that one? I wondered about the sanitation facilities here."

"Sorry you have to deal with that, Rhian."

She shrugged. "Not to worry. Done similar things in some of the countries I've had to visit. Anyway, feel free to eat if you're hungry."

"Thanks, I will. Feeling a bit peckish." He took a couple of handfuls of water, then sat down to eat.

"What did the chef send you this time?"

"Hmm, let's see. Elderly bread, squishy fruit, a root of something, and some nuts. Not bad, all things considered."

She growled. "I'll mention that. Sure it's safe to eat?"

He finished gnawing on a piece of bread and swallowed. "It'll do. Don't make too many waves, Rhian. You should start building up a stock of good will."

This time she directed a growl at him. "Do not ... I repeat ... do not tell me how to do my job."

Bob raised an eyebrow at her response. Rhian noted that his face looked a lot better than last time she'd seen him.

"Just stating the obvious, Rhian. I can't help you right now, and I worry. Yes, you've got a lot of experience with new cultures. On Earth, I hasten to point out. Where you know the language and customs."

"Lots of different languages and customs on Earth, Bob. For me, this is just one more. It's what I've trained for and what I've spent a good many years doing."

Rhian blew out her cheeks and wriggled her shoulders to ease tense muscles. "I know you mean well, but I'm not a child or naive waif. And I'm getting far too much of the 'poor little woman' vibe from the men around here. Oh, I'm putting up with it," she said as she waved a hand. "Don't like it, but I know how to play that game well enough." She gave him a small smile to take the sting out of her words. "Speaking of games, are you sure you should be tormenting the guards so much?"

Bob nodded. "Oh, yes. They see me as the War Demon. That means they need to prove themselves by tormenting me, and that'll just escalate until I enforce limits."

"Did your Dad teach you that?"

"Nope. Learned that myself through experience. This isn't my first time in a cell. Hmm, let's try this." Bob examined the fruit, sniffed it, and took a couple of small bites. He made a face and tossed both the fruit and the samples into his waste bucket.

"There are some fruits here best eaten when soft but this was not one of them. Bleh." He washed out his mouth with a handful of water. "Let's try the nuts." He picked up a couple, popped them into his mouth, and began chewing. "I like these," he said, his words slurred slightly by the mass of food in his mouth.

"Didn't the nuts last time have rather hefty shells? These a different type?"

Bob smiled. "Same type. Used for livestock when I was here, but I developed a taste for them. As for the shells, they take care of that for me these days."

"What?"

"Oh, yes. I was taking the shells and grinding them into a

powder." He pointed at a couple of discoloured spots on the wall. "The rough stone works well for that."

"So, is the powder poisonous or something?"

"Nope. Oh, it'll irritate the eyes and nose as any powder will, but it isn't in and of itself harmful. No, back in the day I managed to cobble together some gunpowder while locked up in a prison. There was even a song about it that was quite popular for a time. Guess it's still around. Oh, don't look at me like that ... I was just having a bit of fun with them."

"Heh. Great-gran always said you were a bit of a brat. Guess you haven't changed. So what else do you do for entertainment? Wait, mind if I sit down?"

"Oh, wait ... I'll pass you this empty pail. It'll do for a stool." He passed it out and Rhian sat down on it. While she was settling down, he continued his story.

"An officer came to question me yesterday. Sat on a chair about where you're sitting. An obnoxious, self-important little man. I stood polite and quiet for a few minutes then did a fast lunge at the bars doing a very loud screech and wail. He jumped up then stumbled backwards over the chair. Not sure, but he may have soiled himself. A couple of the guards hurried to help him up but a couple of the others were smiling. That's useful information, by the way."

"How so?"

"It's indicative of the state of armed forces. An officer unworthy of the title, and a coward at that, plus the undisguised sneering by the lower ranks when he made a mistake." Bob shook his head. "That sort of officer can be more dangerous than a professional soldier ... they allow their emotions to rule judgement. Anyway, it's a small sample but still useful."

Rhian nodded. "Speaking of soldiers, I'm seeing a lot of new faces. Younger faces; very intense-looking, some of them. Several different uniforms."

"That makes sense. This facility would have been staffed

with the equivalent of a garrison guard. Old-timers to keep things going smoothly until something happens. Now the real troops are being moved in. The different uniforms are probably from different countries. That'll probably cause other sorts of tensions, so watch out for that."

"I will, thanks. Saw this sort of thing when I was in the middle of a UN peacekeeping mission. I'll be careful."

They fell into silence as Bob finished eating his nuts and drank some water.

Rhian cleared her throat. "Ah ... joking aside, how are you holding up?"

"Better than I expected, to be honest. I was thrown for loop at the beginning, but you helped snap me out of that. Thank you very much for that."

"I worry about you sitting here alone, Bob. Great-gran said this planet had put some deep hooks into you."

"She was right about that, Rhian. Been doing a lot of thinking and lot of remembering, that's for sure. But it's not knocked me into a black hole like it used to. Maybe it's a side-effect of this new body or maybe it's mature wisdom finally kicking in." He grinned. "In any event, I'll take it."

"You up for answering some questions about the past?"

His grin widened. "As I've often told you, ask me anything."

She flashed a smile before becoming serious once more. "I looked into Quinslax. That led me to Htoumsnni and Stradbog. You warned me, but it was worse than I expected. So bad that I can't help but think there's something nasty behind it."

Bob's smile had vanished by the time she finished. "What did you find out about Quinslax?"

"Very rich, serious natural defences, small army equipped with the very best weapons. Same with the other two."

"How long did the green glow last?"

The question startled her. "About a century or so." Her eyes narrowed. "And the land never recovered. What remained was

131

stunted and deformed." Bob said nothing as she chewed on a lip. "Radiation. No, wait. Something else." Her face went white. "Chemical and biological weapons."

"Correct on all counts."

"Oh, Goddess, Bob. What happened?" Rhian clasped her knees to prevent herself from falling over in shock.

"Long story short? They were all the most tempting targets on the planet, but every army that attacked them died to the last man. No sounds of battle, they just died. That made me very suspicious at the time and I resisted calls to attack them. But you have to understand that armies have a mind of their own and sometimes a commander can only go where he's allowed to go. So we went to Quinslax. It was morning and there was what looked to be a heavy fog. Strange but not unheard of for the area. Then my healing factors warned me of the biological hazards in time for me to keep most of my soldiers alive. At first the affected animals began twitching and frothing at the mouth, then bleeding from the eyes and nose. The troops I failed to get out in time were in the same state. We waited for the winds to blow the fog away, and all we could see were dead things littering the fields and into the forest. Birds, insects, everything dead except the plants. The silence was frightening."

His eyes were unfocused as the memories filled his mind. Then he shook his head and looked at her again. "We moved to a different spot and were hit by another sort of chemical attack, a nerve agent this time. We spent a couple of weeks moving around their borders and were met with a similar response each time. Finally, we probed and met no resistance. I took a squad in and probed inland. Now, we'd not seen any people to this point. None at all. After a half-day's hard riding we came to a village. There were people there ... of a sort." He took a deep breath and let it out slowly. His shoulders slumped and his head hung below his knees.

"Bob?" Her voice was gentle and low.

He lifted his head to look at her. "Oh, sorry. I'd not thought of this in a very long time. Up to that point I thought I'd seen horror, but this was worse. All those people, Rhian. Men, woman, and children infected with something vile and stumbling about. It looked like a fungal growth that started at the head and gradually spread over the rest of the body. We galloped out of the town and to the next one only to find the same thing. We camped out in a forest and waited for dawn to head back. Next morning two of my men showed signs of infection. They had shoved away some infected that tried to grab them. We began heading back but by noon they were fully infected and couldn't ride. Then my healing factors informed me that in the early stages the disease became airborne."

"Oh, no. What did you do?"

His face was calm but his eyes were haunted. "No choice. I killed my men ... they were dead or going to die. At least I gave them and their mounts a clean death. I galloped to the nearest high point and scanned as far as I could. Everything seemed to be infected. There was some movement in the distance, so I galloped off to see what it was. Turned out to be a mass of the infected who'd gathered together in a hideous migration, marching towards the border. It was a slow migration but there was nothing to stop it."

He paused to shake his head. "It was like something out of a nightmare. No shouting or talking or crying. Just the sound of feet marching in a random rhythm. All those people, covered in that fungus thing."

"So you sterilized it all. You had no choice." Her voice was low but firm.

"No choice at all. It had to be stopped. Those idiots had unleashed their ultimate weapon and it had turned against them."

"How did you return to your troops without infecting them?"

"Well, I rode back to the border and just before reaching it

I killed my horse. It was showing the signs. Then I built a large fire and stood inside it. Oh, don't look so horrified. My healing factors dealt with the injuries, but I had to get rid of any infection that was on the surface of my body. That was sufficient to get me safely away from the infected zone."

"Then you burnt it all."

He nodded. "Had a hard time convincing my men, but they understood once they saw the migration coming towards them. It took some weeks, but we managed to cleanse the entire province. It was all but enclosed by natural features, so it wasn't as difficult as it sounds. Just time-consuming and ... horrific."

"One story has you going into the interior after the cleansing."

"Yes. This was a manufactured bioweapon, so I needed to destroy whatever facility created it. Found it and destroyed it. Then found something just as bad."

"Radiation weapons."

"Radioactive dust, to be precise. Half-life of about twenty years, more or less. There was a bunker somewhere with fanatical troops who released it in a frenzy of fear or insanity. What the chemical and biological weapons failed to kill, the radiation finished off."

"What about the other places?"

"The facility I destroyed had some records that indicated a transfer of technology between the three countries. A case of the very rich doing everything in their power to protect each other. Never did find out who created what, and never really cared. I'd grown to hate this planet and everything on it, but I wasn't going to stand by and let a small group of self-centred monsters destroy everything."

"So you stopped them."

"I had to stop them. They had the tech to create those weapons but not to control them."

There was a noise at the door indicating that it was being

opened.

"You have to go."

"Yeah, dammit. Bob ... are we ever going to get out of this place?"

He nodded and grinned. "Just keep putting one foot in front of the other. You're making progress. We're both still alive."

The guards began yelling. Rhian stood up and gave Bob the empty bucket.

As he took it, he pointed at the bucket in the cell. "Oh. Would you mind taking this waste bucket with you? It's traditional in jails to take the old one when giving a new bucket."

She wrinkled her nose and snorted. "It would be my honour, my dear sir. I've taken shit from everyone else here."

* * *

As the days passed, a rhythm began to emerge. Rhian woke up at sunrise, had breakfast with Torstanda, took food to Bob, and then returned to the large office to continue her historical research with Torstanda. The pair of them were making good progress slogging through the historical records, much to the surprise and delight of Torstanda.

"You ask such interesting questions, Rhian," he was moved to say.

She snorted. "That's only because I see things with fresh eyes and a desire to discover the truth, whatever it may be."

"That is true, Rhian, but you have talent. Still, I take your point. Too many people here try to fit the facts into conclusions. Worse, those conclusions are increasingly made to suit the needs of the powerful."

Rhian nodded. "That is often the case on my world as well. But we seekers must strive to serve truth as much as we can."

As Bob continued to urge her, Rhian, for the most part, avoided causing friction. One problem occurred when she tried to get new clothing. The clothes she had obtained from the base were not wearing out so much as they were beginning to smell. Day after day, though, her requests for new clothing went unanswered.

Finally, she exploded and took it out on long-suffering Torstanda. He patiently explained, once again, that the problem was finding the appropriate female clothing for one of her status. Her status was unclear, so no decision could be made. The proper formalities had to be observed. Things had already been stretched beyond accepted norms by allowing her work with him.

After pondering the problem and asking some pointed questions, a compromise was reached. She would be allowed to exchange one piece of clothing at a time, one day at a time. That allowed her to, for example, wear a substitute shirt while her own was drying in her bathroom after washing it. The clothes they provided her were obviously castoffs and from a variety of sources. It made for some interesting ensembles and got her a variety of looks ranging from shock to sneers. She took it all in stride, content to be wearing clean clothes.

Franza posed another problem. Every day he would drop by for an update, and each time he would shake his head and fuss about what a problem this research would pose. To his credit, he did not stop it, and in fact ensured that books and records were made available to them. Rhian grumbled that it was as bad as having her thesis adviser fussing over any paper that had a hint of controversy. When she explained those terms to Torstanda, he laughed and said that things were much the same for many seekers on his world.

Despite the irritants, Rhian was beginning to enjoy her stay. The work was interesting, and Torstanda was a delightful colleague. On the other hand, seeing Bob in a cage was becoming increasingly hard to bear. He remained irritatingly cheerful and was quite interested in her work. As he explained to her one day, "You're finding out things that I never knew. I was in the middle of it, and you're seeing the big picture.

Worse, I spent a long time lost in madness. This is helping me put it all into perspective. On top of that, it really is quite fascinating."

When she reminded him that there was a trial coming up, he just shrugged. "Not here yet. The soldiers gossip amongst themselves and I can sometimes overhear them. The different countries can't agree on a proper format. There's four major powers, each with a cadre of medium powers allied with them. There are a number of smaller states, most of which are nominally non-aligned. In practise they work hard to keep the larger powers from running roughshod over them. In this one instance, though, they have an equal vote and are using it to gain concessions. Lots of international intrigue and power struggles. You need to watch out for that. The soldiers guarding me are certainly reflecting those tensions."

He jerked his head towards the far door. "There's no love lost between the different lots of soldiers. Their interactions are increasingly becoming limited to formalities. The original, older soldiers fraternized despite being from different countries. These new younger ones are harder and keep to themselves. From what I've seen it'll only get worse."

Both Franza and Torstanda agreed with that assessment but had a different conclusion. "This trial," said Franza, "will be a triumph of our modern values over the old hatreds. We have never been so united."

Torstanda cleared his throat. "With respect, Franza, there are still many outstanding issues. The major powers still control the rivers flowing into many of the lesser powers. Building dams has led to many angry words."

Franza waved a dismissive hand. "Minor issues that will be resolved when the Planetary Council convenes." He fixed Torstanda with a condescending look. "Seekers of all nations are rising in influence. The rule of law and the seeking of truth will triumph over those that merely yell slogans."

Torstanda nodded and turned to Rhian. "That is correct,

Rhian. This is an important point in our history. Those frictions that the War Demon speaks of will pass." Rhian nodded in acquiescence, but only to forestall an argument.

In any event, Bob's tidbits of gossip were enough to keep Franza interested in pulling strings to keep Rhian as the daily food-bearer for Bob. He may have disagreed with Bob's analysis, but found the gossip useful enough.

By her count they'd been there for over three weeks when one morning Bob announced that the trial was immanent, probably within a few days. Rhian hurried back and asked Franza about it. He rushed out of the room and came back an hour later in a huff. The rumour was true, and he was quite put out that he'd not been informed through official channels. After ranting for a bit, he turned to Rhian and Torstanda and instructed them to prepare a series of maps for a proper display he could show in court. Both of them were shocked, as this was the first time he'd suggested or even hinted at such a thing. He stormed out and Torstanda said to Rhian, "At last his pride is more important than his powerful friends. We have much work to do."

The next day it was formally announced that the trial would take place the morning of the day after next. The evening before the trial, Franza strode into the office and demanded a briefing. They showed him their maps along with the associated records. One map showed all the event attributed to the War Demon. They had also prepared a series of maps, showing attributed events by year, one map for every year.

Franza grilled them on their methodology and sources of information. At the end of it, he was rubbing his hands with glee. "Oh, this will be the trial of my career. There will be a proper testing of truth in the crucible of justice, never fear. Too many on the Great Council have assumed that they will wave their hands and ignore the law. But the law exists for all and procedures must be followed."

Rhian chose this moment to speak up. "Franza, what is the

procedure on what the accused should wear?"

"What do you mean?"

"Bob ... the War Demon ... is only allowed to have a blanket in his cell. What will he wear to such a trial?"

Franza looked at her with amusement. "I sense that you have a solution."

"Yes. Let him wear the clothes he wore when we arrived. They are the uniform of his people. Not a dress uniform, but more suitable than a blanket."

"Hmm, yes, you make a good point." Then he smiled. "And what will you wear, Rhian? You have such a mixture of clothes these days."

Rhian flushed and reminded herself that she needed this man's good will. "I will wear the clothes I had when I arrived. They are appropriate to my station and gender according to the procedures of my people." She remembered to give a professional smile.

Franza clasped his hands behind him and harrumphed for a moment. "The soldiers have examined the War Demon's clothing many times and found nothing. They have also examined yours, Rhian, when you left them in your room. I suspect you knew this."

"Yes, Franza. It does not bother me. I have nothing to hide."

"Your clothing is very similar to his. This is not our way, but you say it is yours. I will accept this and will tell the soldiers." With that he shrugged. "If they object I will tell them that the War Demon must look the part for the trial. No-one will fear a man dressed in a blanket." He laughed as if he'd made a great joke. Rhian and Torstanda make encouraging smiles and bobbed their heads. Franza left the room still chuckling at his cleverness.

"Is there anything else we should be doing, Torstanda? It is still early."

"No, Rhian. We have done all we can. Let us simply clean up here and make everything ready for tomorrow. We both need a good night of rest for the ordeal tomorrow."

He hesitated for a moment then added, "You know how this will end, Rhian."

She smiled at him and said, "The ending is not written before the game has begun, Torstanda. Tonight we will rest. Tomorrow will reveal the ending."

As they spent the few minutes it took to clean up, Rhian realized that she believed what she had said. To her surprise, Bob's unshakable optimism had rubbed off on her, but she wasn't sure if she should thank him for that or not.

CHAPTER TWELVE
Trial of the War Demon

Daybreak came all too early. Rhian rose and took extra care with her grooming. There was no makeup to put on, for which she was grateful as she'd never gotten into the habit of using it. More to the point, on this planet a woman not wearing makeup was strange enough that it helped to mark her as something alien and somehow unclean. That had served her well given that she was the only woman in a facility filled with men.

She gave her clothes a final brushing. They didn't need it but the busywork helped to keep her calm. No-one had told her what to expect at the trial and she was torn between curiosity and dread. At last she could put off the inevitable no longer. She finished dressing and examined herself in the bathroom mirror with a critical eye. Her image nodded its approval of her appearance, so she went back into the main room. She stood there for a moment trying to calm her nerves when she inhaled sharply and headed to the desk. From within the drawer she took her sheaf of notes and some blank paper. They fit nicely into an inside pocket of the jacket without making an unseemly bulge. With a final look around, she took a deep breath and knocked on the door.

The door opened and the guard examined her carefully before nodding. It was one of the older, original guards who had always treated her as sort of comrade, or perhaps a junior who needed to be watched over. In any case, he seemed satisfied with her appearance and with his fellows escorted Rhian to Bob's holding cell.

A surprise awaited her at the door to the cell area. Instead of the usual buckets, there was a pushcart filled with four buckets of water, a proper breakfast, and Bob's clothes. She pushed the cart through the doorway, straining against its weight to keep it in motion. The expected shove didn't come this time, for which she was grateful.

"Good morning, Rhian," called Bob from his cell. "That's quite a load you've got there."

She nodded a greeting but said nothing until she reached the cell. "Oof, that's heavy. Lots of water. I guess they expect you to wash yourself. And there's a good meal, for a change. Those sausage things are quite tasty, by the way. Oh, and your clothes. Which do you want first?"

"Hmm. Pass the empty bucket first, then the clothes, so I can keep them off the floor. Then the water, I suppose. Food last."

It took several minutes to pass everything through.

Rhian wrinkled her nose. "Glad they're finally letting you have a proper wash-up. You need it. No offence."

"None taken," Bob said as he chuckled. "You're right, of course." He rubbed at his chin with a hand. "Could use a shave, but that won't happen. I overheard them arguing rather loudly about that with someone. The soldiers refused to give me anything sharp. Can't say as I blame them."

"Perhaps the wild, unkempt look might work in your favour."

Bob replied through a mouthful of food. "Not in this case. It's considered a sign of disrespect towards authority to appear with less than perfect grooming. Say, these sausages are excellent. Didn't have anything like these when I was here." He took a bite of bread and looked at it in surprise. "It's fresh and good quality. Wasn't expecting that." He wolfed it down and drank some water.

"Easy there, don't go gulping it down."

Bob wiped at his mouth with the back of a hand. "Nice to have good food. Oh, I hope you're keeping your ability to understand the language a secret as I suggested."

Rhian nodded. "Yes, thank you for that. After a week or so of practise, Torstanda stopped teaching me. I gather it wasn't something he was authorized to do, and he lost his nerve. It was enough to give me the basics, so I was able to fill in a lot of the blanks by reading and listening. I don't think even he knows the level of fluency I've obtained. Can't speak it very well, mind you, but I can understand it well enough."

"Good. Anything new on the maps that I should know about?"

"Not that I can think of. Wish I could have shown you the maps rather than simply describing them."

"The descriptions were more than adequate. I know where I was and when, so it'll be interesting to see what else they're trying to pin on me."

Rhian made an exasperated sound. "I wish you'd take this a little more seriously, Bob."

Bob chuckled. "Can you think of a better time to be less than serious?"

She glared at him a moment then laughed. "No, you're right. Sorry to be a nag. It's just that I can't believe how optimistic you've stayed despite all this." She waved a hand to encompass the cell and prison.

He smiled as he said, "I've been in a lot of tough situations before. Worse than this, I assure you." Then he became serious. "But it's not myself that I'm worried about, Rhian, it's you."

"Well, as Great-gran always told me, when the shit hits the fan, attack the fan. I won't give up hope."

"That's the spirit. I—"

The sound of the door opening put an end to their conversation. Rhian frowned. "That was less time than usual."

"Guess they want to me to get ready for the trial. It'll be starting soon. You better go get yourself something to eat. I suspect it'll be a long day."

The guards shouted what Rhian now recognized as a string of personal insults directed at her parentage, age, looks, and sex. She turned and gave them a pleasant smile as she waved. Turning to face Bob she muttered, "Assholes. But, yes, I need to go. Give 'em hell at the trial."

There were further shouts from the guards so Rhian turned and walked towards them with her head held high and a professional smile on her face. She was damned if she'd ever show weakness to these self-important assholes.

Rhian was escorted to the office and let inside by the guards stationed there. Torstanda as standing at the conference table and he waved her over. "We must hurry. There is little time. First we have a quick breakfast, then we must work." He held out a seat for her and helped her sit.

"Torstanda, please sit. I can fill my own plate, thank you. Now eat and tell me what is happening."

"The trial, Rhian. The time of the trial is now sooner than expected." He glanced at a clock on the wall. "It begins in just over an hour, but we must be there sooner. Franza is very upset about the change and thinks it is a tactic to put him at a disadvantage. He has left to protest and make a big noise." Torstanda grinned. "He is beginning to act as a proper interceder and is enjoying it." Then he frowned. "Now we must eat quickly. Franza wants us to be his helpers and carry all these papers to the trial chamber."

Rhian had been picking at her food while listening then fell to it with a will. This promised to be an interesting day.

* * *

Franza rushed them to get there well before anyone else.

The trick, he told them as they hurried along, was to be set up and looking fresh as everyone came in. He fussed over getting his notes set up just so on the podium dedicated to his use. Rhian and Torstanda sat at a small table just behind him, with all their exhibits neatly arranged. Then, speaking through Torstanda, he said, "Torstanda, I wish for you to have one— no, two—open books in front of you. Have slips of paper marking several spots within each. Rhian, you will take notes. You do not speak the language, of course, but just make a show of it. It is not seemly for a woman to sit there with nothing to do." He turned away before he could see Rhian sneer and roll her eyes, with Torstanda making small motions with his hands trying to get her to stop.

Each of them busied themselves with their own preparations while Franza settled his robes of office to better effect. There was little for her to do, so she passed the time examining the room. It was a large amphitheatre design, finished with the ubiquitous wood panelling. Unlike the rest of the facility, there were no carvings or heraldic displays.

The audience was beginning to file in and were directed to seats that rose up in several stepped tiers. Those people sat on benches. Off to each side were smaller tiers with upholstered seats, which Rhian assumed were for the high and mighty. The front of room was what caught her eye. The structure there consisted of a series of elevated benches, in three levels. The upper layer had four chairs, the next layer to either side of the upper held five chairs each, then the lowest tier on the ends held six chairs each. Hanging off the bench in front of each chair was a flag. Rhian recognized them as the flags of different countries. She leaned over to Torstanda and pointed at the front. He nodded and whispered, "The Planetary Council sits in judgement there. The strongest countries at the top, the middle powers to each side, and the others on the lowest level."

The noise level of the room rose as people filed in, until it reached a point where Rhian could not have spoken to Torstanda without shouting. Franza stood at his lectern beaming and nodding at various people as they came in. To Rhian's eyes he appeared to be quite enjoying himself. For her part, Rhian studied the people with interest as this was her first chance to see the regular civilians of this world. The ages seemed to range from young adults to the very old, with a roughly equal mixture of the sexes. The women, though, tended to sit in groups. Their outfits were quite showy and reminded Rhian of the aristocracy of Europe's 1700s. The men's outfits had more variation than she expected, and were on the flashy side. There were several glances and hard stares directed at her, especially from the ladies who were obviously sizing her up and finding her wanting. She felt rather plain among all the finery and was glad of it.

A gong rang out once, filling the room with echoes of its sound. It rang once more and hidden doors behind the Great Council's tiers opened up. A series of men filed in and began taking seats behind the benches. Their outfits were much more sombre than the rest of the people, but Rhian noticed a lot of embroidery on them that blended in with the otherwise sombre attire. The room grew silent.

When the Great Council were all seated, one of the topmost members drew a dagger. He held it aloft for a moment then rapped the pommel three times on the table then placed it in front of him, with the blade facing outward. In rough unison, the others repeated the ritual. The primary judge, or so Rhian thought of him, looked at his fellows then raised he left hand and said, "Trial begins. Bring forth the accused."

The main doors, which had been closed when the judges entered, opened up but Rhian could not see the entrance with all the people in her way. She did, however, hear the stomp of feet marching in unison. The marching came closer and closer, then she saw four soldiers followed by Bob then another four more soldiers. He was dressed in his uniform and looked clean but unshaven. His arms were bound with a set of heavy-looking manacles. Bob, however, bore them with ease. In fact, he made it appear as if he was a dignitary being escorted by an honour guard rather than jailers.

They marched past Rhian and to a point about five metres from the Great Council, when they came to a halt. Bob halted in lockstep with them, making it look as if it had all been rehearsed. There was a soft buzz from the audience which the chief judge silenced with a glare. The guards spun on their heels and took three steps before spinning once more to face Bob. Their weapons—a rifle with a bayonet on the end—were lifted to their chests in a ready position.

The chief judge looked down at Bob and said, "We are here to judge the one known as the War Demon. His crimes are extensive and known to all. Our judgement shall be swift."

Bob shrugged his shoulders, fluttered his arms, and the manacles fell from his wrists, ending up being held in his right hand. A gasp came from the crowd. Bob extended his left arm and used the manacles to slice across the arm. Tossing aside the manacles, he dropped to one knee, smeared blood from the wound onto his right hand, and used it to draw a half-circle on the floor in front of him. He re-covered the right hand with blood and slapped it on the floor just below the arc.

"I claim Right of Trial," he said in a loud, clear voice. He rose to his feet and extended both arms out from his sides. "I bind myself to the truth with my blood as pledge."

Lowering his arms, he looked at the judges. There was no mocking or laughter in his voice or face. The crowd grew silent. Several of the judges began shaking their heads and others made dismissive motions with their hands.

After a few seconds the chief judge slapped his hand on the tabletop twice. That was enough to bring silence. His face twisted as if he'd bitten on a lemon. "How dare you claim right of trial, Demon? That is a ritual from the old times and no longer applies. We ... ", he indicated the judges on the top tier, "will pronounce sentence on you. That is the way of things now."

The declaration had a startling effect on the other tiers of judges, especially those on the lowest level. One leaned forward and declared, "We of Wilnof still honour the old ways. War Demon or no, he has made the pledge and we grant it." The judge waved his hand to encompass the others on the lower tier, who nodded in stern agreement.

The chief judge looked taken aback for a moment. Then he shook his head. "No, it has been already agreed. We will make the judgement."

The lesser judge smiled without humour. "Her Wisdom granted an equal vote to all judges in case of a trial. Shall we vote on this?" This time his smile held a trace of humour. The chief judge was not amused. He huffed for a moment then turned to Bob and said, "We grant you trial. Do you have an interceder?"

Rhian heard a soft sigh from the crowd that stopped as Franza stepped forward to stand next to Bob. "I have been named interceder and stand ready to perform my function."

The chief judge drummed his fingers on the tabletop then stopped himself with a start. "Very well. We will begin in a few moments." The top-tier judges began a low-voiced discussion among themselves. There was a soft buzz of excitement as the crowd discussed this new development.

"What just happened?" whispered Rhian.

"The Council tried to render a judgement without a trial," whispered Torstanda. "Your friend used an old ritual claim to trial. In those days it was used as a means to ensure that all voices would be heard. But the judgement could only choose life or death. The smaller countries object to being treated as lesser, so they agree with the claim as a show of strength."

The chief judge slapped his hand on the tabletop twice. "Trial will commence."

"Demon," he said, "state your name."

148

"My name is Bob. I have no other."

"When did you come here?"

"In the year 4891 by the calendar of the Plitsfor throne."

"How did you come here?"

"By means of a doorway device."

"Why did you come here?"

"I came to be tested."

"Explain."

"My father trained me to be a soldier, but I had never fought a real battle. He sent me here to learn the ways of war on a planet that was awash in it."

"To what end?"

"To prove myself in battle."

"How old were you?"

"In your terms, about seventeen."

That caused a flurry of conversation that the chief judge had to work to squash. The judge who supported Bob's right to trial spoke up. "How were you to prove yourself? By destroying our world?"

"No. I was to join an army and learn. Your world was already sliding into chaos when I arrived. What you call the Great Collapse."

After taking a moment to look at each of the judges, Bob shook his head. "My father did not know of the Collapse. He assumed that the perpetual warfare that existed here would continue."

"Why did you not leave?"

"The doorway device was only an entrance to this world. To leave, I would have to find the exit elsewhere on this planet. Finding it was part of the test."

"How long were you here?"

"About twenty years."

Another judge from the middle tier interjected. "That cannot be true. We have records of your atrocities spanning decades."

"My interceder can give you the details, but I swear upon

149

my blood that I was only here for twenty years."

"Why should we believe you?"

Bob pointed to the symbols he had created on the floor and said, "I have sworn it."

That caused an uproar of voices from both the judges and the spectators. Above them all could be heard Bob's voice booming out as he said, "Of all the stories, are there any that speak of me breaking my sworn word?"

The crowd, and the judges, grew silent.

Franza spoke up at last. "As the assigned interceder I have investigated the crimes ascribed to the War Demon. While some are undeniably by his hand, there are others that are not. I am prepared to show how I have tested the truth of things. May I proceed?"

The top tier of judges shook their heads and muttered among themselves. After a few seconds, the chief judge looked up and said, "His guilt is without question. Why do you waste our time?"

Franza drew himself up and fixed the judge with a look of steel. "A fundamental principle of our system of justice is that no man shall be tried for crimes he did not commit. Whatever the crimes of the War Demon, he must be judged only on the ones that can be proven beyond a reasonable doubt. I can show that many of the crimes that he is accused of have reasonable doubt."

Once again the top tier of judges shook their heads, but the majority of the others made it plain that they wanted to hear what Franza had to say. Finally the chief judge announced, "You may proceed. The War Demon will sit in the appointed place while we listen."

The guards used their rifles to motion Bob towards a low, wooden chair off to one side. He walked over there as if being led to a throne and sat down. Franza took one of the maps and unrolled it, holding it up with his hands. The chief judge waved him to silence and instructed two of the soldiers to hold up the map. Franza, now in his element, proceeded to explain how he had sorted through all the assumed crimes and found new truths.

While Franza pontificated, Rhian jotted down notes. While writing she noticed that Bob was beginning to fidget. This, to her knowledge, was new behaviour for him. He touched and fiddled with different areas of his clothing until finally settling down with his hand over his mouth. She frowned but kept her head down as she wrote. There was a faint buzzing sound that she attributed to insects, so she shifted slightly in her seat. The buzz became a faint but distinct voice.

"Rhian. Rhian, can you hear me? Scratch your nose."

She paused for a moment, unsure of what to do. After a moment she gave her nose a brief scratch and risked a quick look at Bob.

"Yes, it's me. The uniforms have some tricks built into them. My ship has just entered this system and is two or three hours away. If we can stall things that long we'll be fine."

Rhian scratched at her nose again while giving her head a slight shake.

"Not sure how, exactly. Wait for my signal." He lowered his hand and once again rested his hands in his lap, seemingly at peace.

For the next hour and a half, the court listened to Franza recount his the details of "his" investigations. The assembled multitude was, at first, transfixed by the revelations but as the minutes dragged on they began to show signs of restlessness. Oblivious to this, Franza droned on citing detail after detail. Even Rhian, hardened as she was by endless university committee meetings, felt her own eyes drooping. An angry muttering from the crowd brought her back to full alertness.

"In conclusion," she heard Franza say, "We have erred in our understanding of what Her Wisdom, Kydos, told us. The fault is ours, not hers, of course."

Cries of "false truths" were heard coming from the audience.

151

The chief judge banged his hand on the desk to restore order. The outcries died down, but angry mutterings remained. A judge from the second tier leaned forward. "Are we to understand that the War Demon made no attacks upon the great kingdom of Acirema? How, then, do you explain its downfall? It was the best of us then and is a leader of us all now." He bowed towards the chief judge who acknowledged him with a nod. Cries of "Make Acirema great again" rang out until the chief judge restored order. The judges on the lower tier leaned back in their chairs. Many shook their heads. Some rolled their eyes.

Franza spread his hands and boomed out, "We are better now than we were then and can see with fresh eyes. Her Wisdom gave us the facts. It is up to us to make use of them. The truth, as she showed us, is that many nations, great and small, fell during the Great Collapse for reasons of their own making."

Catcalls greeted this pronouncement, but Franza only raised his voice. "The War Demon's crimes are many, but he cannot be blamed for all our problems. We have made such great progress and can take pride in our achievements." The yelling of the crowd finally drowned him out, and he stood there unsure what to do. Such disrespectful behaviour was outside of his experience. He shot a pleading look at the judges.

For their part, some were arguing among each other, some were nodding along with the various chants, and others were shaking their heads in disgust. The chants had begun with calls about the glory of Acirema, but soon chants extolling the virtues of other countries were heard. This continued for several minutes, then shouting between audience members could be seen. Rhian even saw several individuals shove each other. Several minutes later, fistfights began to break out. Rhian was surprised to see that the first of them occurred among the women. "Like a bloody footie match," she muttered to herself. To be on the safe side, she shoved several pencils into a pocket of her jacket. She'd been caught in riots more than once and wanted to be able to defend herself.

The sharp banging of doors became heard through the dull roar of the crowd. The doors behind the judges were open and soldiers were trotting in. Unlike before, these soldiers all wore the same uniform ... that of Acirema. They created a line behind and in front of the judges. Another group of soldiers came trotting in through the main doors. These wore the uniform of Niatirb, another of the major powers, and staunch ally of Acirema.

The chief judge nodded and one of the soldiers fired several rounds into the air. Within seconds, the room became silent. All eyes were on the judges. Rhian risked a glance at Bob and saw him fiddling with his clothes. She hoped it indicated communication with the ship and not a nervous tick.

"I will have silence," thundered the chief judge. "We will not be misled by false truths. Her Wisdom has guided us in the past as she will guide us now. We of Acirema and our allies ..." he paused to nod at the other top-tier judges, "have decided to summon Her Wisdom. Before leaving, she entrusted us with a communications device. We have used it to inform her that we have the War Demon in custody and await her judgement."

A judge from the bottom tier screamed in rage and others shook their fists. One yelled out, "You have failed to share with us the medicines that Kydos left and now you speak of hidden technologies? How dare you do this to us? We demand a vote on this." The other bottom tier judges were quite vocal in their agreement.

The chief judge made a chopping motion with a hand. "It is already done. The time for voting is over." He pointed at Bob and Rhian. "Bring the War Demon and his accomplice to the doorway chamber."

The roar of the crowd rose to a deafening level and the audience began to move forward. They were met by a solid line of soldiers with rifles raised and fingers on the triggers.

Bob's original guards stood with weapons held to their chests but not pointed anywhere, their faces showing conflicting emotions. A squad of the new soldiers turned to face them with weapons pointed and began barking orders. The original soldiers looked stubborn, then one by one lowered their weapons and dropped to their knees. Four soldiers ran towards Bob and pointed their weapons at him, motioning for him to get up and follow them.

A single soldier ran to Rhian, grabbed her arm, and dragged her to her feet and with him to the far doors behind the judges. He wasn't rough, just very insistent, so Rhian didn't resist. She shot a look a Bob who gave her a single nod before facing forward once more. Just before they were lead behind the judge's platform, Rhian shot a glance over her shoulder. She saw Franza and Torstanda standing where she'd last seen them. It was impossible to say which one of them looked more heartbroken. A shove to her shoulder forced her to pay attention to her own predicament as she stumbled forward.

The group rushed through a maze of corridors that left Rhian feeling disoriented and lost. They dashed through one final doorway and into the room where Rhian and Bob and arrived. As before, the portal mechanism was active and glowing with a soft mother-of-pearl sheen. The only thing new was a suitcase-sized box next to it. It was black and featureless except for a small display on the top, which glowed with a pale blue light. Rhian counted at least a half-dozen men gathered around the portal to greet the new arrivals.

"Has she replied?" wheezed the chief judge. He, and the other judges, were gulping air and sweating as if they'd run a long race. Rhian felt flushed and was panting slightly, but was by no means winded. Bob and the soldiers weren't breathing heavily or even sweating.

"No, my lord," replied one of the attendants. "The device indicates that the message has been received, though."

"How long ago?" puffed out another judge.

"Almost two hours."

"Perhaps she and her organization of peace are engaged in saving another planet?" suggested one of the judges.

The room became silent except for the gasping and wheezing of the judges. That silence was broken when the chief judge rasped, "You there. Demon. Stop fidgeting and stand still. Meet your judgement with honour, if you have any."

Bob became still and stood erect, his bearing that of a prince among lesser beings. Or of a soldier in full command of the situation.

"And what do you know of honour, lord of Acirema? Or you, lord of Niatirb? Or any of you others?" He fixed them with a steely glare as he spoke, each in turn as he scanned the room. All but the soldiers turned away from his gaze, but even they looked uneasy. He turned his gaze to the attendants. "Did you remember to set the unit to reception mode after you transmitted the message? Rotate the control in the shape of a triangle as the instructions said to do."

The attendants looked at each other with growing apprehension. The one who had spoken with the chief judge lunged forward and turned a control and then stumbled backwards. A rich female voice, thickened by anger, boomed forth from the portal.

"...ools. Speak to me. What is wrong with you? The device can be operated by a child. Oh, why am I plagued with such as you?" Kydos uttered a heavy sigh as one who has endured much. "Speak. To. Me."

The chief judge cleared his throat and said in a quavering voice, "Your Wisdom?"

"Finally. Who is this? Speak up."

"I ... that is we ... have captured the War Demon. He came here just as you foretold all those years ago."

"Yes, yes, so your underlings informed me several days ago. Is he dead yet?"

"Ah ... not yet, your Wisdom."

"Why not? Must I do everything myself? Where is he?"

"You Wisdom we did not know what it was that you wished to do with him. We held a trial but there were those who raised doubts about his guilt, so we brought him here for you to deal with."

"Here? What do you mean?"

"Hi, Katie. Been a long time. You've been busy I see." Bob's tone was that of one greeting an old friend.

"Bob? Bob! Why are you still alive? Oh, I see. You've poisoned them against me, just like you poison everyone and ruin everything."

"No, Katie. We need to talk. Your attempts at social engineering here are falling apart and causing serious problems. You need to come here and set things right, otherwise there's going to be another collapse to rival the one I was caught up in."

"Oh, I don't have time to deal with such trivialities, Bob. I was assigned to clean up your mess as part of my rehabilitation." Her voice was light and lilting, but the emphasis she made on the last word made it obvious she was rolling her eyes. "Finished that—adding a few flourishes of my own, as you've found out—and moved on. So many things to do. I'm setting up a new organization and a new network based on these old portable portals. Aren't they just the most wonderful things? Uncle Virgil has made some fascinating modifications to them. He's even better at portal engineering than your father. You of all people should know that ... he's the one who killed you."

Then her voice became harsher as she spat out, "But you just won't stay dead."

She heaved another great sigh that echoed throughout the room. Her voice was once again light and lilting as she added, "So we'll just have to fix that little oversight, won't we?"

A low moan began to be emitted by the portal, and its soft shimmer became brighter.

"Katie, what have you done?" yelled Bob.

"A remote overload. So very handy, don't you think? Our ancestors didn't include that function in these units, but Virgil managed to work around that. Oh, don't worry ... it'll only destroy half the continent. Give it a few centuries, and no-one will know it ever happened."

When the chief judge yelled, "What is happening?" Bob realized that he and Kydos had been talking in their own language.

Kydos laughed sweetly and replied in the local language. "For the sake of peace throughout the galaxy, the War Demon must be destroyed. The doorway device will self-destruct and ensure his death. The sacrifice of you and your world will be remembered by everyone for all time. Please accept the heartfelt thanks of myself and all peace-loving peoples." The communications box began to glow and within seconds had melted into a puddle of molten material.

Turning to Bob the chief judge screamed, "What did she mean?"

"Kydos has set the portal ... the doorway device ... to explode with great force. It will destroy much of this continent. I might be able to stop it."

The noise coming from the portal became more intense.

"I don't have much time." Bob stepped towards the portal, halting as all the soldiers pointed their rifles at him.

One of the other judges yelled, "It is the will of Kydos. The land will be cleansed of the non-believers, and the faithful will rise up to rule over a new world. Blessed be the will of Her Wisdom." Several judges nodded at this and smiled.

"No," yelled Bob. "You and your world will be destroyed. Did you not hear what she said?"

The judges began to argue with each other. Bob turned to the soldiers and said, "The doorway device will explode very soon. I must neutralize it. Please, let me stop this."

The soldiers looked at each other, not sure of what to do.

Several of the soldiers turned and ran out of the room, followed by the portal attendants. The others looked hesitant, then swung their rifles towards Bob.

At that moment he lashed out, knocking rifles and soldiers to one side. Rhian had only ever seen someone move that quickly in the movies. Bob twisted and weaved his way through the soldiers, his arms and feet knocking them aside.

As the soldier next to Rhian raised his rifle she reached into her pocket, grabbed a pencil, and stabbed him in the neck. She knocked aside an arm that was reaching towards her, took her remaining pencil and buried it into another grasping arm. She felt a great pressure against her side and was flung into a wall, hitting it with great force and falling to the ground dazed. When she was able to focus once more, she looked around and saw a tableau of blood and bodies. Bob was standing at the portal, manipulating the controls. The portal was still moaning, but in a wavering fashion, and its glowing was lessened.

"Bob ..." she managed to croak. Her head throbbed and her right side felt as if it were being massaged with broken glass.

He took a quick glance at her then returned his attention to the portal. "Glad to see you're awake ... you took quite a hit. Ship's entering the atmosphere and will be here soon."

"Portal?"

"Still set to self-destruct, I'm afraid. Slowed it down, though. Not by much, but enough, I think."

There was a banging at the doors.

"I locked the doors. Should hold for long enough. Ship arrival in a minute or so."

"The others?"

His face hardened. "I have to stop this. They wouldn't allow it."

Rhian noticed that he was covered in blood and there were several holes in his uniform. "You're hurt."

Bob managed a weak chuckle. "Yes. Need treatment. As do

you. After we fix this, we can fix ourselves."

Rhian felt a tingle at the small of her back and saw Bob look up. "Our ride's here." He walked over to her, picked her up, and carried her towards a wall. She couldn't help but notice that he winced when he picked her up and was walking with considerable effort.

Bob raised his hand to his mouth, uttered a few words in a language she didn't understand, then the roof vanished. That is, it was swept to one side and the debris fell to the floor at the base of a wall. Rhian could see a large shape above them blocking the sky. A dot appeared in the shape and flew down towards them. It landed with a thud not far away and looked to be a cylinder about her size. Bob staggered over and manipulated some controls. The cylinder vanished in a shower of dust to reveal what looked like a space suit.

Bob set her back on the floor and donned the suit over his uniform, wincing with pain as injured areas were pressed. He bent down and shrugged on an odd-looking backpack. There were several short rods there as well which he took and placed around the portal. He coughed several times, and Rhian thought she saw blood on his mouth.

He came over to her, took a slim item the size of a playing card from his belt and slapped it onto her wrist. She felt a wave of welcome coolness emanate from the patch as Bob lifted her to her feet. "Med-patch to help with the pain and shock. Place your arms around my neck, please. Hold on tight."

With an acceleration that made her gasp, the pair of them shot up through the opening, and within seconds were inside the ship. Bob disengaged her arms, lifted her into a carry position, and walked down a corridor. They soon came to a room filled with many controls and several well-upholstered chairs.

"I'm going to put you that chair. No time to be gentle, I'm afraid."

Rhian stifled groan as she was transferred. Bob muttered a

hurried apology before he rushed to another chair and manipulated the controls. The solid-looking surface in front of her rippled for a moment and then she was looking outside. She felt her stomach sink low as they flew into the air. As they rose above the building, she saw the portal rise with them. This was the first time she'd seen anything outside of the building, and she forced herself to focus.

The containment building was surrounded by several rings of buildings, none more than a few stories tall, laid out in decorative geometric patterns. As the ship rose, Rhian could see swathes of green spaces that looked like parkland filled with a riot of colours. The sky held a number of aircraft, whose size and shape reminded her of dirigibles and blimps. As they rose, details shrank but larger patterns appeared. Rhian could see farmlands and forests, then other towns and cities.

"It's beautiful," she whispered.

The colour of the sky changed from blue to a black as they rose above the atmosphere, and the planet became a disk showing the western continent and surrounding oceans.

"Almost. Almost," she heard Bob say in a soft voice.

The view shifted as the ship banked. Seconds later she heard him say, "Good enough."

A moment later she saw a very bright flash and instinctively closed her eyes even though the ship's systems made sure to limit the amount of light it displayed to a safe level.

"FTL engaged," she heard Bob say as she opened her eyes, blinking rapidly in an attempt to stay conscious.

Rhian felt Bob's hand on her arm. She looked up to see a wan smile on his face as he stood next to her. "I'm going to lift you up and carry to the medical bay. Time to heal our own wounds."

"Wait," she said. "Shouldn't we go back and help?"

Bob shook his head, then grimaced with pain. "Can't. The portal's destruction filled the area with energies that'll interfere with the ship's engines for days, possibly weeks." His eyes closed for a moment as he steadied himself before continuing. "That's by design. Any FTL-capable ship would be similarly affected."

"What about the planet?"

"For them, it'll be like a massive solar flare. Probably interfere with communications and power. Possibly alter weather patterns for a short while."

"That's not what I'm referring to, you know."

"Yeah, I know. But there's nothing we can do, Rhian. We've take away the hold that Kydos had. What happens next is up to them." Then he wobbled and held onto her seat for support. "We need to get our bodies repaired. Brace yourself ... and up you go."

He carried her down a short corridor and into a room with a pair of couches. Bob put Rhian into one, spoke a few words in a strange language, then stumbled into the other couch, still in his spacesuit. There was a whiff of something sweet, then Rhian lost consciousness.

CHAPTER THIRTEEN
Locked In Transit

Rhian was enjoying floating down a river, her fingertips glancing along the surface of the warm water. There was the gentle tinkling of bells in the distance, their song echoed by the birds she could see in the lush trees that lined the bank. Without any warning, the tinkling became more strident and the trees vanished into a sudden fog that appeared all around her. The light that once seemed so soft and inviting was now a harsh glare that seemed to come from all around her, despite the fog. She tried to lift an arm to shield her eyes but it, and the other, were being held down somehow. In fact, her entire body seemed trapped in something that allowed no movement. She struggled for a moment then took a deep breath and tried to scream, but all that came out in a soft gurgle of sound. As if in response, the force holding her down lessened. As she cleared her throat and forced herself to calmness, and the holding force lessened even more.

A voice floated in on the breeze that wafted across her but too low to make it out. She cleared her throat again and shook her head to the extent it was allowed.

"Stay calm. Focus on who you are and where you are. The auto-medic won't release you until you appear to be awake and in control of yourself. Do you remember your name?"

"Namph? Ah, name. Yes. Rhian Faernsworth. Doctor of

socio-archaeological research." She paused and made a brief sound of amusement. "Formerly of the planet Earth. Now on a spaceship somewhere between the stars after saving a planet from being destroyed by Kydos. Good enough?"

The fog dissipated to reveal a tech-filled room. Rhian was on a form-fitting couch that was a bit wider and longer than herself, with a sheet covering her. Out of the corner of her eyes, she detected something metallic sliding away out of sight. She took several careful breaths but her torso no longer hurt and her head felt fine.

"Take it easy for a few seconds until the disorientation passes. The auto-medic likes to keep its patients immobilized as it works. Speeds the recovery, or so the theory goes. How are you feeling?"

Rhian recognized Bob's voice. She cleared her throat and licked her lips. "Feel pretty good. Mind if I sit up?"

"Sure. Here, let me help you." He lifted her up while managing to keep the sheet in place to protect her modesty. She noticed that he was wearing fresh clothes.

"How long was I under? How long have you been up? Wait, where are my clothes?"

"The auto-medic destroys the clothes of its patients. I've not been up long. We were both under for just over a day."

Rhian looked around the room. Aside from the two couches, there were only bumps and displays on the wall to indicate any sort of function to the room. "Not much to look at. Thought I caught something moving out of the corner of my eye when I woke up."

"That'd be some of the diagnostic and treatment probes. They get withdrawn when not in use."

"You called this the auto-medic."

"Yep. Think of it as an automated sick bay, if you like. Feeling well enough to stand?"

"Yeah, let's give that a try," Rhian said.

Bob held her elbow as she slid off the couch and onto her

feet. There was no sense of disorientation, so she made a careful wiggle of her head. "Everything seems to be working," she said. Glancing down she added, "Could use some clothes. Your auto-medic thing doesn't have much fashion sense."

"Ah, about that," said Bob with some embarrassment. "The auto-medic doesn't like clothes of any sort on its patients. I added the sheet because I thought it might be more comfortable for you."

"I see. Well, yes. Thank you for that. Now about those clothes you promised?"

Bob laughed. "Indeed. Follow me to your cabin if you will, Doctor." He turned and led the way out with Rhian following, the sheet wrapped around her.

"The auto-medic bay you know, but this is the sign for it." He pointed at a hand-sized symbol. They took a few steps, and he pointed to the left. "Mess." Pointing to the right, he said, "Engineering and cargo areas."

They took a few steps and turned down a short corridor. "Cabins down here—four of them. The control room is directly down the other end of this corridor."

He stepped inside a cabin and motioned her in. "This one's yours. Bed there, bathroom facilities there, desk there with a pull-down chair." He gestured as he spoke. "Clothes on the bed. There were some personal effects found in your clothes. Those got automatically bagged up and I put them in the dresser there."

Rhian stood in the doorway and peered in at the small space. "It's ... efficiently laid out."

Bob chuckled. "That it is. Here, uhm, let's switch places and I'll let you get settled." With that done Bob said, "I'll leave you to it, then."

"No, wait, please. Uhm, could you wait just outside while I change? And keep the door open?"

"Sure." He stepped to one side and stood in the corridor. "This must seem pretty strange to you."

"Not as much as you might think. I've been on ships—sea-going ships—before. This is similar. Well, in terms of size and lack of personal space at any rate."

"Heh. There are stories from the wars that tell of up to four people assigned to each cabin. So consider yourself lucky."

Rhian stepped out and faced him. "Lucky, you say. Any chance that luck might extend to some food? To my great surprise I'm feeling a bit peckish."

"As am I. There's some soup and bread waiting for us in the mess. This way."

Within a minute they were seated in the mess with a cup of soup and a plate of soft bread in front of them both. They ate in silence for a couple of minutes. When she was done, Rhian placed the cup on the table and leaned back in her chair. She picked pieces off the bread and popped them in her mouth. "We were both of us hurt pretty bad. My side and head hurt like hell. I saw holes in your torso. Don't think all that blood on you belonged to other people."

Bob shook his head. "No, a lot of it was my own. Got shot a couple of times, stabbed once, hit repeatedly, and had some internal damage. You had a couple of broken ribs, one of which had entered a lung, and a concussion."

Her eyebrows raised to their limit. "And we're walking around already?"

"Well, we'll both need a couple more treatments but we're fit for light ship duty."

"Light duty as in piloting the ship?"

"Exactly. We're heading back to the base we left. It's the nearest secure spot for us, by quite a few weeks of travel. The ship was just puttering along until I told it where to go. When there's crew on board, the ship prefers them to be making the decisions."

"Hmm. So how did it find us? Thought your control systems weren't supposed to be so smart."

"That's the first thing I checked when I woke up. I need to

dig deeper, but apparently the base control system figured out what the rogue sentience did. Then it convinced my ship that I was in serious enough danger that it should take the initiative and go to me."

"That way you say that it sounds as if that's not quite normal."

He shook his head. "No, it is not. But then, these are not normal times. Still, I'm surprised the ship agreed. On the other hand, it did take several days to be convinced. On yet another hand ... well, you get the idea." Bob gave a snort and shake of his head. "Within the realms of possibility, but a very long shot. Glad it did, though."

"As am I. So, how long is this trip going to take?"

"Just over two weeks. Call it eighteen days. Could shave a couple of days off that if I pushed the engines to their maximum, but I don't like doing that. It's an old, old ship. I've patched it up the best I can, but I'm no expert."

"So what now?"

"Finish our lunch. Eat all of it, by the way, don't just pick it to death. The soup and bread are formulated to help the healing process. Then I'll give you the full tour. After that, a nap. Trust me, you feel fine now but in about an hour you'll be dead on your feet." He flashed her a grin. "I've had a lot of experience with this."

"Bob ... about what happened ..."

He held up a hand to forestall any further comments. "Not now, Rhian. Later, yes, we need to talk. As much as you want. But for this first day of recovery we need to focus on the here and now. It's important."

Rhian frowned and made a soft sigh before nodding her acceptance. She forced herself to smile. "You promised me a tour, I believe. Never been in a spaceship before."

* * *

To Bob's surprise, Rhian adapted to monotony of space

flight much better than he did. The sense of wonder of being on a star-hopping spacecraft faded in a couple of days, but then she settled down to work. In any event, she spent much of the day inside her cabin, writing in a journal Bob had provided for her, coming out only for meals. As she seemed lost in thought, Bob respected her need for privacy. Privacy, as he was learning, was in short supply on the small scout ship.

Finally, in an effort to break the silence that was growing between them, at a meal break he asked her what she was so absorbed in.

"Writing up my remembrances of what's happened. Writing letters of condolences to the parents of Kathy, George, and Niles. Remembering our time together. Trying to process and come to terms with everything that has happened." Rhian uttered a soft chuckle as her mouth settled into a slightly lopsided grin. "Guess I've been wrapped up in my own head. Lots of stuff to process. Sorry."

Bob nodded as he cradled a cup of hot tea in his hands. "A sensible approach. Just don't get lost in remembrances of the past. Find something to ground you in the present. Something that makes you look forward to the future." He nodded as his mouth quirked into a wry grin. "I speak from experience."

"Interesting that you say that," Rhian said. "You seem like a caged tiger, sometimes. You pour through your notes, do research on the data you've accumulated, that sort of thing. But the way you glare at the displays reminds me of a predator on the hunt. And the way your fingers slam down on the keyboard as you type ... hope you brought some spares along."

Her warm smile took the edge off her words, but her eyes held a hint of concern. Even though she was aware of his personal history and long life, to the extent Celcilia had known it, his youthful appearance caused her to think of him as a younger colleague.

"And," she continued, "you seem to be using the medical bay rather a lot. Sometimes several times a day. Is there something

I need to know about?"

Bob gave an embarrassed shrug. "No, not at all. It's just ... well, a bit embarrassing to tell the truth." He paused to take a deep breath which he let out slowly. "Partly it's due to getting treatment for the injuries I acquired during our recent adventures."

He waved off her concerned look. "Nothing serious, I promise you. Everything is all cleared up. No, it's just a habit I've picked up since getting this new body." He gestured towards himself.

"I'm not sure that I understand."

"Well, you now about my healing factors, correct?"

She nodded.

"Not sure if Celcilia grasped what they really were or what they meant to me. Think of them as more of a symbiont than mere tech. That's not quite accurate, but bear with me. The point is that they were always there, always part of me, always communicating. I rarely paid them much attention on a conscious level unless I required some specific information or action. Does that make sense?"

"Yes, I think it does, Bob. They supplied a steady background hum of conversation, and now you miss that."

"That's a big part of it, Rhian. But think about the implications for a moment. The healing factors allowed me to know, to a very deep level, the state of my body practically down to the cellular level. Now it's as if I've gone partially blind and numb. For the first time in my life, I have to be careful how I move, how and what I eat or drink, worry about parasites and germs, and worry about injuries both minor and major."

He rolled up the sleeves of his shirt and showed her the pattern of thin scars on his arms. "See these scars? Most of them came from learning how to use this new body. Training it to the maximum levels that it was capable of ... and finding out the hard way what those limits were. Having scars at all is a novelty for me, come to that."

"Doesn't that healing machine—auto-medic, I believe you called it—deal with scarring?"

"After a fashion. The more rapid the healing, the greater the amount of scarring. I've set the default of the machine to the most rapid setting. It also depends on the extent of the injury...minor injuries will have little or no scarring." Then he grinned. "My dad always said that scars—physical and psychological—serve to remind us of our errors."

While Bob had been talking, Rhian had been studying his arms with interest. When he finished talking, she sat back heavily in her chair and stared at him with her eyes wide. "I hadn't considered the implications of your new body. I ... I keep thinking of you as one of us. A regular human." She blushed and muttered an apology.

To her relief Bob just laughed with genuine humour. "Heh. Well, I always was a regular human. To my way of thinking, anyway. Now I'm more human—more like my ancestors, I guess you'd say." He leaned back with folded arms and an engaging grin on his face.

Rhian placed her hands on her knees and studied him for a moment before speaking. "Yet you have lived for many centuries, according to what you told Great-gran Celcilia. Almost of them with all those enhancements that you'd take for granted and incorporate into your way of thinking, into your automatic reflexes. Then in a blink, you're stripped of them. You've done very well, Bob. Impressively well."

Bob tilted his head in acknowledgement of her praise. "Thank you, Rhian. But it was a case of adapt or die. My upbringing taught me how to adapt, survive, and thrive—and that included doing so with minimal use of my enhancements. This is just taking it to extremes. That's how I've been thinking of it, anyway."

Rhian nodded. "Speaking of adapting, there's something I need to talk with you about," she said in a neutral tone.

"Hmm. Sounds serious. As I always told Celcilia, ask my anything. Can't guarantee an answer, but feel free to ask."

She gave him a small smile. "I can't go home again, that much seems certain. As much as I appreciate your saving my life—twice over—I need a way to build a future for myself. Out here, I mean." She shrugged. "I'm at something of a loss as what that might be, though. Any ideas?"

"Ah. Yes. Been wondering about that, myself. Didn't want to force you to think about that until you were ready."

"Appreciate that and all, but probably need to start thinking about it sooner than later."

"Any thoughts?"

She grinned at him, and he realized that he probably wasn't going to like this.

"I'm a trained historian and researcher, with years of experience. I'm good with languages, living among different cultures, and enjoy travel. Galloping amongst the stars, like some of the fictions on Earth talked about, sounds pretty good."

"Uhm ..."

She didn't give him time to get any more out before she continued. "The biggest problem with travel—and I've done a lot of it in quarters more cramped than this ship—is finding something to do. As I said, I'm a researcher who's good with languages. Think I proved that while researching during your trial. As for new languages, how about I learn yours?"

"Uhm ..."

"Once I've got a handle on the language, I can help you with any research or data analysis you might need. That's a large part of what I do, you understand. Digging through archives and records looking for cultural changes and patterns of behaviour or whatever. You've got data coming out of your ears, if what I've glimpsed is any indication. More than you can deal with. Or, perhaps, even know how to deal with. You need an assistant. And I happen to be in the market for a new job. Seems like a good fit."

"Uhm ..."

"You've been saying that a lot, Bob. Try using your words. Or just say 'yes'."

Bob sat back in his chair, pinned by the intensity of her gaze, and pondered her suggestion. As he pondered, he stared intently at her, which she met in equal measure with her own calm equilibrium. Nothing was said between for a minute, then two. Then Bob gave a short, sharp grunt.

"An interesting suggestion. But impractical."

"Nonsense," she replied in curt, no-nonsense tones. "State your objections, sir. This is a time for plain speaking."

In spite of himself, Bob found himself rather liking his new companion. In many ways she was like his old friend Celcilia, but grown in experience and wisdom.

"You have a glimmer of what it is I do and how dangerous it is. Forgive me for saying so, but the deaths of your colleagues should be testament to that. I was barely able to keep Celcilia alive. I am less capable now of keeping you alive."

"Granted and accepted. Great-gran was at her physical peak when she met you. I, on the other hand, am a middle-aged woman. In pretty good shape for someone my age, but middle-aged, nonetheless. I can't play the soldier, I will grant you. But there is more to your objection than physical security, isn't there?"

She paused for a moment and looked at him with her head cocked slightly to one side.

"Secrecy," she said after a few seconds of thought. "At your core you are a soldier, a military man. Secrets are your bread and butter, the learning and keeping thereof. You're afraid I'll learn something you want hidden. Or maybe you're just so used to working on your own that trust comes hard."

In spite of himself Bob's mouth quirked in a slight smile. "True enough, I suppose. On all counts. As you say, though, there are secrets. Some kept by habit and some by necessity.

Learning them, or even the hint of you learning them, could place you in harm's way."

"You mean make me a target of Set, Kydos, and others like them?"

Bob nodded.

"So keep the big secrets from me. That's only reasonable. All I'm asking for is a chance to do something useful. What's the alternative? Dump me on some primitive planet and try to integrate with a primitive tribe? Or a high-tech world where I'll have to hide my alien origins and never fit in? Neither sounds terribly appealing, to be honest." She paused for a couple of seconds before adding, "And I need time to process everything that's happened. You may be used to bouncing from world to world, but I'm not. This ship is a perfect place to catch my breath, as it were. But I still need something to do. Something useful."

Bob tapped at his thighs with his fingers. Finally he inhaled deeply and let it out with a whoosh. "Fine. We'll start with language skills. I'll have the ship set you up with access— limited access—to its systems. I'll look to see if there's some learning programs in there, but suspect there probably are."

"Thank you." Her relief and gratitude were obvious.

"I'd like something in return, though."

She quirked an eyebrow at him.

"I'd like you consider allowing me to read Celcilia's book." To her surprise Bob blushed as he spoke. "I know it's supposed to be secret and all, but she was a good friend during a rough time in my life and I never got to spend enough time with her. Would really like to learn more about her and how she thought about things."

Rhian was touched by the depth of emotion he was displaying for her ancestor. "Uhm, sure. It's not so much secret as something we learned to keep hidden from the rest of the world." After a moment she chuckled. "Secrecy as a habit. Like yourself, I suppose. Yes, I'm sure she would have wanted you to read it."

Then she winced. "But that'll have to wait until we get back to the base, I'm afraid. All my kit is there, including the book."

"That'll be fine," said Bob. "It'll give me something to look forward to." He grinned at her. "Does it have a name?"

Rhian grinned back. "Great-gran never named it, and none of us could agree on what to call it."

"What did you call it?"

"I was always rather partial to 'The Precepts of Celcilia'."

Bob gave a hearty chuckle. "Oh, I'm sure she would have made some rude comment about that."

Rhian chuckled along with him before answering. "I'm not so sure about that. She became quite the practical philosopher over the years. Her observations and advice became quite pointed and acerbic the older she got. She was never one to suffer fools gladly, was Great-gran."

Bob allowed as that had always been the case.

Rhian gave Bob a calculating look. "In truth I'd be interested in getting feedback from you on it. We've never been entirely sure about what was history or speculation, what aspects of her philosophy were influenced by you or her Order, that sort of thing."

"Hmm," was his only comment.

Rhian hastened to add, "We know that she was influenced by a great many sources. And, as you'll find out, her greatest injunction was to 'take all advice with a grain of salt, even mine'."

"Now that sounds like the Celcilia I knew," said Bob with a grin. "Any other big rules to live by?"

"Just one," replied Rhian with a grin. "Assumptions lead to mistakes. Mistakes lead to failure. Failure leads to death."

"Ah, that's one I learned from childhood and probably quoted to her more than once. But it never gets old."

Their conversation was interrupted by the soft trilling sound.

"Problem?" asked Rhian getting to her feet.

"No, that's an alert signal, not a warning alarm. The ship's detected something important enough that it wants a human to look at it."

He gave a jerk with his head. "Control room."

Rhian followed with some excitement. Aside from a very brief tour, and their frantic rush to escape the planet, she'd not spent any time in the control room. They entered the control room and Bob pointed to one of the three crew chairs. "Sit at that station." As for himself, he sat down in the main control chair and manipulated the controls.

Rhian sat down with care and wiggled to signal the chair to adjust itself to her. Within seconds it had moulded itself to her. She gave a soft sigh. These chairs were the most comfortable she'd ever experienced, and she never tired of sitting in them. Turning her attention to the screen, she saw what appeared to be a star chart with quite a few additional markers. Bob turned his chair to look towards her.

"Training time. See the controls at my station? This group here are duplicated on yours."

Rhian studied her controls for a moment, nodded, and pointed at the area on hers being careful not to touch anything.

"Good. Now watch what I do." Bob touched three controls and rotated a fourth with exaggerated slowness. "Do that with yours. Don't worry, you can't hurt anything if you make a mistake." Then he added with a grin, "Mostly."

"Hah hah." She reached towards her own control panel and performed the required manipulations. Her screen blinked and showed something different than before. This time there just a handful of stellar representations, but this time one of them was blinking and a side-panel popped up to show more information. Unfortunately she couldn't read the language, so it was just so much gibberish—*for now*, she thought to herself.

"I gather there's something special at that location. Can't tell what it might be ... can't read the language, you know." She said the last with a slight glare.

Bob acted as if he was impervious to her glares and simply nodded. "We'll get you up to speed on that, never fear. Those controls you fiddled with set the display to show the ship's current item of interest. Worth doing that every so often even during a routine trip. Anyway, the ship's picked up a distress beacon. One of ours ... my people, that is. Nothing specific, just that something in that planetary system is broadcasting it."

"Another ship?"

Bob nodded. "Ship or base. Could be in orbit or on the surface of something. It's an emergency beacon—on or off is all that sort of thing does."

Rhian noticed that Bob was tapping an index finger against his leg. "Something bothering you about it?"

"Indeed. The ship picked it up here." A marker appeared on her display. "Given its signal strength, we should have been able to pick it up here." Another marker popped up, some distance away from the first.

"Ah. Can't tell if that's a big distance, but I gather it's enough to worry you."

"Yeah, about half a day's travel." He shrugged. "Might be some sort of natural cause for that, but that's be pretty rare. Possible but unlikely."

"A trap, perhaps?"

"But by whom? It's an awfully specific sort of trap, if it is one."

"Kydos? She turned that planet against you. That was a long-term project just to get back at you."

"Yes and no. It's strange, but she spent a lot of time there doing good works." He waved a hand. "Oh, yes, she played up my bad reputation to use as a catalyst, but I suspect she needed something powerful enough to get their attention in a short period of time."

Rhian's eyebrows shot up. "You're defending her now?"

"Hmm, not so much defending as trying to understand.

Remember that planet of hers where I found Celcilia? That entire structure was built around Kydos and her own goals. On top of that she'd organized worshippers across several worlds and centuries with herself as the focus. This time it appears that the planet wasn't even part of her organization ... she mentioned something about rehabilitation, you'll recall. Yet she expended considerable time and effort helping them get back on their feet and focused on cooperating with each other. That's ... not what I'd have expected from her."

Rhian gave a grudging nod. "That's true, and probably more than you know. I discovered out that she'd founded schools and hospitals plus social structures to tie them all together across the different nations. She was revered, Bob, and referred to as 'Her Wisdom' for good reasons. On the other hand, she set up the social mechanisms to deal with you if you ever showed up in your current form. Not to mention at the end, she was ready to throw all that away just to see you dead. That was unexpected."

Bob shrugged. "That's Katie. Very smart, very good at planning and organizing, but could nurse a grudge for decades until she exploded with rage. Been that way since she was a kid."

"And yet you dated her."

"What can I say? I was in my 'damaged goods' phase and raising hell in my own way. She thought that my temporary insanity was 'cute'."

He shrugged once again. "I was younger then."

"Uh huh," said Rhian in a neutral tone. "In any event, let's ignore Kydos for the moment and focus on the here and now, shall we? What about this distress signal? If I had to guess, I'd say it wasn't on our present course."

"Well spotted, Rhian, and quite correct. It's about, oh, four or five days away and roughly perpendicular to our present course."

"Do we have the supplies to make the detour and get back

to base?"

"Good question, and yes we do." His expression was unreadable.

Rhian sighed. "You want to investigate."

His expression didn't change.

"Bob, if I weren't with you, would you investigate?" Her voice was firm.

This time it was his turn to sigh. "Yeah. Those beacons mean someone is in trouble. One of my kind. It could be bait for a trap, so we'll be careful. This ship was designed for sneaking around, so I'm pretty sure we'll be safe. Not guaranteed, though."

Rhian studied the display for a few seconds before turning back toward him. She grinned and said, "Like yourself, I love a good mystery. Besides, it'll give me more time to learn your language and ship systems."

CHAPTER FOURTEEN
The Burden of Prophesy

The next few days passed by in a whirl of focused study for Rhian. As Bob suspected, language tutorials were available. In addition, the auto-medic proved to have a mode for enhanced learning. Those sessions were useful to build up her vocabulary, but tended to give her a slight headache. In the end, though, it was her talent and experience that allowed her to obtain a good grasp of the language in a short time. Learning the ship's systems allowed her to practise those new skills.

"Anything in the ship's records about our destination?" asked Rhian. "I've not been able to find anything in the records."

Bob shook his head. "Nothing aside from basic astrophysical information. A bit smaller than Earth, but the gravity is about the same. Hmm, the core is denser than Earth's, so I guess that's why."

"Does this mean it was never used by your lot?"

"Possibly, but not necessarily. There's no record of a portal being established there. On the other hand, the records from the Great Wars have a lot of gaps. We'll just have to wait and see."

"By that I assume you mean a stealthy approach."

"Indeed. And there's enough time to train you in the basics

of that."

Rhian groaned. "I've got more than enough on my plate with the language studies, thank you all the same."

Bob was unmoved. "This'll give you a chance to do some practical translation work. And get you used to thinking in non-scholastic ways." He waved a hand. "It's a dangerous galaxy out there. The more you know about keeping yourself safe, the better off you'll be."

"Yes, yes," said Rhian with sigh.

"You just hate it when I'm right, don't you?" Bob said with a grin. "Celcilia was the same way. I suspect it's genetic."

In response, Rhian stuck out her tongue and blew a raspberry at him.

For his own part, Bob tapped at some controls for a few moments. "There, I've given you access to some relevant records on tactics. Just skim them to get a feel. Oh, and review the basics of navigation as well. When you're done that, take a look at the astrophysical data for the target solar system as well as the planet itself."

"Excuse me?"

He turned to look at her. "We're sneaking up, remember? Think of it as being exposed on a flat plain where we need to take advantage of every scrap of cover. Instead of trees and shrubs, we use comets, asteroids, and occultations."

Rhian frowned. "Hmm. Didn't think of it in those terms. Figured the ship's stealth tech would hide us."

Bob gave her a 'more in sorrow than in anger' look as he said, "Rookie mistake. Stealth tech minimizes our signatures but doesn't eliminate it. Always best to use it but not depend on it."

"That from the Precepts of Survival?"

"Nope, that's my Dad. But it ties in with making minimal use of tech ... a lesson I had to learn growing up."

The trip to the mystery planet took all of the six days that Bob had estimated and most of a seventh. As promised, he snuck in using all the tricks of his extensive experience. He taught them to Rhian along the way, but for her it was akin to watching an elite athlete. The sport might be playable by anyone, but the accumulated skills and nuances would be out of reach without considerable effort and training. To her surprise she found the process intriguing and she was an apt pupil with a keen eye for the subtleties of stealth.

They paused on the planet's natural satellite, on the side currently facing away from the planet.

"What would you do if there wasn't a handy moon to lurk on?" asked Rhian.

"Pretty much all human-inhabitable worlds have one. Might be larger or smaller than your own planet's. Some rotate and some are tidal-locked." He grinned. "Always a good idea to pause just before barging in, though. Gives us a chance for one last check of ourselves and the ship. Loosen up, eat a snack, take a nap ... whatever it takes. Notice how tense your shoulders are?"

Rhian gave her shoulders a shrug and gave a small wince. "You're right. Hadn't noticed that. Guess it's from hunching over and staring at the displays for so long."

"That's correct," Bob replied. "Sneaking is a tense business and it pays to be aware of that aspect of it."

Rhian winced as she moved her shoulders around to loosen them up. "Good advice. Alright, what's the plan? How do we sneak in from here to the surface without being seen? Nothing to hide us."

"Indeed. This is the most dangerous part of the process. First, we do a passive sensor scan. I'll have the ship send out a probe to peer over the horizon. The moon's mass will mask the energy used for that manoeuvre. I like to wait a full planetary day for that, so I can check for potential problems on the entire surface."

"Didn't we do scans on the way here?"

"Yep, but now we're closer than before. That'll let us work

at a higher resolution. While we're waiting on that I'll kit you out in a light-duty environmental suit. Ideally we'd have days or even weeks to get you fully trained, but a few hours will do for the basics. That'll allow you to survive and function in complete vacuum or toxic atmosphere for several days."

"Several days? Uhm, I'm no expert in such things, but the spacesuits of Earth need to be custom fitted and require all sorts of invasive plumbing for, uhm, body functions."

Bob laughed. "Mine are better ... one size fits all. Suit up naked, then let the suit take care of any requirements. The neck section holds spigots for food and water. Body movements power the recycling process to supplement and conserve the power units. Not as bad as it sounds. Let me launch the probe then we'll both suit up."

To Rhian's surprise, the environmental suit was as comfortable as promised. Once adjusted, it fit like a glove and offered complete freedom of movement. The only problems she encountered were with the helmet and the gloves. The gloves, while excellent, were still not as responsive as bare skin. As for the helmet, she had problems getting the hang of putting in on and off.

"Oof," she opined after a training session. "In the movies they just press a button and the helmet flows out of the suit and around the head."

"We've got those," said Bob with a disapproving grunt. "And so do a number of other human cultures. Too many points of failure, to my way of thinking ... and that of my ancestors. Lift helmet, drop onto neck interface, lock in place, and you're good to go. Reverse the process to remove it. If necessary, one can raise and lower the visor, but best to keep yours locked and sealed. Look, you've got the basics so let's leave it at that for now. Show me where you stow the helmet at your action station."

Rhian nodded and slid her helmet along the guides of her chair. She'd noticed similar guides throughout the ship, including the cabins and had wondered what they were for. Now she knew.

"Now sit in the chair, put your hands on the controls ... now put on your helmet."

She did as ordered and managed to get the helmet on with a minimum of cursing. To her annoyance, Bob had managed to get his own helmet from across the room and put in on before she got own fastened. He tapped at the side of his helmet then pointed at the controls at his wrist. Rhian choked down a curse and tapped the control that engaged the communications circuit.

"Well done, Rhian," she heard in her helmet. "The only thing to remember is to engage the communications as soon as you've put on your helmet. Well, in most cases, but we'll ignore exceptions for now. Trick question: we've got an atmosphere in the ship now, but what would happen if it were vacuum?"

"Uhm. The suit would get stiffer?"

Bob sighed. "You didn't read the manual. No, don't try to deny it. The suit feels only marginally different in vacuum. I'm hoping you never experience it, but I'd rather you know about it than not."

Rhian swallowed an angry retort then nodded. In truth, she was more annoyed with herself than with Bob. He was trying to condense the hard-won experience of centuries into a very short time. It was just that it had been such a long time since she'd been so new at something.

"Enough for now," Bob declared. "De-helmet, rack it on the chair, and let's see what the probe's picked up so far. Bring it up on your screen and describe."

Rhian's face was a study in concentration as she tapped at the controls. She lacked the nearly instinctive grace that Bob had with them, but was getting better. After peering at the results for a few seconds, she said, "Nearly half of a planetary rotation since we started scanning. Astrophysical data corresponds to the data records so far. Haven't seen the source of the beacon, though."

Bob shrugged. "That's why I wait a full rotation. Sometimes you get lucky and sometimes you just miss it. In this case, though, I suggest a meal and a nap."

Rhian opened her mouth to argue then nodded. They'd already put in more than a full day's work. "You're right. Think I'll just keep the suit on, though. Feels quite good."

"Good idea. I suggest a light meal and then a nap. That'll get us rested and ready for the infiltration phase."

* * *

Rhian awoke, glanced at the chronometer, cursed, and stumbled out of bed. She paused to splash some water on her face before heading out to the control room. To her annoyance Bob was already there studying the displays.

"Why didn't you wake me sooner?" she demanded.

"Duty station," was all he said.

She sat down and tapped at the controls. The planet had gone one rotation and was well into another. "Sorry," she muttered as she rushed to see what she'd missed.

"Don't apologize ... you needed the sleep. Now, tell me what you see."

"Uhm ... beacon located. Beside that ocean. No structures that I can see. Wait ... that's interesting."

"In what way?"

"Looks like a landing pad. About a half-kilometre from the beacon."

Bob nodded. "Not just a landing pad, but the sort of location I'd choose if I was going to land on an unknown planet in a situation like this. Defensible yet with ready access to the beacon."

She turned to look at him. "Meaning?"

"Meaning we're expected. Or, rather, I'm expected. Very strange."

"A trap?"

"Can't tell without going in." He grinned at her. "You ready for this?"

In response she grabbed her helmet and put in on. "Aye, aye, captain."

The trip to the planet took just over an hour. It would have taken less time except that Bob had engaged the full stealth capabilities of the vessel. Once in orbit, he took almost as long to descend to the target area on the surface.

"Need to go slow in an atmosphere," Bob explained. "All too easy to show up in any number of ways, stealth or no stealth."

When they were within a kilometre of the landing zone Bob used the active scanners at minimum power to examine the area. They showed only natural materials with no sign of any other tech. After a few seconds of thought, he made the decision to land. The ship settled down in the target zone with no problem. The ground was flat, and the rocky surface held the ship without crushing under its weight.

Bob got out of his seat and went to Rhian's duty station. "It looks safe enough. Look, if the situation goes bad then hit that control there. I've set the ship to take you to my home base. You'll be safe there." He paused to look at her. "You OK with all this?"

Rhian nodded. "We've discussed this. You need to investigate the beacon. Truth be told, I'm wanting answers to this mystery as well." She smiled at him as she said, "Good luck."

"Thanks. I'll keep the comm channel open." He put on his helmet and went to the airlock. There he donned some lightweight armour, a combat belt with a pistol, and an anti-grav pack. It was a compromise that offered the best combination of agility, protection, and firepower without being too intimidating. Like all compromises, it failed to excel at anything in particular but it was a combination that Bob had used to good effect in the past.

He stepped into the airlock then went outside, closing the

doors behind him. Locally, it was early afternoon. The sky was overcast with clouds dark enough to give a dismal feeling to the area. There were a few holes in the clouds, but the fleeting splotches of sunlight only served to emphasize the overall gloomy feel of the place. The terrain was rocky with little vegetation other than a grey, slimy form of lichen.

"Outside and ready to proceed," he said.

"Very well. Anything of interest?"

"Nothing you can't see from in there. Proceeding on foot to the beacon."

That was something Rhian had problems understanding. Bob had an anti-grav unit that would have allowed him fly to the beacon in little time, so why not use it?

"Stealth," he had told her. "Anti-grav uses the alternate energies, and those can be easily detected. On foot I look like part of the landscape, more or less. The comm link is a whisker beam with nearly imperceptible leakage."

Bob trotted to the beach where the beacon was located. The footing was quite good, considering the rocky terrain, and he made good time. Neither the ship's systems, nor his own, could detect anything that might be a problem. He slowed his pace the closer he got to the location of the beacon. There was lots of cover for a stealthy approach, which he took full advantage of. If this was a trap, it was a very odd one. Finally, he was in view of the sea. It had a unhealthy-looking oily tinge on the surface.

"At the location and don't see ... wait."

Bob spotted a small cube that was pulsing with a faint mother-of-pearl glow. His instruments indicated that it was the beacon he was looking for and nothing more.

"Found it. Approaching the beacon. Seems like a normal device of its type."

He bent forward to peer at it. The pulsing glow stopped. "Huh," said Bob. "Don't think that's supposed to happen."

At that moment a frothing began on the surface of the ocean

a dozen metres from the beach. Bob took a step back and took a defensive pose but didn't reach for his gun ... there'd be time enough for violence if necessary.

The frothing became more intense, as if being boiled from below. There was a darkness gathering beneath the waves. A darkness that grew in size until at last a figure emerged.

Bob stared at the figure that had arisen from the depths. It was several times his size, with an oversized head that had a great number of tendrils covering it—several of which were writhing. Bob held his ground without displaying any outward signs of flight or fight. The figure looked vaguely familiar, as if a memory had been distorted.

He waited until the figure became relatively motionless before asking, "Who are you? I came in answer to your signal."

The figure turned to face him. Its eyes were milky and faintly luminescent. Sounds came from where its mouth should have been, but they sounded like the strangled sounds of a fish out of water. Then his communicator began to crackle and buzz. Bob frowned and tapped at the controls. After several attempts a voice emerged from the static, speaking in the language of his own people.

"I greet you, young Bob. It has been many years since we met and I fear that the years have not been kind to me."

"Uncle Lou?"

"Yes, child. It is I who summoned you. I knew you would be passing near here after your last adventure. Congratulations on successfully facing your greatest fear, by the way. Your young colleague was of great assistance, of course. She will be so again. Your choice of friends does you credit."

Bob's head jerked back as he automatically came to attention as old habits took hold. "Greetings, Uncle. Thank you. Yes, it has been a long time. I was but a child when my father brought me to see you. Not to this planet, though."

"No. I moved some time after we last met. It was necessary

for my studies."

"Studies? Are you referring to your philosophical studies of the shared mental links between all humans?"

A ragged sigh issued from his communicator. "A poor way to describe such a rich and difficult subject, youth. Think of it, if you will, as a sea upon which we all float. Not a physical sea, but rather one of subtle energies and interactions therein."

"If you say so, Uncle. It wasn't a subject that I spent much time investigating."

"Or any time at all, I suspect."

There was a burbling sound that Bob recognized as laughter, and he added his own chuckling.

"No, sir. My father's teachings emphasized more practical matters."

The large head nodded in agreement. "He recognized the truths behind the Precepts of Survival better than most. But he accepted that there were things beyond his ken, even if he had little use for them himself."

Bob refrained from sighing through a great effort of will. "Uhm, Uncle, you said you summoned me for a reason? I don't wish to seem rude, but I'm in something of a hurry."

Lou stared at him with large, luminescent eyes as several tendrils moved in complex patterns. "Attend my words, youth. There are things you must learn and understand, and there is little time left to me. Your colleague inside your craft is monitoring our conversation and hearing it in her own language."

"Oh. Thank you, Uncle, but—"

Lou continued as if Bob hadn't spoken. "Stick your hand into a body of water then remove it. Ripples from your actions expand outward. As well, your very presence will also affect how the environment interacts with the water. All those ripples and changes interact with each other as well as other influences. Those dynamic patterns of interference linger for those capable of seeing them and from them extracting the

187

original events."

Intrigued despite himself, Bob blurted out, "Like a hologram?"

"Yes, but much more complex and exquisitely more difficult to interpret. Many different types of radiation, operating on different timescales depending on their speed of propagation. Detecting and integrating them was the work of eons. Interpreting them was the work of many more."

"Ah. Are those tendrils part of that? They look painful."

"Indeed they are. They are a modified version of sensor wands integrated with my sensorium. They allow me to directly interface with the mechanisms embedded into the planet's structures."

"Why underwater?"

"Cooling, primarily. The mechanisms work better at a constant temperature. Some off the offworld sensor arrays employ liquid helium."

"All that to tap into the—what did you use to call it—the Sea of Dreams?"

"Oh, there is far more to it than that, young Bob. Even more that I, with my eons of experience, realized until relatively recently."

A look of concern crossed Bob's face. "That sounds dangerous, Uncle Lou."

"Rewards are purchased with risk, child. You, of all people, should know that. And the rewards of this endeavour are boundless, even if the price is high."

"I'm not sure that I understand, Uncle."

Lou continued as if he hadn't heard him.

"I can now sense the ripples of events in all the bands of all the energies, including the alternate energies, throughout the galaxy. The Sea of Dreams is but a minor aspect of that, as it turns out."

Lou's body swayed slightly as ripples of spasms ran up and down it for several seconds before stopping. Bob's hands clenched as he watched, unable to help—this did not bode well.

"The Seas of Dreams offers, at best, snippets of thoughts. A widened perception simply increases that tantalizing trickle into a fathomless raging ocean. Dreams, communications, the movement of ships, the murmurs from every locus of technology ... all of it. I now see further and deeper than even the Changed."

"How do you process that sort of deluge of information?" said Bob as the implications began to sink in.

"At a cost," whispered Lou. Then his voice strengthened. "It is only in the last century or so that I've been able to correlate the fragments into a useful if woefully incomplete form. I watched as you destroyed the portal network. I listened to the scream in subspace after you sacrificed yourself to save a planet. I heard the whispers of your rebirth as you employed the ancient forbidden technologies."

"Ah, about that, Uncle Lou ..."

"It was a necessary event, youth. Possibly driven by the urgings of the subconscious threads that binds all humans."

"Are you talking about fate?"

Lou shrugged his enormous shoulders. "Call it what you will, but I sense something other than blind chance to your revival in your current form. Humanity needs you, Bob. Only you can save it."

"Excuse me, Uncle Lou? I'm just one man with limited resources. Why not contact the Conclave and let the Changed deal with whatever the problem is." His voice took on a bitter edge. "It's not like they're talking to me these days. Nor are any of the un-Changed."

Lou raised an arm until a finger pointed at the sky.

"There are those of our own people who are trapped behind a shield that has become a cage. A dagger forged to protect has now been turned against us."

"Shields? Daggers? What are you talking about, sir?"

"Do they teach nothing of history anymore? I am referring,

of course, to the Veil of Tears."

Bob's mouth dropped, and he closed it with a snap. "Well, yes, I suppose the Veil could be thought of as a shield. Although it was a cage into which an Enemy from the Great Wars was lured."

Lou nodded. "Yes. A cage using some of our own people as bait. They were the sacrifice to lure the Enemy into the area and then trigger the release of the energies that created the Veil itself. Nothing physical can pass through it, nor any form of communication."

"Are you saying that the Enemy has returned?"

"No. They are long gone, to be replaced by a deadlier menace."

Bob tried to scrub at his head but hit his helmet. Getting straight answers out of his uncle had been a problem that better minds than his had failed to accomplish.

"Alright, but what sort of menace is this? And wouldn't the Veil keep it contained?"

"Nothing lasts forever. And there are always ways to bypass any prison. You of all people should know that."

"OK, fine, but—"

"You must enter the Veil and neutralize the threat."

"The Veil is impenetrable. You said so yourself."

"There is a way, but one that can be used only by the younger races. A narrow tunnel pierces it, to be traversed soon lest it close once again."

"Psh. A tunnel? How can I traverse those destructive energy fields that no-one else can? I'm ..." He paused as a look of wonder crossed his face. "I'm merely human now, aren't I? Like our ancestors who created the Veil."

"Yes, Bob, you are. And only you have the tech and training to do what needs to be done. Only you can do it in time."

Bob's face hardened. "No. I'm done with that sort of thing. Let the Conclave figure it out."

Bob's outburst was interrupted as Lou began to spasm and

gasp. Cracks appeared in his body—some had a glow deep within them while others oozed fluids. Sensors in his suit warned of a buildup of various energies.

"Uncle Lou!"

A stentorian voice, edged with pain, came from his communicator. "Knowledge comes at a cost, youth, and now I must pay the price. My time is short and the end will be explosive, both personally and for the planet. Run to your ship as quickly as you can. There is little time. Go." The last came out as a pain-filled gasp.

Pausing only for a fraction of a second, Bob attempted to engage the anti-grav but found that the surge of energies prevented its operation. He turned and ran towards his ship.

As he ran, he heard Uncle Lou speak, his voice raspy. "Return to the base of mystery—many answers are contained therein. The foul sentience has been purged. It was created as a result of the new enemy within the Veil."

What followed were bursts of static interspersed with gasps of pain that tore at Bob's heart. Just as the ship came into sight Lou said, "I am so sorry, Bob. This task is a terrible burden, but you will be able to rest after this. I can promise you that much." After that came two bursts of data, then silence.

The airlock opened just as he ran up, and he raced into the ship. "Close the airlock," he yelled as he ran towards the control cabin. Several heartbeats later found him leaping into the control seat, boosting the ship without bothering to strap in.

"Airlock closed and ship secure," said Rhian with a gasp. The artificial gravity was insufficient to entirely compensate for the sudden surge of acceleration. "Sensors indicate a large accumulation of energies taking place across the planet. What about your uncle?"

"Dying and taking the planet with him. Not his fault."

As the ship cleared the atmosphere, Bob curved its trajectory to place as much of the planet between them and

Uncle Lou. On the planet's surface, Lou writhed as energies built up within his body and back into the submerged facilities throughout the planet.

"So much to tell you, but now it is too late. Beware of ..." was all they heard on the ship's communication system before the explosion.

The planet's bulk shielded them from the worst of the explosion and provided them with enough time to outrace the shock wave. As soon as practicable, Bob activated the FTL drive and headed back to the base. He sat there staring into the eye-searing interplay of energies that was subspace. Rhian let him sit there for an hour before speaking.

"Thought you told me never to stare into that mess. Said me it'd give me headaches and bad dreams."

Bob let loose an explosive sigh and hung his head. After a moment he wiped his eyes but kept looking down.

"He was the last of the Eldest Ones who'd not undergone the Changed. Possibly even the eldest of us all." He turned to look at Rhian. "You heard? He said he was broadcasting our conversation to you in English."

She nodded. "I heard it. One channel was the original and another had the translation. I recorded it all." She paused for a moment. "Are you alright?"

"Yes. No." He leaned back at let his breath out in another explosive burst. "I don't know."

After a moment he snarled, "He had no right."

"Excuse me?" asked Rhian in an even tone.

"Dumping this so-called great quest on me." He scrubbed at his mouth with a hand. "Maybe it was all something out of a deranged mind."

"Do you really believe that?"

Bob fumed in silence for a moment, then exhaled sharply as he shook his head. "No. Not really."

He turned to look at her. "There's something strange going on within the Veil. My own home base has recorded the reception of intermittent garbled signals from within it over the eons. Not often, but often enough to be something other than chance or mere noise."

"So what, exactly, is this Veil of Tears thing?"

"During the middle of the Great Wars, we came up against a terrible enemy that was on the verge of defeating us ... eliminating us, in fact. It was decided to create a trap. An oh so clever trap. We—my ancestors, that is—created the illusion that the core of human civilization lay within a specific region of space. To do that, several world's worth of people volunteered to populate that area and create the technological infrastructure. Then the Enemy was allowed to discover the hitherto secret core of humanity. Their battle fleets swarmed into the area. Once inside the prepared area, the Veil was raised. It's an energy barrier fuelled by exploding stars and planets. Nothing could get in or out. Nothing physical, no communications."

"And the people inside?"

Bob closed his eyes and said in a voice raw with pain, "Left to deal with the Enemy as best they could. If they could." He opened his eyes and looked at her. "Their sacrifice saved the human race. But after that the Veil was always referred to as the Veil of Tears. It is said that my ancestors—the ones who survived—cried for a century. Or so the story goes. Anyway, that sacrifice is drummed into us from an early age."

Rhian was silent for a moment. "I'm sorry, Bob. That event is obviously of great importance to you."

"No, you don't understand. That sacrifice, all those people ... if Uncle Lou is correct, it was all for nothing. Only delayed the inevitable. Or worse, created the destruction of humanity that it was designed to prevent."

"But your uncle said it was possible for you to fix things."

Bob waved a hand in dismissal as his gaze looked at painful memories only he could see.

"Stop that self-pitying nonsense, Bob. Stop this very

instant," Rhian said in crisp tones. He turned to look at her.

"I'm quite serious," she said. "From what I understand, your uncle sacrificed himself to give you this information. He was the only one capable of obtaining it, and it seems that you are the only capable of doing something about it."

He just stared at her.

"Well," she continued, "for starters, what was that squawk of data he sent? It means nothing to me."

Bob sighed and decided to humour her. He leaned forward to his data terminal and tapped at it. A few seconds later her frowned.

"Well, what is it?"

"Hmph. Well, there's two parts to it. The first is the address of a planet. The second is some sort of code ... perhaps a pass-phrase or something."

"A planet? Where is it?"

"Give me a second," Bob muttered under his breath as he typed away. A few seconds later he let out a satisfied grunt and leaned back. "There—a planet. Not too far from our current course, actually. It's, oh, a couple of days from here."

A chirp from the console interrupted him. He peered at the display and shook his head. "That code? It's a high-level pass-code dating back to the Great Wars from the time just before the Veil was activated."

"A pass-code for what?"

"Don't know." Then he turned to her and grinned. "Maybe that new planet will hold the answers."

* * *

The next morning found Rhian gazing intently at her console as she chewed on her lower lip. She exhaled sharply and sat upright as she turned to look at Bob. "Mind if I ask a question? It's a bit personal."

Bob leaned back in his chair and gestured for her to continue.

"Great-gran mentioned that your kind were forbidden to interact with you. Is that still in effect?"

"As far as I know. Haven't actually met any of the Changed since my re-birth, and none of the un-Changed, except for Uncle Lou. Well, there's Kydos, but that wasn't so much an interaction as an attempted murder."

"Ah. Alright, so why did your Uncle seek you out and speak with you?"

"Hmm, yes. Good point, and one of the things I've been thinking about. As I told Celcilia, even among my kind Uncle Lou was considered a bit odd. Or perhaps 'eccentric' might be a better word. In any event, he focused on his studies and kept mostly to himself so far as I know. Anyone foolish enough to interfere got smacked down hard. Not one to suffer fools or interference in his affairs was Uncle Lou. He was one of the eldest of us and did things pretty much his own way."

"So is that prohibition still in effect?"

"Don't know."

Rhian digested this for a minute. "The others ... the un-Changed, I mean ... do they avoid you or simply refuse to talk to you? Sorry if this is a sore point, but I'm trying to reconcile Great-gran's notes with what you're telling me."

Bob shook his head. "Not really a sore point; more of a mystery. After I, ah, was re-born shall we say, I went back to shutting down the remainder of the portal network. Discovered that there was nothing left of it, and I had no memory or records of doing it myself."

"Could you have done it between the time you left your base and the time you died? Oops, sorry. Didn't mean to be rude."

Bob waved a hand. "Not rude at all. It's a strange situation and the language to describe what happened gets twisted. But to answer your question, I kept careful records about planned ops as well as what happened during them. I never went after more than one portal at a time. Even if, for some reason, I made a change to my last mission it wouldn't have involved more than a few portals at most. No, someone—or several someones—destroyed them."

"Would the portals have been destroyed when someone joined up with the Changed? As part of an initiation perhaps?"

Bob shook his head. "Never saw that happen before I died."

"What if the portals weren't destroyed but just turned off?"

"They don't work like that, Rhian. Once deployed they become a fixed transit point. More than that, any portal can check on the status of any other portal. To make doubly sure, I took the ship to a couple of the closer portals ... and even those trips took several months each. In each case the portals had been destroyed. Not explosively, just ... well, 'melted' is the best word I can use to describe it."

Rhian was silent for nearly a minute. "Uhm, did you ever go back? To that last planet you visited before you ... well ... died?"

"Nope. Too far away to waste the time. The portal didn't respond to queries, so I am quite sure it was destroyed. Now enough idle chit-chat. You have a lot to study before we get to our destination."

"Yes, sir, Captain Bligh."

Bob considered that for a moment. "Wasn't he the one whose crew mutinied because of supposed cruel treatment?"

Rhian gave him her sweetest smile. "That's the one."

CHAPTER FIFTEEN
Embers of Old Flames

As they approached their target, Bob had Rhian plot their stealthy course into the system. She was becoming frustrated by the number of mistakes she'd made.

"Beginning to wish I'd payed more attention to my astronomy courses," she grumbled. "Feeling like a right fool, what with all these mistakes I've been making."

Bob shook his head. "Not true. Oh, you've made tactical mistakes but they've been small ones."

Rhian grimaced. "Like that time I stalled the engines on approach to that outer moon?"

"That's a ship-handling operational mistake. For someone who's had such limited time on a ship, you are doing very well. A couple of those mistakes have been from not understanding the language sufficiently well. Even there, I see you've been reading up on some of the historical accounts of these ships. Some of those are pretty dry reading at the best of times."

"You're quite right about that, Bob." Rhian shook her head. "After-action reports seem to be the same dry stuff throughout recorded history on all worlds. Still, I thought I'd had the basics of ship handling down pretty well. Those old reports talk about months of intensive training for basic instruction, with years for full mastery. Didn't believe 'em."

Bob flashed a smile at her. "In truth, I made that same

mistake when I first flew this ship. The basics of ship operations are so simple that it's easy to overlook the subtleties. I suspect the same's true for a lot of things. Speaking of basics, though, we're coming up to our target's moon. Approach the far side then hover in synchronous orbit. I'll take it down."

A few minutes later they were on the surface, nestled in a small crater that shielded them from direct view.

"Deploy sensor probe for passive scanning?" asked Rhian.

"Yes, please. Have a good idea what we're going to see, though."

Rhian released the probe then turned in her seat. "Care to share?" she asked in arch tones.

Bob waved a hand. "Specialist knowledge. The passive scans we made sneaking it revealed the presence of the alternate energies. You saw those?"

Rhian nodded.

"Well, those specific energies are from a quiescent portal ... a fixed portal that wasn't part of the original network. Which means what, trainee?"

"Hmm. Private portal?"

"Exactly right." Bob leaned back in his chair and absently tapped his nose with a forefinger. "Don't know whose, either."

"Still in use or abandoned?"

Bob made a sour grunt. "Not sure. Might be abandoned now, but that could change in a blink." He ceased tapping his nose and began drumming his fingers on the arm of his chair. Then he stopped and looked directly at Rhian. "Check that location Uncle Lou gave us. Where is it on the planet's surface right now?"

Rhian tapped at the controls for a few seconds. "It'll be local morning there, so just past the terminator. The probe will be seeing it any time now. Ah, there we go." She tapped at the controls and a display of the planet appeared on her display. "There ... the probe is detecting the alternate energies in the region of those coordinates." She pointed at the display. Bob checked his own work station and tapped at the controls for a few seconds before leaning back in his chair to stare at a bulkhead.

"You'd go in now, wouldn't you?"

"Eh? Excuse me?"

"If you were on your own you'd be flying in without waiting your usual planetary day. I know that look."

"True enough." Bob said with an embarrassed shrug. "Been wrong before. Got the scars to prove it, too. Still, Uncle Lou gave us this location just before he died. It was important to him that we have it."

"Any ideas of who might own this place?"

Bob shook his head. "Private planets weren't always talked about. Usually were, if only as a display of ownership to prevent misunderstandings. But there's nothing else of interest in any of the stellar systems near here, and this is a pretty mundane-looking world in a mundane system."

He took a deep breath, let it out slowly, then gave a firm nod. "Gear up. After that we'll check the probe. If nothing's amiss, we'll go in."

"Yes," said Rhian, emphasizing her enthusiasm with a fist pump. At Bob's raise eyebrows, she laughed. "Great-gran often talked about her grand adventures with you. After a lifetime of academia, to my great surprise I'm quite enjoying all this, too."

Bob grinned at her enthusiasm for a moment then became serious. "Did she ever regret it?"

"No, Bob, she did not," Rhian said in a firm voice. "Missed you, of course, but as a dear friend whom she worried about. She loved her time gallivanting about galaxy—her who was born with nothing and had only hard times ahead of her. After you brought her home, she loved making a life for herself and her family. She made sure all of us felt cherished and strong enough to take on anything. That part's not in her book, but it's the most important gift she passed on to all her descendants."

Bob looked at her for a second, then nodded and left the room. Rhian smiled fondly at his departing form then followed him out. There were adventures to prepare for.

* * *

Bob landed the ship about a kilometre away from the portal, nestled in a small valley away from casual observation. That was the easy part. The hard part was convincing Rhian to stay in the ship.

"Too dangerous for an initial foray ... as you are well aware," he said in a firm voice.

"Pfft. I'm armoured."

"Pfft, yourself. That's a minimal environmental suit. What your own space agencies called a skin-suit. Remember Uncle Lou's world? Think you could have gotten back to the ship in time? No, let me do an initial recon." When she opened her mouth to object he hastened to add, "This is a military situation. And as you've mentioned to me numerous times, you aren't a soldier."

To take the sting out of it he added, "You'll be out and about soon enough. I promise."

"Uh huh. And there's you, with the same suit I've got. A few extra goodies, I'll admit, but no extra armour."

Bob tapped his belt. "A minimal kit but enough to let me fight my way back to the ship if need be. I've got the training to make this work, and you don't. I need you to keep the ship ready to back me up."

Rhian snorted. "The ship can do that without me. That's what it's designed for. But, alright, I take your point. I'll monitor and record. We also serve who sit and wait." The last came out as resigned sigh.

Bob was about to make a smart-ass comment but instead just said a heartfelt, "Thank you, Rhian. I'll go to the portal and come right back again. That's all."

He turned and went to the airlock and exited the ship. The sensors said that the air was breathable but he kept his helmet on. He'd been doing things rather more 'by the book' since starting Rhian's training. Not necessarily a bad thing, he reminded himself as he jogged towards the location of the portal. He was halfway there when Rhian broke radio silence.

"Bob, I'm picking up energy readings. Alternate energies but not portal-related. Behind the hill next to the portal. No, wait ... it's moved. Near you, now. Watch—"

The rest of the transmission was drowned out in a burst of static.

Bob dropped to a crouch but kept his hands away from the pistol. He heard the *crack* of snapping branch to his right, and spun around in time to catch a glimpse of a blur that vanished behind a bush. There was a *crack* to his left but he simply stood up and spread his hands. "I come in friendship and seek hospitality."

"You say the words ... and those with an atrocious accent that almost defies understanding ... but you sneak in unannounced like a thief," said a booming voice.

"My name is Bob. I was sent here by Uncle Lou. I mean no disrespect, but did not know this planet was inhabited."

"You speak in half-truths, as you have always done. I know you of old, young Bob." A figure came from behind a copse of trees. It was half again Bob's height and of proportional width, well-muscled, and with a flowing beard that covered much of his chest.

"Hello, Uncle Th'or. I didn't know this was one of your worlds. Fancy meeting you here."

"Hmm. Well, it is a new one. Still, how came you to be here?" The words sounded like the rumble of thunder. "No, wait. Let me guess this riddle. There is no public portal and ye've not used my private one. Oh, wait ... a ship? Yes, it must be a ship. What kind? I didn't sense it coming down. Oh, do tell me." His face radiated the eagerness of a dedicated enthusiast.

Bob recalled that Th'or had been something of a tech buff in his early days. "Uh, yes," he replied somewhat hesitantly.

Th'or laughed. It was a deep booming sound that came from the soul. "Playing it cagey like your father taught you, I see. That is more than fair. Aside from my personal interest in such things, I've found a small mystery of my own here. It's a small hardened structure, hidden behind a locked stasis field. Too small to be a base, though."

"Perhaps a cache?" suggested Bob, confused by the turn of events but trying not to show it. "Our ancestors set up such things during the Great Wars. Not many left, though. Have you opened it?"

"No, the stasis lock still confounds me. Been pecking away at it now and then to pass the time. Built my house over it to make things convenient." He waved a large hand. "It's a good site—water, forests, and game a-plenty. Nice view, too. Care to take a look?"

"What's going on here, Uncle Th'or?"

"Whatever do you mean, Bob?"

Bob resisted the urge to give in to anger. Instead he took a deep breath and let it out slowly. "Please, Uncle, I am neither a child nor a fool. We've not seen each other for centuries, most of our kind have embraced the Philosophy of Change, yet here you are acting as I'd just stopped by to pass the time of day." He paused for a moment then asked in a soft voice, "Where are the others ... your wife and daughter?"

The man before him seemed to age in an instant. "Gone. Accepted the Change. I chose to stay with the old ways."

"Here?"

"Yes. Fresh start on a new planet. The old home held too many memories."

Bob didn't know how to respond. The old rituals no longer seemed to apply, and he didn't know what to say to the older man.

"My new home is just over that hill," said Uncle Th'or, breaking the silence.

"Excuse me?"

"You seemed lost in thought, young Bob. Much is lost but much remains—never forget that. I built my home over the place of mystery. You said that you seek hospitality ... I offer it for you and your friend."

"My friend?"

"I sense another presence on my world. Oh, don't look so surprised. This world may be new to me, but it is still mine. Please, join me for refreshments. I insist."

Th'or raised a hand above his head, with fingers extended. There was a hint of strong energies in the air. He closed his fist with a snap and Bob heard Rhian's voice in his helmet. "Bob ... Bob ... the ship is moving. Should I activate weapons?"

He tapped a control on his wrist and said, "No. Stand by. Let the ship go where it goes."

Then he glared at Th'or. "I want her kept safe. She in an innocent in this."

"Lad, I don't harm innocents. You know this."

"I know that the man you used to be would not."

The two stated at each other for the space of several heartbeats. Th'or broke the silence. "That is still the case. But I am an old man who has been alone for too long. Is it too much to ask for a bit of company for a short while?"

Bob watched as the ship sailed overhead in silence towards some unknown destination. "I suppose not, Uncle. But I must state for the record that she is under my protection."

The look Th'or gave him was one of sadness. "Lad, you are in no position to offer protection to anyone, even yourself."

He turned and began walking in the direction ship had taken. Bob hesitated for a moment then followed, regretting that he'd not followed Rhian's advice to equip himself better.

* * *

203

Bob and Th'or walked in silence to the old man's home. As they walked past the portal, Bob saw that it was shrouded within a lovely grove. He gave an approving nod and asked Th'or about it.

"Aye, even though it's a private portal, I decided to upgrade the grove protection aspect. Something that your father helped me with, to be honest. We still speak now and then despite him having adopted the Philosophy of Change."

He paused for a moment before adding in a soft voice, "He regrets the angry way the two of you parted ways."

Bob shrugged, his face impassive. "We both said all that needed to be said between us ever again."

Th'or said nothing. He gave a sad nod and continued to lead the way.

They rounded a hill and came upon a structure. "Home," said Th'or with pride.

Bob saw a single-story building similar to Uncle Sid's on Earth, but on a somewhat grander scale. Where Sid's had been plain and meant to blend in with the forest, this one had simple, but bold, lines. It appeared to be made of wood that had been polished to such a fine degree that it resembled marble. Bob's ship sat to one side, in parallel with the building. The airlock was about a dozen metres from the doorway.

"Nicely done piece of work, Uncle Th'or. You did this all yourself?"

"Indeed I did. Needed something to keep myself occupied. This did the trick for a while. Got some ideas from Sid."

Bob nodded. "Thought I recognized his influence. This is similar to his house on Earth, if somewhat fancier and better finished."

"Indeed. Although he was trying to blend in so as not to be noticed. I am not so constrained."

"Hmm," said Bob. "And yet my sensors couldn't detect it."

Th'or shrugged. "Old habits. Ah, here we are." He paused in between the airlock and the door. "Invite your friend. Go ahead ... I promise not to harm her."

Bob hesitated only a moment, then nodded. It would be dangerous to not accept such a promise at face value. He keyed the suit's comms and said, "Come on out, Rhian. You'll be safe."

A handful of seconds later the airlock opened and Rhian stepped out. She paused for a moment then walked over to meet the two men. Her manner betrayed no sense of alarm or concern. Upon reaching them, she stopped and made a formal bow. "Hello, honoured sir. My name is Rhian Faernsworth. I'm not sure if you can understand me, but I am very pleased to make your acquaintance."

To the surprise of both Rhian and Bob, Th'or returned the bow and replied in perfect English, "Welcome to my home, Rhian Faernsworth. Please, won't you come in?" He gestured towards the building and the door opened. He led the way and the others followed him. Rhian raised her eyebrows at Bob, who returned a small shrug.

They passed through the door, which shut itself after them without a sound. They passed several rooms which, to Rhian's eye, appeared to be the equivalent of sitting rooms. Th'or led them down a curved hallway and to another door that opened of its own accord. Inside was a good-sized dining hall. There was a long wooden table with eight wooden chairs around it, four on each side, with one a much grander one at the left-hand end. Th'or held out one of the chairs for Rhian, who sat down with a smile and a nod of thanks. He motioned Bob to sit in a chair on the other side of the table. For himself, he sat in the ornate chair at the end. There was an elaborate place setting laid out, with plates and cutlery. Richly carved goblets sat in front of them, filled with a liquid.

"Wine," said Th'or lifting a goblet. "Perfectly safe for humans." He gave Bob a hard stare and made a soft snort.

Rhian took a small sip, smiled, and took another. "It's very good, sir. Thank you."

205

"Please call me Th'or. I'm glad you like it. What do you think of it, Bob?"

Bob took a small sip then frowned. "I've tasted this before but can't remember when."

"Think harder." Th'or's voice had taken on an icy edge.

Bob sighed and placed the goblet back on the table with care. "It was some time ago, Uncle. Last time I saw you, I think." He sat back in his chair and leaned it back slightly.

"Oh, so you do remember." Th'or's voice was quiet with a hint of menace. Rhian kept very still, hardly daring to breathe.

"It was a long time ago, Uncle. I was very young. So was she."

"That's no excuse, Bob. You took her away. Some hurts are not forgotten." With that he picked up a knife from the table and flung it at Bob with such force that Rhian could barely see it.

In response, Bob kicked his chair back, causing it to fall onto the floor. The knife passed through where he'd been, but not by much Rhian noted. Bob rolled and bounced back to his feet. Th'or roared and tossed a plate at him. Bob turned to one side and the plate sailed by, missing him by no more than a hair's breadth.

"Uncle Th'or—" Bob began but stopped when he saw the older man leap down the table towards him. Bob spun on the balls of his feet and slammed his hands against the arms of his oncoming opponent. The force of that blow cause Th'or to slide past without touching Bob.

"We don't have to do this, Uncle."

"Defiler of daughters!" roared Th'or as he lunged towards Bob. Bob took his own plate and tossed it in front of him onto the floor. Th'or stumbled as his foot landed on the plate causing his leg to skid to one side. Bob danced out of the way as the older man stumbled. Despite the stumble, Th'or swung an arm that Bob avoided by blocking, ducking, and allowing the force of the blow to drag him along and toss him several metres through the air.

Bob hit the ground, tumbled, then bounced to his feet. His left hand was held up in a placating fashion, while the right snatched at his belt. Th'or growled and bounded forward. Bob's right hand shot out to throw something as he followed through by squatting low to the ground and letting his spin carry him off to the side. The substance that he'd thrown hit Th'or in the face and began to expand into a rope-like mass.

Th'or huffed and tried to pull it off, but it stuck to his hands and soon expanded into another rope-like mass that enveloped his hands as well as his face. The dual masses began to drip and soon drooped down his legs, which also became covered with the substance. Bob stood to one side, ready to repel another attack, puffing from the exertion. Rhian sat frozen in her chair, unsure of what to do.

To their surprise, Th'or began chuckling. The chuckle turned into full-throated laughter that lasted for nearly half a minute before he got it under control.

"Tangle rope," he managed to wheeze. "Oh, where did you find this? Thought it only existed in the histories." He shrugged and twisted but only managed to make the ensnaring tangle worse.

"Uhm, Uncle. Do you ... ah ... require assistance?" asked Bob. "I've some of the neutralizing spray with me."

"No, no," came the muffled reply. "I got myself into this. Want to see if I can get myself out."

Through the web of tangles Rhian saw motion around his face. There were several bursts of light as clumps of the substance fell away. That was followed by a writhing around his neck and shoulders as the sensorium was extended. Rhian was fascinated by the sight, as she'd only had her ancestor's description of it to go by. A set of tendrils, of varying lengths from stubs to hand-length, emerged and began to glow. The web of ropes peeled away and dropped to the floor with a dull thud. Within a dozen seconds Th'or was free and clear.

"Truce, boy," boomed Th'or. There was a large grin on his face as he turned to face Bob. "You're still the tricky and devious lad you always were. Your father's son for sure."

Bob cleared his throat before answering. "Thank you, Uncle." He looked unsure of what to do next.

"Oh, sit down, sit down, the both of you," said Th'or who re-took his own place. He gave Rhian an engaging smile. She gave a slight nod and lifted her goblet in salute.

After Bob resumed his place, Rhian shot him a hard look. "I take it you dated his daughter and that it ended badly."

Bob gave his head an embarrassed shake. "We were both very young."

Th'or chuckled at his discomfiture. "That you were." He turned to Rhian. "My daughter was a bit older than Bob, you see, but was of a more ... flighty nature, shall we say. To be fair to Bob, I was never sure who had corrupted whom."

Bob developed a great interest in his goblet and took a healthy drink from it.

Rhian wasn't smiling. She turned to Th'or and said, "He's matured since then. Mostly."

Th'or gave a hearty laugh as he raised his goblet in salute to her before taking a large swallow that drained half the glass.

"What happened to her, Uncle? We lost touch."

"That's a polite way of putting it, Bob, and thank you for making the effort." He turned to Rhian as Bob's gaze returned to his goblet. "Her affair with Bob didn't last, of course ... such things never did. She drifted around and ended up with Set and his crowd. You had contact with her there, I think, Bob."

Bob nodded. "Briefly. She'd tried setting herself up as a god on a minor planet. I put a stop to it. Wasn't hard to do ... her heart wasn't in it. She even thanked me before she left. Last I saw or heard of her."

Th'or nodded. "She came home after that. As you say, her heart wasn't in it nor anything else. Oh, nothing to do with you, Bob. Like so many of her generation she was lost and looking for a purpose in life. Then the Eldest Ones started offering the Philosophy of Change and she went out of curiosity. It helped her and many like her. Even those that you didn't, ah, encourage shall we say."

Bob chuckled as he gazed into his goblet. After a moment he frowned and raised his head to look at Th'or. "You were testing me just now, weren't you? Why?"

Th'or met his gaze with a steady one of his own. "To see if you were still yourself. Heard about your death and rebirth. Heard the word 'abomination' tossed about, too. Needed to see for myself." Then he grinned. "As I said, you're still your father's son." With that said, he became serious. "So what brings you to this planet at this time, Bob? An honest answer, please."

Bob looked away for a moment as he took a deep breath to calm himself. "Uncle Lou gave me this location. Told me a very strange story. And then ..." He turned to look at his uncle. "He's dead, Uncle Th'or. Burnt himself out with his researches. Called me to his planet just before he died." He shook his head. "I still can't believe he's gone."

"He was one of the Eldest Ones, Bob. Very old and no-one lives forever. Still, I am sad that he's gone." He turned to look at Rhian. "Were you there?"

She nodded. "In the ship. He spoke to me in my own language. I'm sorry for your loss."

"Thank you. He was a good man, and I shall mourn his passing. You never had a chance to get to know him, did you, Bob? Before he got all wrapped up in his researches, I mean. Did you know that he used to be a pretty good singer? Oh, yes. Did full polyphonic musical accompaniment using the tympanic membranes that were part of his aspect. He never had children of his own but he used to love amusing them, your father and myself included." Th'or shook his head and had a small smile of remembrance on his face as his eyes looked far away. "Hard to believe we were that young once, though."

He looked at Bob and said, "Then he got wrapped up in his work and all that came to an end. Still, he was a good man, Bob, and a wise one."

Th'or raised his goblet and said, "In memory of Uncle Lou." Then he drank it dry. Bob and Rhian raised their goblets and drank in salute, although they each took only a sip.

No-one said anything for nearly a minute. Th'or broke the silence. "He called to you and told you to come here, did he? Must have had a good reason." He scratched at his head. "Nothing here except an old man. Oh, and that storage facility I was telling you about, Bob."

"You said it was locked and sealed."

Th'or shrugged. "A small bending of the truth until I knew the truth of you."

His eyes took on a faraway look for a few seconds. "Your ship is an old scout craft, type Sharp Claws Five, is it not?"

Bob nodded. "Yes. A Mark Eight, to be exact."

"I thought so." He gave a satisfied nod as he added, "My favourite type."

He grinned at Rhian as he said, "That was the type mentioned most often in the stories I heard when growing up. I once even went so far as to memorize all the available documentation and manuals for them. Bob's father and I got quite deep into that until he decided to become a portal specialist. You're very fortunate to be able to serve on such a fine vessel."

His gaze returned to Bob. "That sealed facility was a weapons cache meant to resupply scout craft on long-range patrols. It includes a strap-on cargo module. Ever seen one of those?"

Bob shook his head, but it was obvious from his excited look that he knew what it was. He leaned forward. "How is it configured?"

Th'or grinned. "For a long-range recon. Most of it's given

210

over to cargo, but there's a couple of spare cabins to give the crew some extra personal space. Includes a power booster, speciality recon gear, and lots of assault weapons. A standard general-purpose load." He cleared his throat as if about to ask a delicate question. "Ah, do you know how to attach this to your ship, Bob?"

"No, Uncle. There'll be manuals in the ship's records, I'm sure."

Th'or shrugged and spread his hands. "Not as easy as that, I'm afraid. As I mentioned, your father and I delved quite deeply into the manuals. There's a bit of a trick to it and then the engines need a slight re-tuning to adjust for the extra power and change in configuration."

He cleared his throat. "Ah, I could do that for you. No, no ... no bother at all." He gave an embarrassed smile. "Truth be told, I've been itching for something useful to do for some time. I'd be honoured to be able to be of service to you."

Bob hesitated only a moment before giving a formal nod. "I thank you for your offer of assistance, Uncle, and accept it with thanks."

"Excellent," cried Th'or as he clapped his hands together. "You two stay here and rest, while I make the preparations. There's suitable fresh food in the storage locker over there and more wine next to it." He got up and strode out of the room, his brisk walk faster than the others could run. Th'or had just turned the corner when his voice boomed forth, "Please let your ship know I'm coming."

Rhian waited until she could no longer hear his steps, then leaned forward and whispered to Bob. "Is that wise?"

Bob shrugged and took a swallow of his wine. "He offered honoured service. I would've needed a very strong reason to refuse that." At her raised eyebrow he added, "One of our customs."

"So what do we do?" she asked.

He gave another shrug and stood up. "See what's in his

larder. Hope it's different than ship rations."

"Oh, those aren't so bad. Had worse in my day."

"True enough, I suppose. Still, my experience, and the stories of my ancestors who crewed those ships, makes a point of eating fresh food whenever it's available. Long trips can get boring."

"Thought an advanced society like yours would have practically perfect food replicators."

"Getting the basics is easy ... tuning them to create the equivalent of fresh food was something only the very talented could manage. That's why we stopped using them after the Great Wars, for the most part. I'm not that talented, as you've come to experience for yourself."

Rhian grinned and drained her wine. Bob smiled and said, "You might want to take it easy with that."

"Pfft. I'm British. We know how to drink. But I take your point—what's there for food?"

Bob inspected the offerings. "Nibbles, for the most part. Let's see ... various types of bread, cheeses, cold meats, some fruits."

"Will it be safe for us?"

Bob hesitated a moment then shrugged. "He made a point of saying that it was suitable for us."

Rhian nodded. "And it would no doubt be an insult to not take him at his word, correct?"

"You're learning. Still, I'd stay away from the fruits. Everything else is cooked or processed in some fashion, so should be safe enough. Want a refill of the wine?"

The food, to Rhian's mind, was delicious. There were a variety of spices used in everything, but with a light touch. Bob found something that resembled beer, so they switched to drinking that. Their conversation was, for the most part, light and of inconsequential matters. One thing had been bothering Rhian enough that she asked, "How did he move the ship?"

Bob smiled. "Did you take note of the energy readings and

their spectrum while it was happening?"

"Uhm, sort of. It was all rather sudden and unexpected," she said looking embarrassed.

"Not surprised at that, Rhian. Anyway, take a look at the records when we get back. You'll find that it was a standard tractor beam."

"Really? He held up his hand and the ship moved in lockstep and ..." she wound down as a thoughtful look appeared on her face. "Misdirection?"

"Yep. It's the sort of thing he used to do to entertain us kids. Whenever one of us would start to catch on, one of the other adults would create a small diversion to draw away our attention. We all got wise to it eventually, but let on like we didn't. The adults seemed to get such a kick out of it that we didn't have the heart to ruin their fun."

Rhian laughed. "I used to think that adults created childhood events to amuse themselves as much as to amuse the children. Interesting to see that it seems to be a cultural universal. Did I ever tell you about the time that Great-gran Celcilia tried to teach us kids how to juggle?" That was the start of a long series of recollections of their childhoods and they didn't notice the passage of time until the echo of approaching footsteps could be heard.

Within seconds Th'or strode into the room, his presence dominating it. "Oh, lad, that was a pleasure such as I've not had in many a century. My thanks to you for allowing it." He came up to the table and sat down in his chair. Bob pushed a bottle towards him. Th'or nodded his thanks and drained it. "Tinkering is thirsty work," he said as he winked at Rhian.

"I spent decades poring over those old manuals but today I got to put my hands on that magnificent vessel. It was an honour to be part of such storied history, Bob, and I can't thank you enough for that. The pod integrates perfectly with the ship, and everything is tuned to factory specifications."

His eyebrows furrowed as he looked at Bob. "You'd not

gotten the tuning quite right on some of those systems, you know."

"Thank you, Uncle. That was very kind of you."

Th'or waved a nonchalant hand as he leaned back in his chair. "It's what I spent a lifetime learning to do, lad. Like your father and his portals." Then he leaned forward and became serious, his hands folded together on the tabletop. "But you've a hard task ahead of you, I think. Uncle Lou would not have sent you here on a whim." He hesitated a moment before continuing. "It's not for me to know, of course, but I wish you and your companion all the best of luck in what is to come."

Then he stood up. "I get the feeling that time is not your friend, Bob, and shall not keep you any longer." He nodded at Rhian, then Bob. "You've made an old man very happy. I want you to know that, the both of you." He spun on his heels and began walking. "Let me show you the way out."

Rhian and Bob looked at each other then shot to their feet. Bob grabbed his helmet and hurried after their host, with Rhian in his wake. Th'or lead them through the corridors and back outside where the ship was parked. It sat higher than before to accommodate the extra girth that now encompassed the lower half of it. It reminded Rhian of a pregnant guppy.

The airlock was some ways up in the air, and a staircase was extended from the new pod to compensate. They paused at the bottom and clustered in an embarrassed huddle.

"Don't like goodbyes, Bob. Done too many of them these past few years." He bowed to Bob and said, "May your journey be a credit to your ancestors." He then bowed to Rhian and repeated his words. With that he spun on his heels and strode back to his home and was soon out of sight.

"That was—" began Rhian.

"Time for us to go," said Bob. "Let's up and away, shall we?"

Within a minute they were airborne and heading into space.

* * *

214

Th'or watched as the ship rose into the air and flung itself into space. When he decided it was far enough away, his form melted away to reveal a tall pearl-white ovoid. A second ovoid approached him.

"Will he succeed, Uncle?"

"I hope so, Freddie. In any event, we've done all we were ordered to do. Time to return to the others. There is much preparation to do."

"Yes, Uncle," came the diffident reply.

"Something bothering you, lad? Are you upset that you were chosen for this task? It was part of your healing process, as you well know."

The one referred to as Freddie would have grinned if his form allowed such a thing. "Uncle Th'or, please. I hold Bob no ill will. His besting me in combat was the best thing that happened to me in a very long time. I owe him my thanks for giving me time with Aunt Freida and Uncle Sid."

At a glare from the other he added, "Well ... and perhaps a bit of a kick in the pants for being an asshole about it. Anyway," he hurried to say before Th'or could interrupt. "Anyway, as good as he is with portals, I'm a better ship tech than him."

"Hmm. Meaning what, young Freddie?"

"Heh. The ship now runs like new." He paused for a moment then continued in a happy tone that had an element of pride. "And the engines are better than that. I figured out how to make them work at better than twice their rated speed. That's more than three times faster than the ship could do before Bob came here." Then his tone became serious. "He'll need that."

"So what's bothering you?"

"This whole business, actually. This is a job for us, the Changed, not a single person. Bob deserves better than this."

Th'or gave the equivalent of a deep sigh. "You have a point, lad, but I helped the Conclave come to this decision. Uncle

Lou set things in motion without informing us until the last minute. We could do nothing but help that plan along, I'm afraid."

"But we could—"

"Do what, Freddie? All we know is that there's something stirring inside the Veil. We can't tell what that is and there is no way for any of us to get there. Uncle Lou says it's something bad and sent Bob to somehow investigate. His message to the Conclave was as short and mysterious as any he'd ever sent, but it was clear the intent was for us to give him a cargo pod and to include a crate of readers and extra power cells to the standard load. No-one knows any more than that, so we decided to give a bit of help on the off chance that it was something serious. What more would you have us do?"

Freddie was silent for a moment. "I don't know. But I still don't like it."

"On that we agree, lad. Oh, and best not be mentioning that extra work you did to the engines. The Conclave wasn't too happy about having this much interaction with Bob. Your going above and beyond won't sit well with them."

"Me? You're the one who socialized and reminisced about old times. And I saw how well you stocked that cargo pod. There's enough there to stock a small forward base." He paused for a few seconds. "On the other hand, Uncle, you have a point. It was made very clear to me that our help should be kept to a bare minimum."

"As was made clear to me as well. Let us just say that the term 'minimum' can mean different things to different people. That would, I'd suggest, allow us to truthfully report back to the Conclave that we followed their instructions exactly."

"You mean we should lie to them?" Freddie said in a voice that had a touch of the mischievous in it.

"I'm shocked that you would even suggest that, young man. We are, as you well know, evolved well beyond the need to lie. You and I will simply tell them what they need to know. No

216

more, no less."

"I bow to your superior wisdom, Uncle."

"Now, Freddie, just as Bob has his path to follow, we have ours. Shall we be off?"

They began to emit a radiance that outshone the sun for a few seconds, then they vanished.

CHAPTER SIXTEEN

Back to the Beginning

Bob set the ship's course to rise out of the system's ecliptic while staying in sub-light.

"Something wrong, Bob?"

"Hmph? What? Oh, just taking things easy while I get the feel for the modifications that Uncle Th'or did."

"So why the frown? Do you not trust him?"

"Oh, I think we can. Trust him, I mean." Then he turned to face her and grinned. "Just being careful, is all. I've learned the hard way to take things easy after a major overhaul."

"Are you referring to ships or bodies?"

Bob laughed. "Applies equally well to both. In this case, however, I'm referring to the ship."

"Ah. Looks like you're drawing less power than before." Then she frowned. "But the velocity is ... wait. That can't be right." She turned to Bob. "Oh stop grinning at me ... I'm still getting the hang of these systems."

"So what's the problem, trainee?"

"Not a problem," she snapped. Then in a milder tone she added, "Although it does appear that we're using less power— a lot less power—than the ship used to require to achieve and maintain this velocity."

"Very good. Uncle Th'or did say that he tweaked things. I guess this could be considered a tweak. Anything else?"

Rhian studied the controls for a minute, her frown deepening. "Everything. I mean, it's all working better than it ever did." She pointed at a series of controls. "See there and there? Everything is working to spec the way the manual says it should. No offence."

"None taken, I assure you. But you're correct. Everything is working to spec, and in some cases a bit better."

"I notice you've not activated the FTL drive yet."

"That's right. Getting us out of all the local gravity wells before I try it. At minimum power, I might add." He looked at the controls. "Should be fine to try now. Care to do the honours? Set it up for a minimum jump at minimum power. I'll stand by to shut things down, just in case."

Rhian tapped at the controls. "There. Minimum jump at minimum power set up. Course continues along our current path. Sensors show nothing in our way."

Bob nodded. "Looks good, Rhian. Nicely done. Jump when ready."

She nodded. "Ready in three...two...one...and go. And done."

They both studied the controls.

"Oops," said Rhian. "That's further than expected. A lot further. Are you sure I set things up correctly?"

"You did. If this small jump is any indication, the FTL engines are more efficient than ever. Better than the specs say they should be, in fact."

"By how much?"

"Not sure without more testing." He grinned and turned to her. "Ready to go again? Set up for twice the distance of the last test."

An hour later found them sitting in the mess enjoying a light meal. The ship was back on course to their destination base.

"You sure it's safe to walk away from the controls like this?"

Bob shrugged. "At this point the ship can handle any problems faster than we can. Probably a good idea to set up formal watches, though. My people used to stand watches that were, oh, about five of your hours. Makes it tough to sleep until you get used to it, but it's only for a few days."

Rhian nodded. "Good idea. So what's the final top velocity?"

"Looks to be better than three times what it was before Uncle Th'or did whatever to the engines. That's way beyond what should be possible, by the way."

Rhian was silent for a moment. "Doesn't all this strike you as strange, Bob?"

Bob nodded. "Oh, yes. In more ways than one. I might have been able to accept tuning the engines up to their designed ratings ... although that would have involved new parts that I've never been able to find. More than that, these new engines integrate perfectly well with the ship's controls. Not sure how that's possible, given that they must be operating on a whole new level."

He frowned as he looked at her. "Ships are tightly integrated systems, you understand. Changing one thing means changing a lot of other things, especially on the controls side. These new changes operate as if the ship had been designed for them. That takes a lot of talent. Specialized and experienced talent. I suppose it's possible his technical expertise extended to that sort of thing."

"Not only that, but he seemed to do it willingly," added Rhian. "No mention of the shunning you were under."

Bob nodded. "Glad you picked up on that. Yes, that's strangest thing about all this. There's more going on here than we know about."

"When did you see him last? Was he one of the ones you had to, ah, convince to accept training from the Changed?"

"No," said Bob as he shook his head. "Never came across him or any of his family while I was destroying the portal network. His worlds were among those I failed to get to before I died."

"Were you on good terms with him? Aside from corrupting

his daughter, I mean."

Bob had the grace to blush. "In my defence, it was something of tie as to which of us corrupted the other. Anyway, to answer your question, my family never had problems with his. In fact, he and Dad were childhood friends and stayed friends. So far as I know, anyway."

"So what do we do about this new-found assistance? Do you think he did it as a favour for your father?" asked Rhian.

"Take it at face value for now, I think. If what Uncle Lou warned us about is true, we're going to need all the help we can get. As for Dad, he's always been pretty much a 'sink or swim' kind of parent."

"Uh huh. So why are you drumming your fingers? You only do that when you're pondering a deep mystery, and there's plenty of those here."

"Yes there are, Rhian. Did you notice that he never asked about your background or why you were travelling with me?"

"I did. Would have thought that a lonely old man would have wanted more details—for entertainment if nothing else. Then there's how he pretty much shoved that cargo pod onto us."

Bob nodded. "Yeah. So very handy that he just happened to have that." Then he sighed heavily. "On the other hand, Uncle Th'or always was a technical sort and Uncle Lou told us to meet with him, so perhaps it makes sense." He ran a hand through his short hair and scrubbed at his scalp. "I don't like coincidences. Especially when they're being tossed at me like this."

"So what do we do?"

"Not much we can do. We need to head back to the base anyway, but now we've got something to look for when we get there." He grinned. "Lots of mysteries to investigate."

Rhian grinned back. "It's always good to have a plan."

* * *

The trip back to the base took less than a week. The new

221

engines weren't even pushed to their limit, something Bob was loath to do that without more experience using them. The system defences challenged them as soon as they dropped out of FTL, but accepted Bob's command identification without any problem. Bob took a full day for a leisurely approach to the base itself, and they were challenged at several points along the way. He assured Rhian that it was standard procedure.

Before landing at the base itself, they were challenged one final time before being allowed to approach and land. Once down, Bob manoeuvred the ship into a cavernous hanger. It was, as he explained to Rhian, the lesser of two evils. He didn't yet fully trust the security of the base, but the hanger offered better physical security than sitting outside.

Once the ship was secured, they changed into skin-suits and helmets, then disembarked into the base itself. Their first stop was the commander's office. Bob spent nearly half an hour making queries and examining all the displays before he declared the base to be secure.

"Whoosh," said Rhian as she removed her helmet. "Glad to be out of that. Suit feels comfortable enough, though. Now what?" She paused as she realized Bob still had his helmet on as he stared at the displays. Rhian tapped a control on her suit and said, "Hello, hello. You said it was all safe."

Bob waved a dismissive hand and kept staring at the displays. Several seconds later he leaned back and removed his own helmet. "Just checking some more things. The artificial sentience is gone ... not a trace anywhere in any of the subsystems."

"So what was all that extra typing about?"

Bob shrugged. "Tied the ship into the base's control systems to do a security check. Want to make sure the AS didn't leave any programmed surprises for us. So far so good, though. This area, the mess, and the crew quarters are verified as safe by the ship. Will know about the rest in an hour or two."

"Is that why you've kept your helmet on?"

He grinned at her. "Nah. I don't notice it any more, really." At her surprised look he laughed. "I've spent a lot more time with this gear than you, Rhian. Part of my training was to spend a week floating in space with just a skin-suit." At the horrified look on her face he hurried to add, "Not recommended, I assure you. On the other hand, some of the larger suits can be quite comfortable for long periods. I infiltrated one target's bases that way once while I was eliminating the portal network. She'd ringed the portal with an elaborate defensive grid. I drifted in to the planet over the course of a month, like a piece of space junk."

"Eww. Seriously?" She shuddered. "I get the shivers just thinking about it."

"Rather relaxing, in its own way," he said. "Best part was the anticipation." Bob grinned in a way that reminded Rhian of a cat on the hunt. "A culture in the habit of travelling by portal tends to ignore any other means of transportation."

He got a satisfied look on his face as his eyes focused on something far away and long ago. "Good times."

Then he snapped back into focusing on the present. "But for now, let's head back to our old quarters, shall we? The displays show everything there as being undisturbed, and the ship confirms those records. You know how to work the supplies network for clothing and such. If anything—and I mean anything—strikes you as not right, call out. Otherwise, let's meet in the mess in an hour? Will that give you enough time to settle in?"

Rhian considered that for a moment then nodded. After the confines of the ship, the expanse of the base seemed quite inviting, if a bit unsettling. Her feelings of unease vanished after a shower and change of clothing. The uniforms of the base were similar to the ones offered on the ship, but she found that she relished the change. The room itself seemed a strange combination of familiar and new. On the one hand it was her first non-Terrestrial experience, and those memories were quite powerful. On the other, after spending so much time on the ship and learning about Bob's culture, it seemed far more familiar than it had. The various displays and controls no longer seemed alien ... in fact, she was beginning to accept them as something normal. Glancing at the clock, she noticed it was nearly time to head to the mess, so she headed out.

As expected, Bob was already there, reading from a data tablet. He looked up as she entered the room and rose to his feet, smiling in greeting.

She smiled at him as she sat. "What's on the menu today? Scrambled eggs and gruel again?"

"Nope," Bob said with a grin. "Managed to tweak things better ... with the help of the ship." He got up and went to the kitchen area, returning with a pair of trays. He placed a tray before her, then returned to the other side of the table with his own tray.

"Smells good," Rhian said appreciatively as she sniffed at the steaming dishes. "Dare I ask what it is?"

"That, my dear Doctor, is a meat dish of which I am quite fond, plus several other tasty items. Very similar to what Celcilia and I ate when we visited the Five Stars Empire. Thought you might like a taste of history."

Rhian grinned at him, surprising herself with how pleased she was with this gift. She sampled a bite from every dish before attacking the meat dish in earnest. "This is quite good," she mumbled around a mouthful of food. She swallowed before adding, "How close is this to what Great-gran ate?"

"Pretty close," Bob said. "The spices aren't quite the same, but as close as I can make it. Glad you like it. Would have served it before, but the ship's equipment isn't up to the task."

"Uhm hmm. Yes, that's tasty. She tried to duplicate it over the years, but was never happy with the results. Which reminds me ..." Rhian reached into a pocket of her jacket and handed Bob a bound book about three centimetres thick.

"Great-gran's book. I've got it in electronic form, never fear. Have also all but memorized it."

Bob took the book from her and carefully examined its exterior. The cover was a dark blue, with no writing on the cover to indicate what was within. He opened it up and glanced through, pausing at a dozen random pages. He paused several times in his reading. Finally he closed the book and brushed at his eyes.

"Thank you," he said with a bow of his head. He cleared his throat before continuing. "This means a great deal to me."

Rhian was touched by his display of emotion. "I hope you enjoy it as much as I have." She grinned. "As much as all of her descendants have. We trusted Great-gran to tell the truth, but it all seemed so fantastical." She looked around. "She would have loved this, I think."

To her surprise Bob chuckled. "Not sure that I'd agree with you about that, Rhian. Oh, she loved the wandering about the stars, despite the danger and the pain it brought her. But by the end she was happy enough to get home, I think."

Rhian grinned back at him and pointed at the book. "Read it. She had a good life, but there were times she missed it, the star wandering. T'were a number of us got itchy feet from those writings, myself among them. She inspired a great many of us to be our best selves, too." She looked around the room once again, and her face took on a sad look. "She also taught us that sometimes adventures are paid for with pain and loss."

She was silent for a moment then inhaled sharply as her focus returned to the present. "So where do we go from here?' Her voice was clipped and precise.

"We rest," was Bob's prompt reply. "We've been through a lot, and there's worse to come, I suspect. Take things easy for the rest of the day, have a good night's sleep, then a fresh start in the morning."

Rhian nodded. "Sounds like a good idea." Then she grinned. "Do we have time for a proper tour? Never saw much here the last time."

That got a laugh out of Bob. "There's more to see than can be seen in a week of exploring, I assure you. But, yes, by all means let's do the grand overview. It'll do us both good to get a feel for this place."

They spent the next several hours wandering about the base and only saw a fraction of what it contained. As Bob had promised, there was enough there to keep a team of explorers busy for a week or more just on an overview. Rhian began the tour looking at things with the eyes of a trained archaeologist, but after the first hour settled for being an observant tourist.

The first place Bob took her was to the main control centre. It was laid out like a large half-circle, with a half-dozen chairs in the centre surrounded by over a dozen arranged in an arc around them. Each chair had a data console in front of it, and the walls were filled with displays of various sorts.

"It looks like a cross between the control of a nuclear reactor and a movie depiction of a space ship command centre," she said, grinning as she looked around. "Why do you spend time at the commander's office instead of here?"

"Better overview," was the prompt reply. "These stations are for specific departments, the ones at the centre for the duty officers. These offer a more detailed, and finer, control of things but the commander's office oversees it all." He pointed at a display to the right of the centre of the arc. "That's the security function, there. See the displays of the planetary and solar system monitors?"

Rhian peered at them. "Huh. Pretty close to what the ship has. Don't understand it all, but can get the gist of it."

Bob nodded. "Exactly right. Similar tech, just separated by a few centuries. We didn't change much over that time. Anyway, seen enough? We'll be coming back here in the coming days. I want to show you something. You'll like this."

She tried to get more out of him, but he refused to say anything more as he led her through another maze of corridors. He opened a door, grinning, then motioned for her to go in. The room was dimly lit except for a glow from a large pit in the centre. Rhian walked towards the pit, which had an instrumented railing around it. She peered into it and let out a gasp. The pit was about ten metres in diameter and filled with stars. After a few moments she realized that it was a three-dimensional depiction of the galaxy. Even at this scale, there were confusing conglomerations of stars that seemed to merge together, with some gaps and other structures. Rhian walked around the perimeter of it trying to take it all in.

"Use one of the stations on the perimeter," she heard Bob say. "Just look into the display and see if you can figure out the controls."

Rhian paused at one of the stations and peered through what appeared to be a smoky pane of glass. There were a number of controls below it. She studied them for a moment then cautiously tapped at them. The pane changed to show stars. Manipulating the controls allowed her to swoop in and out of the portion of the galaxy seen by the pane. Tapping other controls brought up a series of tags associated with various features displayed on the plane.

"I know colleagues in the astrophysics department who would literally kill for access to something like this," she said as she turned to look at Bob. "This is ... addicting," she said as she manipulated controls to zoom about the galaxy.

"Also good for coordinating interstellar warfare," he replied. "Want to see that function?"

Rhian shook her head. "Some other time. I'm enjoying the purity of stars too much."

After letting her investigate for half an hour, he suggested moving on. With reluctance she agreed.

"Did you ever see something like this?" she asked as they walked out of the room.

"Similar," he said. "Some larger, some smaller. Had one half this size at home when I was growing up, with more powerful ancillary controls."

He waved a hand back at the closing door. "In battle, there would be someone at every station. Co-ordinating friendly fleets was a logistical nightmare. Distances are vast, and faster-than-light drives don't shrink it by much." He shook his head. "Battles took years, or even decades, to come into focus. Usually there were multiple battles on multiple fronts, and all sides trying desperately to figure out what happening much less control it all."

Rhian turned to look at him as they walked. "But your side—the humans—had faster ships and portals."

Bob nodded. "That's true. The portals gave us better intelligence and the means to move small forces around very quickly." He shook his head. "But fleets take time to move, however much faster ours were than theirs. And they had many more ships than we did, more often than not." He paused for a moment. "Do you recognize what's down that corridor?"

Rhian peered down and glanced at the signage. "The hanger we landed in, I think." She paused for a moment then pointed at a doorway further down. "What's that?"

"That goes to the maintenance shops. I'll want to take a look at that eventually, but not now. Next stop is the armoury, then on to what the maps indicate as the research area."

The armoury held little interest for Rhian, though Bob enjoyed poking about. The research area consisted of a large number of offices. Some were for single-person use, others for multiple persons, and others held tables that seemed to be for meetings. There was little of immediate interest there, so Bob suggested they head back to the mess for a meal.

"You seem a bit disappointed, Rhian," he said.

"Hmm," she said as she nodded. "It all seems so ... functional." She blushed and added, "Sorry."

Bob laughed. "It's a working base, you know, filled with military people and clerical staff and researchers."

"Researching what, exactly?"

"Not sure," said Bob as he frowned. "That's something we need to look into first thing tomorrow." Then he brightened. "But first, we need to have a bite to eat. How about you lead the way to the mess this time?"

Over the meal ... Rhian wasn't sure if it was a late lunch or dinner ... they discussed what they'd seen during their tour.

"Is this a standard base?"

Bob shrugged. "Not much is known about these bases. Oh, we know the basics of course, but only through the records ... and those are incomplete at best. So very few survived, and even fewer intact ones. This is the largest intact one I've heard of." He looked around before continuing. "Still, most of it seems standard enough, from what I know."

Rhian smiled. "Then why are you frowning? Something not quite right?"

"Yeah, but I'm not sure what. Oh, nothing bad, just a small itch in my mind."

"Hmm, I've got a similar itch, I think." At Bob's enquiring look she added, "Spent much of my professional life on archaeological digs and poking into places with hidden secrets. There's more here." She waved a dismissive hand. "Oh, sure, our tour just touched a fraction of what's here, but that's just it ... we saw what we were meant to see." Then she yawned. "Sorry."

Bob gave a thoughtful nod. "You've made a good point about seeing what we were meant to see. Anyway, let's call it a day, shall we? We're both a bit foggy and need a rest, I think. Or at least a chance to stare at the walls and enjoy some mindless down time. Set your alarm for local dawn, and I'll meet you a half hour later for breakfast."

They said their goodnights and went to their respective rooms. Rhian cycled through the musical records until she found something resembling a classical symphony and listened to that for an hour before turning in. Bob spent the time reading Celcilia's book. He suspected it would be a long time before he got another chance.

CHAPTER SEVENTEEN
Search for Answers

Rhian rose at the crack of dawn—or at least what her personal data tablet said was local dawn—and spent some time getting ready to face the day. Looking at her face in the mirror, she was reminded about her first morning here and how close to breaking she was. "We've come a long way, old thing, haven't we?" she said to the reflection. The reflection's grin looked genuine, which she took as a good sign.

She arrived at the mess to find that she was the first one there for a change. After waiting for a minute, she shrugged and prepared a meal for herself. She spent the time alone reading from her data tablet. There were so many new things to learn, but she had decided to focus on learning to use the base's data systems. They were similar, but not identical, to the ship's systems. She had finished the tutorial overview and was planning a series of training exercises when Bob entered.

"Oh, you're up. Sorry I'm late," he said as he headed to the kitchen to make up a meal for himself.

"Well, good morning to you, too, Fearless Leader. And here I thought I was ahead of you for once. Something wrong?"

Bob delayed answering until he had settled down at the table opposite to her. "Nah. Stayed up reading Celcilia's book then got a few hours sleep." He made quick work of half his meal before speaking again.

"Got to thinking about what the rogue sentience said when it sent us off. For one thing, it claimed it was going to destroy the portal. Turns out it had ... we forgot to check that yesterday. My bad."

Rhian shrugged as she replied, "Well, we've been using the ship so much that I'm not surprised neither of us thought of that."

After a moment she got a thoughtful look on her face and was silent for the space of several heartbeats. "Hmm, now that you mention it, wasn't there also something about finding a new testing area within the records of your original opponent? I always wondered why it sent us to the Hell Planet."

Bob nodded. "An excellent point. That was the second thing I checked on this morning. Turns out to be a half-truth. It had breached data systems of my opponent's ship but only managed to access some of the unsecured records, such as from data tablets. The core system, and all the primary records and ship controls, was still intact. I had my ship take a crack at it but turns out that little ship has very good security locks. That'll take time to overcome, so I set the base control system to work on it. It'll be done when it's done. Maybe a day, maybe a month, but it'll get done in the fullness of time."

"So you're not worried about it harbouring anything of significance? Did you do a physical search?"

"Not safe to physically enter until the security system gets cracked. Possible to do, of course, but very unwise." He shrugged. "Whatever secrets it holds, I don't think it has anything to do with our mission. Speaking of which, what's that you're reading?"

Rhian tapped on data tablet. "Reading up on how to access the base records. It's not quite the same as how the ship does things." She leaned forward. "We need to set up a proper office space for us to use. The user guides I've been reading imply that the researchers were expected to have and make use of a fairly sophisticated setup. Perhaps those office we passed through yesterday would be a good place to check out. Or have you something else in mind?" She grew concerned at the blank look on Bob's face as she spoke. "Bob?"

"What? Oh, sorry, I was thinking about what you said about setting up a proper office. Yeah, that's good thinking." He gave an embarrassed grin. "I'm so used to working with minimal controls that I forget about the fancier stuff that can be available."

"What about your home base? You've not said much about it—I understand the security necessity of that, never fear—but doesn't it have fancier data systems?"

He shook his head. "Only to a limited extent. Although, to be honest, I never had a reason to require sophisticated research so I never pushed them to their limits." He grinned as he added, "I'll probably need to brush up on the systems here, too. Yes, that office area is probably a good place to start. You finished with your meal?"

When Rhian nodded, Bob took the remains of both meals back to the kitchen area. He bent down, fiddled at a storage area, and returned carrying a large box which he plopped on the table with a triumphant grin.

Rhian looked at it carefully, then narrowed her eyes as she looked at him. "Don't make me guess what's in it. You know how much I hate surprises."

Bob laughed and removed the contents, one by one. "Figured we'd be busy exploring today, so had the synthesizers make us up some field rations of sorts. There's water, tea, meal bars, and some of those biscuits the ship makes that you like. One set for each of us."

That got a chuckle out of Rhian. "Perfect rations for researchers. You planning on carrying the box all the way?"

"Nope. Only as far as our quarters. We've both got carrying gear that we can pack with these supplies and anything else we might need."

"Any chance I could get something like your combat belt?

233

I've noticed that you've got some handy attachments for things like data tablets and water containers."

"I'll pick up one for you this later this morning, if you like. Shall we be off?"

A half hour later found them wandering about the office area, looking at it with a critical eye. At first they were disappointed, as it appeared to be nothing more than an administrative area with little of practical use. Then Rhian noticed an unfamiliar sign that led to a locked door. Bob's command authorizations got him inside, and before entering he ensured that Rhian would have access as well.

This area proved to be where the real work was done. There were a series of offices arranged around a central communal area. Each office was four metres square, and packed with control consoles and a large desk. It was all laid out for easy use by a single person. The communal area held a half-dozen small tables, each with three minimalistic chairs, and a couple of sofa-like things. Best of all, there was a small kitchen area with a couple of food synthesizers. Bob tested them and found them to be in working order, although only the water dispenser produced a palatable product. He promised that tweaking that up would be near the top of his priority list, if only to get tea and snacks.

There was a short corridor that led to another office area, but those offices were of lesser quality and seated two or more people in each. The communal area for this area consisted of a minimal food synthesizer tucked into a small alcove. "This area was probably for the assistants," opined Rhian, and Bob agreed.

Going back to the main area, they selected a pair of side-by-side offices for themselves. Bob checked out the equipment while Rhian watched. It turned out that her help was necessary, as she'd been reading the tutorial manuals. Within an hour, each had a working set of controls. The only glitch came when it came to using the systems to access data, as it required Bob's command authorizations. Or, rather, it required that the person sitting at the controls have command authorization. That meant that only Bob could use them.

After querying the system for a minute, he turned to Rhian. "I need to get you an authorization identification chit. Sorry, but I didn't think about that before we came here."

"Can you set it up on my data tablet?" she asked as she waggled it.

"Nope. Need a special physical passkey. Not unknown for a research project, I suppose, but strange that such a degree of security is required here. There's no hint that what was being worked on required that level of security. Hmm, that's going to require us to go back to my command office."

Rhian shook her head. "Why don't I stay here and look around while you get that chit sorted out? I've got authorization to be in this area, just not to access the control systems. I could look around and check out what's in their desks. That might give us an idea of what they were working on. Any reason the base won't let me do that?"

Bob tapped at the controls for a minute, then leaned back. "You're right about that ... once in, you are authorized to wander around." He turned to look up at her. "You going to be OK being here on your own? You sure?"

"I'll be fine," she said, waving a dismissive hand and grinning. Then she became serious. "I need to do this, Bob. I can't be your shadow, afraid to sneeze. And, truthfully, I do know how to do this sort of thing."

At Bob's concerned look Rhian gave him a wry grin. "You might recall that I've got a lifetime's experience at poking about ancient sites." She looked around before adding, "Although nothing quite like this. So, yes, go. We've got our comm links."

He nodded, both concerned and relieved. "Alright. I let you know my progress. Yes, yes, you're experienced and all. But keep in mind that is primarily a military base, and we've only just eliminated a hostile threat that was controlling it. Anything you want me to bring back while I'm out?"

Rhian shook her head and made shooing motions. Bob grinned at her and left at a brisk walk. She heard his footsteps grow fainter, then vanish. The room seemed to grow smaller for an instant, then she grinned and spun on the balls of her feet with her arms outstretched. It was something she did at every dig or site, the first time she entered it. The thrill of potential discoveries always excited her, and this little show of exuberance helped to centre her. The ceremony complete, she placed her backpack on the floor in the centre of the room and took out a notebook and pen.

She spent the next several minutes making a rough, but accurate, sketch of the area. Each office had an identifier, which she added to the sketch. The preliminaries done, she took her data tablet and used it to take a scan of the area to provide details the sketch didn't have. Only then did she do another walk around the area, noting each thing of interest on her sketch, and making new sketches as necessary. This wasn't to make a detailed drawing—details could be captured by the data tablet—but to record an accurate overview. Rhian was so absorbed in her task that she lost track of time until she heard a soft chirping from her comm link.

"Hi, Rhian," Bob said. "Sorry I didn't check in before this. I went to my office, but it turns out I had to go to the supply area for the required chit. I'd like to have a chat with whomever left this base in such a disorganized state. You doing OK?"

"Oh, yes," Rhian said in a distracted voice. "Finishing up a preliminary sketch of the site. Found a cabinet with office supplies ... notebooks and such. None of the pens work, though. You might want to grab some of those. Or pencils. Or both."

"Good find. Anything else?"

"No. Oh, yes ... do you have anything like sticky tape? We'll probably want to attach temporary labels and notes to things. And barrier tape, to mark off areas. And some means of measuring distances."

She heard Bob chuckle. "This isn't a dig site, Rhian."

"Maybe so, Fearless Leader, but there's a mystery here for us to solve. The best way to figure out something of this size and complexity is a systematic examination. Yes, we're on a tight schedule, which means we've only got one chance to do this properly. This initial look-around gives us a better sense of what's here. With that done, I can focus on the individual offices and check for clues there. Now, we each have our jobs to do, so I suggest we get to it. And don't forget to check it on a regular basis. You're not on your own anymore."

"Yes, ma'am," Bob said. Rhian could hear the humour in his voice. Then he became serious. "You're quite correct about my forgetting that I'm not on my own, and I sincerely apologize. I'll keep in better touch." His voice took on his normal good humour as he said, "And that goes for you, as well. Don't get so absorbed that you lose situational awareness."

Rhian opened her mouth to make an angry retort, then shook her head. "You're right. We both need to remember where we are. Let me know when you get to the stores room, OK?" Bob acknowledged and terminated the connection.

"Teamwork, old thing, teamwork," she muttered to herself. "And don't forget this place has jaws that bite and claws that tear."

Rhian finished her the initial survey and was beginning to document the contents of the first office, the one they had assigned to Bob. The thing that struck her was how tidy everything was. The whole area was tidy, in fact. Also, there were no personal items anywhere that she had seen ... no pictures or drawings or notices. The desk in front of her was bare of any item not related to accessing the control system. Uttering a small sound of puzzlement, she knelt to begin opening and examining the drawers of the desk.

"Hi, Rhian. I'm in the stores room. It's a bit of mess, so it'll take me a few minutes to find anything. You OK?"

"Yes, thanks. Just about to start looking through the desk drawers. Say, I've noticed one oddity here and it applies to the rest of the base, I think. Have you seen any personal items anywhere? I've not seen any official posters or notices, much less personal items."

"Hmm, you're right. Hadn't thought of it in those terms until you mentioned it. Might be due to an orderly withdrawal, but it's something to keep in mind. Also, according to the records of the time, high-security projects often discouraged having personal effects at work areas. We should check out the personnel quarters later, though. Might find something there."

"Oh, good thought. Hold on while I take a quick look here. No, nothing at all in any of the drawers here. I'll let you go while I check the others. Let me know when you finish there, please." Bob acknowledged and terminated the connection.

Rhian had checked most of the other offices, with similar results, when Bob called to let her know he was heading back to the command office. By the time she'd checked the rest of the offices, Bob was in his command room and activating her security chit. Fifteen minutes later he entered the research area and found her at a desk writing up her notes.

"I come bearing gifts," he said, dropping four carry-all bags to the ground. Rhian smiled and turned around with an expectant look on her face.

"First of all, I brought you a small combat pack. It's got more storage than yours—which is looking a bit worse for wear, by the way—and meant to be used with the gear we'll be using. You can have a larger one, if you like, but I chose this as it's not much larger than yours. Also brought several combat belts plus a selection of pouches. I like to have several, each with a different setup, plus spares, but that's me. All that's in this one carry-all." He pushed it towards her. "Which is also something useful to have around."

Bob hesitated for a moment, then opened up a second carry-all. "Speaking of useful, also brought some weapons, including a couple of pistols. Did you want one?"

Rhian shook her head. "I'm not a soldier, Bob. I've carried pistols in the field when required, but always hated them. Don't know how to handle your guns and don't want to learn."

He nodded. "Fair enough. Now, I also brought some knives and small toolkits. Those you will accept and keep on your person at all times. No, don't shake your head at me. This is a command order, and no fooling. The knives are small and inconspicuous ... I don't expect you to carry around a large combat knife. You will keep one on every combat belt and in an outside pocket of every pack. This is non-negotiable, Rhian. Seriously. Same thing with the tool kits. There are various types of those, and they are always useful to have. Again, keep a small kit with the small knives. The other took kits you can choose as you wish, but I'd recommend taking at least one of the larger ones to go onto one of your combat belts. Oh, and some small first aid kits. Just in case."

Rhian made an annoyed sound that was almost like a growl. Giving her head a sharp shake, she said, "Fine. You're right. I'm not happy about weapons, but ... you're right. The knives and toolkits make sense. So what's in the other two carry-alls?"

Bob pointed at the third one. "Specialist tools, sensor wands, scanners, a couple of spare data tablets, a larger first aid kit, and some hand tools."

"Hand tools?"

He grinned. "You'd be amazed at how useful a hammer can be."

That got the hoped-for laugh out of her and lightened the mood.

"Why the first aid kits? Why not just pop into the medical bay?"

"For minor scrapes and such, I just slap some salve on or

put on a bandage. We'll be poking about and better to have it on hand than not."

"Good point. Guess I got spoiled by the ship's resources."

"All too easy to do, I assure you," he said. Pointing at the fourth carry-all, he said, "Those supplies you asked for, or at least the closest equivalent I could find. You might want to poke about the stores area yourself and see if there's something there that catches your eye." He paused for a moment to fish inside a pocket. "Oh, before I forget, here's your security chit."

Bob handed Rhian a thin slab about the size of a credit card. The surface shimmered in a faint rainbow of colours, and it had a metallic feel to it.

"Keep this on you at all times, either in a pocket or a combat belt. Your jacket has a pocket on the inside that'll do for that, as do the belts."

"What level of authorization do I have?"

"Enough to access pretty much anything short of command functions. That's read-only access, by the way. You'll only be able to write to your assigned work station ... it's different than what we have on the ship. I assigned you two work stations ... the one we chose for you and the one next to it. So be careful what commands you issue on these stations." He waved an arm to indicate all the stations.

"You'll be able to access all of the other work stations as a supervisor. That means read-only access to everything that's on them. The only exception is my station there ... that's assigned to my command codes, and those automatically lock out anyone else."

Rhian accepted the chit and put it into her jacket. After a moment's thought she removed it and put it into a shirt pocket in case she removed her jacket. The card poked into her skin. She sighed and said, "Hand me a belt would you, please? I may as well get used to it. And, yes, I'll stock it with whatever you suggest."

Several minutes later she was twisting her hips to check the feel of the combat belt. It held the obligatory knife and first aid kit, the security chit, and pouches that held her notebook and data tablet very nicely. The weight was well distributed, and the only thing that interfered with sitting was the tablet. All in all, it fit well and made for a convenient way of carrying around equipment. She took a look at the small tool kit and agreed that it was probably a good thing to have, so that got added to the belt.

"Well, that's me all kitted out," said Rhian. "Now what?"

"Snack break, I think, then we'll get to work on our office work stations," said Bob.

After some tea and snacks, they went to the office assigned to Rhian. She sat in the chair and managed to access the system with no problem. "Works a treat," she said. "Think I'll run through some of the tutorial exercises to get a feel for it. Need help with yours?"

"No, thanks. I'm going to set up a couple of them, actually. Want one linked to the ship so it can download the research records ... those seem to be separate from the rest of the base. You keep following your instincts."

Rhian nodded absently as she concentrated on gaining mastery over this new system. She was aware of Bob bustling about in the background, but gave it little thought until realizing that her muscles had stiffened from sitting too long.

"Oof," she groaned as she stood up and arched her back. Glancing over at the next office, she saw Bob glaring at the screen as if attempting to get answers by sheer force of will. Not bothering to stifle a grin, she wandered over to his office.

"Problems? I think I've got the basics down well enough to help."

Bob shook his head. "Thanks, but I've just uncovered another mystery. The data records have been sanitized."

"Excuse me?"

"I've got the ship tied in, and it's been doing a quick look.

Remember a couple of weeks ago I mentioned the odd strange signals from the Veil that my home base has picked up over time? Checked the sensor logs here and they show nothing for those time periods. And by 'nothing' I mean as if scrubbed. Not just deletion of the raw data, but also of anything that might possibly have referenced it."

Rhian nodded. "Hmm. Like the total lack of personal items here. I've never seen a withdrawal of forces that left an area so clean, have you? Every historical site I've examined has something, if only bits and pieces."

"I agree," said Bob. "You checked this office, you said, but not the one for the lesser ranks. I think I want to check that."

Rhian held up a hand. "Have you checked the crew quarters?"

Bob shook his head.

"Fine," she said, "You start on those while I check here. I'll check those other offices and these other control systems. You got me thinking about the one I'm using ... it's got nothing personal in it, either. Not notes or correspondence or data, as if reset to a fresh-from-the-factory state. Was so busy learning how to use it that I pushed that off to one side."

They spent the next several hours exploring on their own, meeting at the mess for supper. Rhian dropped her carry-all with a grunt and went to prepare a meal.

"You find anything that you didn't mention over the comms?" she asked, dropping down into a chair at the table.

"Nope, just more mysteries. The place has been scrubbed, for sure. Remember I mentioned the stores area was a mess? Well, I looked at it again, and it's not so much a mess so much as if certain things got removed in a hurry. Can't even find out what, either. Checked out all of the officer quarters and they're clean. Looked a few of the lesser ranks quarters and they're clean as well." He began eating his meal with gusto.

Rhian shook her head at her companion's dedication to keeping well fed before picking at her own meal. After a minute she raised her head and said, "You mentioned more mysteries. I gather you found more things of interest."

Bob nodded as he took a large drink of his tea before answering. "Indeed. The base seems pretty big, right? Well, I checked out the environmental control and discovered they're set up for a facility at least twice this size. Similar thing when I checked out the power station controls."

"Redundancy? Your people are big on that, as are you."

"I took that into account. There's more here, somewhere." He paused for a moment as if considering whether to impart more information. "My home base was similar. Rather too small for what it should have been. Turned out the bulk of it was hidden behind a stasis screen. Not so much for security, as an attempt to contain a problem."

Rhian quirked an eyebrow at him. Bob looked far away for a moment, then gave a deep sigh.

"This isn't secret so much as ... an historical embarrassment, I think you'd call it. My home base was the site of an experimental program to create artificial bodies ... but you've already guessed that much. It was also the site of the first contract with an alien avian race we call the Ravens. Long story short, as soon as the contact team returned to the base, a virulent plague broke out and killed everyone. To prevent it spreading, the base commander disabled the ships and portal, then sealed the bulk of the base behind the stasis field."

Rhian considered this for a moment. "You think this information is dangerous for me to know?"

Bob shook his head. "Shouldn't be, I suppose. Set worked with the Ravens, you see. Or, rather, they worked through him, offering him the means to control his followers. They were also somehow allied with the Refuser Faction. That plague, like some of the controlling drugs they supplied, was one of the few things our healing factors couldn't recognize. Nearly killed me before I figured out how to neutralize it. Pretty sure the Ravens meant to use it against us at some point, distributing it via the portals. Also pretty sure they were the ones testing plague weapons on various planets, like your own Earth."

Rhian's eyes went wide. "Your Uncle Sid stopped that, according to Great-gran."

"Yes," said Bob as he nodded. "His sister stopped another. That was after their family destroyed an invasion fleet that wiped out everyone except the two of them. It was after that the mind control mechanisms began showing up through Set's organization."

"So you think this base was a victim of the Ravens?"

"No, there's something else here, I think."

"Is all this just a facade, do you think?" she said waving a hand to indicate the base.

"Hmph. Awful expensive facade during a time when there was little to spare for such things. No, there's been a lot of people here at one point, doing something or other of importance. Just not sure what that might be. As for hidden areas, those'll be tough to find if the hiding was planned."

Rhian tapped her fingers on the table as she thought. "My suggestion is that I dig into the data records, and you focus on the physical structure of the base. There's data to be had, so perhaps I can get a feel for where the gaps are." She grinned. "Archaeological research deals with a lot of gaps, some hidden on purpose and some lost to the ravages of time."

Bob grinned back. "A historian on your planet once explained to me that history was like a tapestry, with historians following the various threads and looking for patterns."

"Wise man. Well, let's start checking out those threads, shall we?"

"Tomorrow," Bob insisted. "It's late and we've had a full day. Fresh eyes will see better than ones clouded by fatigue."

"True, true," Rhian chuckled. "See you at dawn."

Dawn found them at breakfast, planning their next moves.

"I'll join you in the offices for a bit before going off on my own. I want to set up a couple more of the control consoles to interface with the ship. Also want to tie in one or two of those lesser consoles in the subordinate offices for comparison."

Rhian nodded. "Good idea. I've got some ideas on how to search the records for gaps and forbidden areas. Your idea of multiple consoles is a good one, and I'd like to have another one or two for my own researches."

Pushing their food to one side, they spent the next half-hour discussing options and avenues of investigation.

CHAPTER EIGHTEEN
Tunnel of Prophesy

Once back at the offices, Bob ended up staying over an hour with Rhian, setting up consoles for both of them. He also did a quick pass-through checking for stasis fields, with no success.

"Didn't think to find anything here, but worth checking. I'll be back to join you here for lunch."

He was actually a half-hour late, but came bearing a proper meal in addition to snacks.

"You look happy," said Rhian. "Find something then?"

"Not as such, but there is most certainly something else here. Still need to figure out what and where. Think I'll spend the afternoon in the command office ... that's where secrets got discussed, if not stored. You have any luck?"

Rhian nodded. "I did, but like yourself just the verification of something hidden. The scouring of records left its own patterns, if one knows how to look. It's not just the sensor logs that have odd gaps. The stellar cartography records have some oddnesses, too. Not so much deleted records so much as clusters of minimal records. That is, the data for those stellar areas gets awfully minimal and vague. When we were travelling, some of the ship's records were minimal, but these are more minimal than that. I may have thought of a way to check other records for references to those stellar areas to see if anyone ever referenced more details for them."

"Oh, that's clever, Rhian. Any records to indicate the sort of research was going on here?"

"Thank you. No, nothing. I'm hoping to get hints by poking around the astrometric data."

They finished lunch and went about their separate tasks.

After several hours of fruitless effort in the command office, Bob was regretting that he hadn't brought a hammer with him. It wouldn't have solved anything, but would have at least offered a means of venting his frustration. A call from Rhian broke into his disgruntlement.

"Bob? I may have found something. Join me in the map room, would you? You know, the room with that big view of the galaxy we saw during our tour."

"You went there on your own? Alright, be there in a couple of minutes."

Bob jogged there and barged in quickly enough to inadvertently startle Rhian, eliciting a small gasp from her.

"Oh, it's you. You could have knocked or something," she chided him before turning to face the volumetric display of the galaxy. "Here's the galaxy. Now, I'll dim the stars a bit and add ... this."

The stars blinked then took on a range of intensities that differed from their original. Rhian held up a hand to forestall questions.

"Before you ask, I'm varying the intensity of each star to show how much information we have in our records about it. The brighter the star, the more information."

Bob stared at the display, trying to take it all in.

"That's using the data from the ship," continued Rhian. "Now, here's what it looks like when I use the records from the base."

The display blinked then reformed. There was the same assortment of brightness except for one very dim volume off to one side.

Rhian continued to talk, explaining how she'd gotten the idea. She stopped when she saw the look of shock on Bob's face.

"Bob? Does this mean something?"

He stood staring at the map for several seconds before responding. Still looking at the dim area, he pointed at it and said, "That's the Veil of Tears. That's the area my ancestors created as a trap." He turned to face her, his face now devoid of emotion. "This base must have been studying it, for some reason. Perhaps it was part of the group that created and raised the Veil."

"But then why try to erase that?" interjected Rhian. "Deleting references to the technology, sure, that I can understand. But why pretend they know nothing about the stars within the Veil?"

Bob's brow furrowed as he turned to stare at the map for a minute. His fingers tapped a slow cadence on the railing. Then he turned to Rhian with a broad smile.

"This might be the key we need. Let's get back to the command office." He turned and jogged out of the room.

"Hold on," Rhian yelled. "Not all of us are soldiers, you know."

She heard the sound of his feet come to a stop. "Sorry," came the yelled reply. Rhian grinned and hurried to join her friend. A minute of fast walking later, they got to the office. Bob rushed to his chair, while Rhian dropped into a guest chair. She worked at catching her breath while Bob worked the controls.

"I'm checking on all references to the Veil," he explained. "Hmm, most are scrubbed." He tapped at the controls at a furious pace. "Most, but not all."

Several seconds later one of the walls turned black, then flashed red several times as the built-in display activated. In response, Bob tapped a few more keys, then slapped his hand on the desk display. A female voice began speaking, then paused. Bob tapped more controls before responding. Rhian didn't understand all of it, but recognized it as being similar to the process Bob had used to claim control of the base.

The large screen on the wall changed to show a complex symbol with the image of a hand in the middle. Bob got up, walked to the screen, and placed his own hand on the image. A cylinder, slightly larger in diameter than an outstretched hand, extended out. Bob placed his hand on that and winced. The cylinder retracted into hiding once again as the display on the wall screen changed to a series of hypnotic Escher-like patterns. Rhian saw blood dripping from the cylinder as it retracted, and removed the first aid kit from her belt. When Bob returned to the desk and sat down, she opened up the kit and passed it over to him along with some tissues. He smiled his thanks as he cleaned his hand before applying salve and bandages.

A soft chime sounded, and all the screens in the office lit up with the original complex symbol on all of them. The female voice spoke again. "Human genome verified. Human nerve responses verified. Human blood match verified. Match with base commander verified. Security records unlocked."

Bob and Rhian stared at each other for a moment. He shrugged then turned towards his console and began typing. A blur of data began appearing on the screens throughout the room, each screen showing something different. They watched it for several seconds, then Bob turned to the controls and began typing. The barrage of images slowed, then stopped.

"Command confirmation required before researcher access allowed," said the female voice.

"Command authorization by base commander," said Bob in a clear voice. "Full read access granted to research stations authorized for use by supervisor level personnel. Confirm."

"Command confirmed. Access authorized." The female voice became silent.

Bob let out his breath with a whoosh before turning to grin

at her. "You found the key, Rhian. Not sure what it's the key to, but now we can find out."

Rhian returned his smile with a tentative one of her own. "Quite the show. Uhm, that blood-letting looked painful. Is that normal?"

He shook his head. "Never heard of that, to be honest. The blood sampling is normal enough, of course. But perhaps the pain was part of the process." Bob laughed at the disgusted look on her face. "They were working on something big and important here. I suspect they wanted to impress that on anyone who wanted to authorize access to it." He wiggled his fingers and winced. "May want the auto-medic to look at this later. The mechanism sliced into me fairly deeply." Then he smiled. "Right now, though, we need to find out what the big secret is. Why don't you head back to your office and dig into the details of what it is. I'll stay here and try to find out where they've hidden it. Sound good?"

Rhian rose to her feet, an eager expression on her face. "Excellent. We should get in touch in, say, half an hour? I suspect there's a lifetime of mysteries to unravel here, so let's try not to get lost in it all."

Bob nodded and turned towards the console and began typing. Three quarters of an hour later he was startled by a call from Rhian, asking him to meet her at the map room right away. He got up, feeling guilty about not calling her, and trotted off. His hand ached, but he pushed that issue to one side. He arrived to find Rhian at the controls with the look of a cat who had just eaten the canary. Without a word, she pointed at the map.

He walked up to the railing and looked down. The map was back to normal, except now the Veil and the area around it were highlighted by shades of angry red. There was a purple line stretching from the Veil to a location on the other side of the galaxy.

"That's us," said Rhian pointing to where the purple line

terminated at a solitary star. "That's the Veil," she said pointing to the other end of the line. "The cloud-like structures around it represent the deadly energies surrounding it. You can just make out a deeper shade of red that's the shell of the Veil structure itself."

"Very nice," said Bob. "What's the line?"

Rhian grinned. "That, my friend, is a cosmic tunnel linking us with a destination within the Veil. It's not a portal, but something else entirely. Unlike a portal, it is large enough for a ship to pass through. That's what all this is for." She waved an arm to indicate the base. "They were investigating the tunnel. There was this base ... and another on the other end." She grinned at Bob's startled look.

"That's most impressive, Rhian, especially given how little time you had to work on this."

She gave a modest shrug. "Thank you, but not really. I came across some summary reports, skimmed those, and decided you needed to know this straight away. This display here is one of their canned demos."

Bob leaned forward and rested his elbows on the railing. "A cosmic tunnel, you called it. Hmm. Interesting tech." He noticed that Rhian was still grinning. "Alright, let's have the rest of it."

"You'll love this, I assure you," Rhian said. "The tunnel wasn't made by humans. This base, and the other within the Veil, were set up around something left by whomever built it." The look on Bob's face made her giggle. "All that from skimming the summaries. Oh, this is going to be so much fun, Bob."

Bob grinned back at her, then winced as his injured hand brushed across the railing.

"It's the auto-medic for you," said Rhian in a stern voice. "And then some supper. I know we're on the clock here, but we need to treat this like a marathon." He allowed her to hustle him out. She was quite correct ... this was too big to take in all at once. Some food and rest would allow them to deal with it properly.

Their breakfast the next morning found them in good spirits and eager to press forward. Afterwards, Bob joined Rhian in the research offices. He set up all his stations to access the new files and made sure the ship began downloading copies of everything it could. The base's security systems grumbled at the ship's access to the secret information, and required several interventions by Bob before they calmed down.

Rhian showed him where the new data was located, and Bob began with the summaries she had mentioned. After almost an hour of intense study, he pushed himself away from the console and stood up. He stretched to work out the kinks then went to Rhian's office.

"Finished so soon?" she said, grinning up at him.

Bob shook his head. "I wish. There's a lot to go through, but I think I've got the basics. The project summaries mention an ancient facility of some sort that the base was built around, but don't give the details. Those, I think, will be found in the command records dealing with details of the facility. You keep drilling down from here, and I'll head back to the command office. We'll keep in touch ... at the very least we should meet for lunch, I think."

Rhian nodded. "Agreed. I'll continue to drill down through the different levels of summaries. We need to learn enough to begin to start asking the appropriate questions." Then she grinned. "This beats digging up shards of pottery and trying to guess what they were used for."

Just before lunch, Rhian got a call from Bob telling her to meet him at the hanger. There was a slight edge to his voice that concerned her, but she decided to hold off on questions until she met him. It took her several minutes to walk to the hanger, and she was puffing a bit from pace she'd set. Bob was leaning against the wall, then stood when he saw her approach. His left hand was bandaged.

"What happened to your hand?" she puffed out.

He held it up and waggled it slightly before dropping it down. "As Uncle Lou said, learning comes at a price. In this case, a bit of blood and pain was the price of gaining access to the facility itself. Or, rather, the keys to the facility."

"So all this here is just a shell?"

"Not at all. It's the necessary infrastructure for the people doing the research. It also serves to protect the ancient alien equipment." Bob opened the doorway and led the way into the hanger.

Rhian nodded as she followed him. "They called it the 'terminus'. So why meet here? I see you need the auto-medic, but there's one on the base, isn't there?"

"Yep. Don't trust it yet, though. The ship knows me inside and out, literally. Also, we need the ship to get into the facility."

"There's no way to get there without it? That seems strange."

Bob chuckled. "There's a doorway, but it has to be opened from the inside. Just another layer of security. Although I can't say that I blame them for any of it."

They reached the ship and went inside. After a brief visit to the auto-medic, they went to the control room.

"Strap in," said Bob. "We're not going far. Our destination is one of the other hangers, marked as 'inoperable' on the maps the base sent us when we arrived."

"Not so inoperable, I gather."

Bob slid a trio of security chits into slots in his console. "Oh, it's inoperable, all right. Suffered a catastrophic failure and is quite impassible. Unless one has the appropriate pass codes, which I've just given the ship."

The ship lifted up on its impellers and moved forward as the outside doors opened. Bob guided the ship outside and around to the other side of the facility.

"It doesn't look like much, does it?" said Rhian. "I suppose that's rather the point, though."

"Indeed it is," Bob replied. Then he pointed at the structure. "See that melted and ruined spot? That's where we're going."

"Look like a jumble of debris," said Rhian, tapping at her controls. "Sensors confirm that, too. We going to blast our way in?"

Instead of answering, Bob just grinned and tapped at his controls. The ship moved towards the structure, then just before it hit, the debris field wavered then disappeared. Bob guided the ship into the now vacant space and moved into a hanger that looked similar to the one they'd left. He tapped more controls and the entranceway was once more filled with debris. A second later the floor disappeared and Bob guided the ship down the new shaft. After several seconds of travel, the shaft opened up to reveal a cavernous space carved out of the rock. Bob grounded the ship and spun his chair around to face her.

"The terminus you spoke of is further down one of the side tunnels, but the control area is here. Thought we'd check that out first."

Rhian gaped at him for a moment before recovering her equilibrium. "Ah, yes. Uhm, was that debris field real or an illusion?"

"Oh, it was real enough. Got sent into hyperspace to allow us to pass. Similar tech to what happens to the portals. The hanger above us is now filled with debris as well. This place is sealed and protected by passive and active defences."

"Is there breathable air here?"

Bob nodded. "There is, but it's a bit lower in oxygen than Earth, has an off-putting odour to it, and the temperature is on the chilly side. In any case, we'll be suited up and wearing helmets. If nothing else, these old bases can have some nasty surprises when equipment fails."

They donned their skin-suits and exited the ship, locking it behind them. As they walked to the control area, Bob said, "Did you find anything of interest while I was shedding blood to find this place?"

"I did. That ancient alien race predates any known intelligent species by some millions of years, human or otherwise. The site was stumbled upon by a human portal survey crew. It's a pretty nondescript planet in a nondescript part of the galaxy, but your ancestors were looking to set up a series of forward monitoring stations. I can't tell if it happened during a time of peace or war but it was well within the time spanned by your series of wars. Narrowing that down is on my list of questions."

"Interesting. I'd suggest that it happened around the time the Veil was erected, probably before. Anything else?"

"Not much. Found references to astronomical data and analysis of the science behind the tunnel. Just dipped into that briefly, but it's nothing I can understand. I'll send you the links to those."

"Thanks, I'll take a look at those when we get back. And here we are." Bob had led them to a doorway that remained locked until he used one of his new security chits.

"Paranoid buggers, those ancestors of yours," Rhian muttered as she entered.

The door opened onto a short hallway that led to a large room filled with several dozen control stations. Across the room from them were a series of large windows.

"Don't touch anything," warned Rhian.

Bob just looked at her.

"Sorry," she muttered. "Force of habit when entering a new site."

In response, Bob grinned and pointed at the window. They walked towards it until stopped by a railing and gazed out. The lighting was dim, but they could make out a vast cavern, with a large hemispherical depression in the centre.

"I'm guessing that's your terminus," said Bob. He turned and walked around the room while examining the equipment. Rhian examined one work station but recognized nothing, so she went back to the window and tried to understand what she was seeing.

After several minutes Bob joined her. "I think this is all just monitoring equipment. Nothing here seems to be for controlling anything, much less your cosmic tunnel."

Rhian pointed at several points along the perimeter of the depression. "Those areas looked interesting so I took some sensor scans. They only responded to scans using the alternate energies. Also, there's something strange about them and the tunnel itself. I'd suggest that we consider the possibility that they're related."

Bob nodded. He'd taken his own scans, but was pleased that Rhian had taken the initiative to do her own studies. "See anything else?" he asked her.

"Aside from those large tunnels that appear to lead back to where we parked the ship, no. Did you see any controls to open up the passageway to the base?"

"The console that was supposed to control that is gone, and all the circuits leading to it melted. I think that access route we hoped to find got eliminated when they shut this place down."

They spent a half hour taking a closer look at everything but found nothing of interest. On the way back to the ship, Rhian expressed disappointment that they hadn't found much.

"Not at all," insisted Bob. "We've found the terminus and the way to it. You've got some sensor readings of it that show something of interest. Use those readings to search the research records, and I suspect that'll turn up something of use to us. Think of this as one of your archaeological digs. We've got a lot of shards of pottery, and those reading may point to something that'll tell us what they were part of originally."

Rhian turned to look at Bob, a pleased look on her face. "That's good advice, thanks. It just shows that I'm going to need your help with this. You know the science side of things far better than I. I, on the other hand, am quite good at digging through masses of data and finding correlations. Perhaps you need to tell me what to search for while you do the analysis on what I find."

"Good plan," said Bob. "As a secondary project, I'd suggest you delve into the history side of things. This ties in with the Veil, somehow, and that might be important."

They reached the ship and returned to the main portion of the base. After a brief meal they went to the research offices and resumed their work.

After a couple days of effort, they had a good handle on the theory behind the tunnel. A couple of days after that brought them to the point where they knew how to operate it.

Over breakfast Rhian said, "It's time to sit down and do an overview of this, I think. We've been bashing away at this for days and you've not told me what I'm looking at."

Bob leaned back in his chair, a mug of tea cradled in his hands. "Fair enough. I've been working you pretty hard, and I apologize for not keeping you up to date." He paused to drain his cup before placing it on the table. "With your help, I understand how this tunnel works, or at least the basics of it so far as my ancestors knew. It uses a technology we called a 'transit tube'. It's something we never got to work because of the inherent instabilities we never conquered. The advantages over portals is that it can move large masses, like ships. Once the link is established, it can operate over longer distances than a portal can."

"Instabilities? Is it safe to use?"

"Yes and no. Oh, don't look at me like that ... I'm not trying to be obscure. Yes, it works when conditions allow for it. The problem is, conditions aren't always favourable. As for the operation, that's pretty easy. Or, rather, easy after teams of my ancestors figured it out after many years of effort. I can get us to the other terminus inside the Veil." He paused for a moment, then grinned. "There's a couple of small points about the operation. First, as your sensor readings hinted, control is based on the alternate energies, which is why it took my ancestors so long to figure it out. Secondly, both the terminus and the transit tube itself involve some pretty complex energies, and from what I can tell that would interfere with both the embedded tech my people have as well as the abilities of the Changed."

"So only regular humans can use it?"

"Yep. Just like Uncle Lou said. And conditions for its use are just right. Won't be for long, though."

"Interesting," said Rhian. "Well, I've not found out anything tied the Veil as such, though I'm still looking. On the other hand, I've found some speculation that some of those Great Wars of yours were caused at least in part by other races who were aware of the tunnel."

"Really? So they didn't know where it was, but were afraid we had found something? Afraid enough to go to war?"

Rhian shrugged. "That's what some of the speculations were. I can't speak to how accurate they were, of course."

"So why was this base abandoned?"

"Haven't found that out. Oh, it was set up before the Veil was erected, though. Not sure if it was decades or centuries, but some time before. It was definitely abandoned after the Veil was created. Again, not sure if it was decades or centuries." She paused as Bob stared into space. After several seconds of silence, he took a sharp breath and looked at her once more.

"See what you can do by, say, lunch. Focus your efforts on finding out more about the terminus within the Veil."

"And you?"

"I want to get a better understanding of the factors that inhibit the tunnel's operation. I think we'll be taking a trip in it very soon."

* * *

They skipped lunch to continue working, then met for a late supper in the mess. As they ate, they discussed what each of them had found.

"According to the records, the device could only be operated safely only under very specific conditions," said Bob.

"Oh, like the stars aligning every few thousand years?" teased Rhian. "That's what all the best fairy tales speak of."

Bob sighed and shook his head with exaggerated sadness. "You mock the mysteries of the ages? Oh, ye of little faith."

They both laughed for a few seconds. Then Bob smiled and said, "That's actually not far off. Not alignment of stars or planets, as such, but other things. It was in operation a long, long time ago until a series of natural novas and supernovas occurred. The shock waves of those, and their interactions, caused the transit tube to become unstable. If I'm reading these research notes correctly, there's a lull in those interference patterns occurring right now."

"What, you mean the transit tube is usable? For how long?"

"Well, that's what it seems. As for how long, those shock waves take years—even centuries—to develop and interact. We seem to be in a quiet period. Won't last long, though. Weeks or months, if these models are correct. There'll be other windows of operation for years to come, but hard to predict too far in advance."

"Well, Uncle Lou said we had to traverse a tunnel to get behind the Veil of Tears. So how do we do that ... is it like a portal?"

Bob shook his head. "Nope, and that's a good thing. We can take the ship with us, it would seem."

"Excellent. It'll be a good base of operations for us."

"Yeah, about that, Rhian. Are you sure you want to do this? It's going to get very dangerous. More than you can imagine, I suspect."

"Your uncle said that both of us were to go. Besides, what choice is there?" She had an eager smile on her face. "It's either sit here with nothing to do or go on a tremendous adventure to save the galaxy and all of humanity. Decisions, decisions."

"You really are Celcilia's descendant, aren't you?" Bob tried to frown but ended up laughing. "All right, but we do this properly. It'll take a day or two to prep properly and get a bit of rest."

"How long will the trip take, do you think?"

"Not sure. A week or two I think, assuming those ancestors of mine knew their business. The records get a bit sketchy about that, I'm afraid. Between the war and a few breakdowns in the record systems here over the eons, there's not as many details as I'd like."

"Enough so you'd risk your life?"

"Yes, but..."

"So we go. Let's get about those preparations, shall we?"

"Aye, aye, ma'am."

CHAPTER NINETEEN
Into the Void

It took just over a day to get ready. Bob would have preferred to take longer, if only to give Rhian a bit more training and to examine the base more carefully. He settled for downloading a copy of its records to his ship. As for the base itself, he commanded the control systems to warn any ships that might appear to stay away. Any ships that failed to respond with his identification code were to be fired upon with lethal force. He would have liked to do more preparation of the base, but time was against him.

The activation of the transit tube was something of an anticlimax. He and Rhian took his ship and entered the vast chamber where the mechanism was embedded. After activating the controls there were several minutes of no visible activity, although the ship's sensor's indicated the buildup of energies. Then without any warning a faint blackness appeared above them, which slowly solidified to become a swirling maelstrom of shades of black. A minute later it blinked (or, at least, that is how it appeared to Bob) and became ... nothing. Not the mind-searing blackness of an activated portal or anything else Bob had seen. Sensors failed to register anything positive about it at all, just a void that reflected and emitted nothing at all.

Bob looked at Rhian who was intent on examining the

readouts at the main sensor panel.

"Any indications of what that might be? The summary readouts show nothing but a void that isn't there, if that makes any sense," she said in a puzzled tone.

"That's what everything here seems to be indicating, from what I can see. That's what the records said to expect. In any event, whatever it is appears to be stable. All set?"

She shrugged. "We don't have much of a choice, do we? Time to go and save the galaxy." She turned to him with a large grin on her face. "Beats giving lectures to bored undergrads."

Bob laughed and commanded the ship to enter the void. At the first touch of the surface of the whatever it was, the entire ship snapped into some other place.

"We're moving," said Rhian in a tense voice. "Don't know how, given that the ship's engines are off, but we appear to be moving."

"Uhm, I forgot to mention that part, didn't I?" said Bob in an embarrassed tone. "Once entered into, the transit tube takes care of the rest."

She turned to him with an annoyed expression. "Oh ta for mentioning that minor point." Then she brightened. "Feels smoother than the ship's FTL drive, though."

"Well, we were a bit rushed, you know," said Bob. "Still, I'm very impressed with the speed of the transit. Even with our improved engines the trip would have taken the better part of an Earth year. And then we wouldn't have been able to breach the barrier. Anyway, we've got nearly two weeks to go. That'll give us a bit of time to tidy things up before arrival. I want to give you some more training on ship's systems. Some weapons training couldn't hurt, either."

Rhian wrinkled her nose. "Weapons? I'm a scholar, Bob, not a soldier. Told you that before."

"Not looking to turn you into a soldier, Rhian. Just want to make sure you know the basics of some things that might come in handy. Like how to load, fire, and ensure that the safety is on for a couple of the basic weapons. Nothing fancy, I assure you."

She sighed. "Oh, very well. You may have a point. Would much rather dig into the data records your ship carries. Maybe some of the records from that base we just left has answers."

Rhian paused for a moment. "Which brings me to a question that's been bothering me. How, exactly, are you storing all that data on this ship? You're carrying eons of data from that base alone, and you've told me about how the ship has eons of data from other sources. Then there's the problem of cataloguing and retrieval. That's been a large part of my professional work, and for the life of me I can't understand how you do it."

Bob nodded. "An excellent point. Physically, the ship uses the alternate energies and other tricks to fold a lot of information into a smallish space. Hmm, think of the ship's data storage as similar to that used by the portals. Does that help?"

"Not in the slightest. Although Great-gran mentioned that the portals held a lot of information about each planet they were on ... geography, languages, history, and so forth. So the ship uses something similar?"

"Right. Similarly for the data processing mechanisms ... lots of processing power. The trick, as you alluded to, is getting at it. The cataloguing is automatic. Turning all that raw data into information and cross-tabulating it is the tricky bit."

"It always is," Rhian said. "Glad to see that some things are universal. So how about we dig into the records of that base and—"

"Nope," Bob said in a stern voice. "First we make sure that everything is stowed properly. We were pretty lax about storing it before leaving, but that won't do now that we are under way. Then training. No, don't give me that look. Properly stowing things will only take a day, if that. Weapons training will only take a few hours. Doesn't your culture have a tradition of obeying the ship's captain without any backtalk?"

* * *

The time in transit was filled with more work than they had time. Bob gave Rhian basic weapons training. She showed little interest and less proficiency, but was soon able to handle basic hand weapons without being a danger to herself or allies. Another day was spent in further training on the ship's systems to make sure that Rhian at least understood the basics what to do in an emergency. Another day was spent training her on how to gain full access to the ships data storage, and there she finally came into her own. She dove into that with a zeal that impressed Bob, who left to do his own research. There was a lot of information to integrate and examine.

Several days later during a shared meal Rhian tossed a data tablet on the table towards Bob.

"Something isn't right."

"Only the one thing?" answered Bob with a smile.

She refused to raise to the jibe. "Your Uncle Lou said that the transit tube was the only way in, correct?"

Bob responded with a slow nod.

"Alright, but I was looking at those interactions of forces that prevented the tube from working. Pretty pictures and all, but something bothered me. I looked more closely and it appeared that there were cracks in both them and the Veil itself. Or maybe weaknesses. In any event, it's damned strange. If I'm interpreting the data correctly, a ship should be able to wend its way inside. Care to take a look?"

Bob gave a noncommittal grunt as he took the data tablet and left to go to his own data station.

At the next meal, he returned with a grim look on his face.

"You were right. Those channels do form a way into the Veil. Not a pleasant trip, though. Just getting to the Veil would take a long time, as I once told you. Those cracks in the structure of the Veil aren't gaps so much as lessened intensities of the barrier energies. Those would allow a ship to travel at FTL but at greatly reduced speeds. It would take weeks or even months to traverse the barrier. Those energies would interfere with my kind, even the Changed. It'd be a painful trip ... possibly lethal."

The frown on his face bothered Rhian.

"There's more, isn't there?"

"Yeah. Uncle Lou said that only regular humans like ourselves could traverse the transit tube. I'm not convinced that's the case, though. From what I can see—and I'm not an expert in such things—it appears that it should be possible to create an insulating field of energies."

"Meaning?"

"Meaning that any of my kind—enhanced or Changed—should be able to get through."

"There's a lot of supposition in that, you realize?"

"Such as?"

"Well, first they'd have to know about the transit tube. Then they'd have to know where to find it. Then they'd have to get through the defences you set up. Quite the chain of coincidences." She paused for a moment. "Those channels of weakness in the Veil seem a more reasonable route. Far more visible to those that know what to look for."

Bob nodded. "Still, Uncle Lou said that I was the only one who could do it. He's cryptic but not prone to lying."

Rhian paused in thought for a moment. "No," she said in a soft voice. "He said you were the only one with the appropriate combination of skills who could do it in time to prevent catastrophe." She paused for a moment. "And basic human form—don't forget that."

They both fell silent. After a few seconds Bob broke the silence. "Oh. I think I know what he meant." His face fell as he spoke.

Rhian raised an eyebrow to encourage him to continue.

"We aren't the only ones. I'm merely the only one with the

mix of skills who can get there in time to prevent whatever that catastrophe is. But there are probably others on the way, or perhaps already there. Problem is, they aren't there to stop the catastrophe. This could be very bad, Rhian."

"Now, let's not get ahead of ourselves and create problems where none exist, Bob. For one thing, your Uncle Lou said that you'd be in time. For another, he said you'd be able to defeat whomever may or may not be following us. Or ahead of us. Whatever. The point is, he may have been referring to hostile forces that exist within the Veil."

Bob chewed on a lip for a moment. "Yeah, perhaps. That's one scenario. Why don't you take a look and see if we've any data indicating what forces might be waiting for us. Oh, and don't forget to work on your language skills. If we run into sources of information within the Veil, there's a good chance that we'll be able to read it. By the time the Veil went up my people had the language pretty much fixed and it didn't change much after that."

Rhian nodded. "And yourself?"

"Check for the possibility of others following us. And make sure the ship is battle-ready."

"Why do you assume that anyone following us is hostile?"

Bob gave a grim chuckle. "Given my experiences, it's safest to assume that no-one capable of following us into the Veil is friendly towards me."

With that less than comforting thought, they sped towards their unknown destination.

Author's Afterword

Although authors are to blame for the final product, none of us are an island when it comes to inspiration and assistance.

The original inspiration came from pictures posted on Twitter as writing prompts ("write a story based on this picture"). I started making up strange and silly responses around a character named "Bob". I'd especially like to thank @DougWallace1973. He not only posted interesting pictures, he encouraged my silly micro-stories and jokes.

Many thanks to my beta readers : Janice, Lynn, and Trit. Your encouragement helped keep me going.

The cover image is based on a woodcut by Virgil Solis (1514-1562) entitled "Classizing Landscape With Three Figures". The astronomical image added in the background is from an image of the Ghost Nebula credited to T.A. Rector/University of Alaska Anchorage, H. Schweiker/WIYN and NOAO/AURA/NSF.

About The Author

Brian retired from the software development rat race to take up the carefree life of an author. He lives with his wife and two cats in Ontario, Canada.

For the latest news about this and forthcoming books, the occasional commentary on life, or to leave a comment (we love feedback), check out Brian's blog at

www.BrianGreiner.ca

Books by Brian Greiner

All books are available as e-books and paperbacks
from :
> kobobooks.com
> amazon.ca
> amazon.com
> overdrive.com

The Ascending Darkness series
> #1 Darkness Creeps Forth
> #2 Darkness Comes Reaping

The Accursed North series
> #1 The Werewolves of Winter
> #2 The Final Doom

The Saga of Bob series
> #1 Ancestors and Descendants
> #2 Dagger of Eons
> #3 Burden of Consequences
> #4 Barrier of Tears

Ancestors and Descendants

Bob has spent much of his life crisscrossing the galaxy
trying to protect people from the ancient evils, horrors,
and demons that lurk among the stars; fearsome creatures
that consider humans as mere nothings, if they bother with
humans at all.
Some call them monsters.
Bob calls them family.
Now he has discovered evidence of an insidious and
corrupting influence spreading across the galaxy,
threatening his family and all of humanity. Unsure of who
he can trust, Bob must fight to uncover the truth and find a
way to save everyone. He will discover there are no perfect
solutions, and all come with a price.

Dagger of Eons

There are horrors and evils that lurk among the stars. Bob
has spent centuries trying to protect humanity from the
worst of them, especially from the schemes of his older
brother.
Now humanity's ancient enemies are rising once more to
exert an insidious and corrupting influence. On the run
and with time running out, Bob must sift through the
layers of mysteries and find a way to stop the destruction
of all he holds dear.
Desperate times call for desperate measures; measures that
will demand a high price.

Burden of Consequences

Actions have consequences.

Bob has always been willing to accept responsibility for his own, but now he's being forced to assume the burden of others. Reduced to being merely human, he's being pursued across the galaxy by a rogue AI, a planet of fanatics out for his blood, and his own people. His many enemies think he's now weak, vulnerable, and ripe for exploitation. They've forgotten that Bob has spent centuries learning how to deal with opponents more powerful than himself.

It's time for Bob to remind them who they're dealing with as he investigates a mystery that threatens humanity.

Barrier of Tears

Bob has saved humanity throughout the galaxy on numerous occasions, and successfully battled against fearsome opponents.

For his efforts, he was forced to be reborn as merely human. Despite his greatly diminished powers, a new challenge has been thrust upon him. An ancient refuge has been turned into a prison, and a force that once protected humanity is poised to destroy it.

Once again, Bob must dive into mysteries that span the galaxy, uncovering and decoding clues. Once again, he is opposed by secretive and powerful forces, some human and some not. The chances of success are low and his chances of survival even lower.

There are many types of barriers. Bob will discover that the least substantial can be the most deadly.

Darkness Creeps Forth

A terrorist attack that leaves Toronto's financial district in shambles and the country's economy vulnerable. An investigative reporter who uncovers a major national scandal and then dies of apparent natural causes before his story can be published. Investigating these seemingly unrelated events draws small-time private investigator Yancey Franklin and his friends into a century-old web of corruption and deceit that threatens the security and independence of Canada. In a desperate race against time, Yancey and his friends rush to prevent an attack by a ruthless opponent on an ageing secret military facility in northern Ontario that holds a deadly secret.

Darkness Comes Reaping

Small-time investigator Yancey Franklin has thwarted the plans of a ruthless enemy to unleash biochemical weapons in Northern Ontario. Now he is on the run and trying to uncover the secrets behind a century-old web of corruption and deceit that strives to eliminate Canada as an independent nation. In a desperate race against time, Yancey and his friends struggle to stay alive as they rush to stop their enemy's latest plan – the deadly "Harvest of Souls".

The Werewolves of Winter

The werewolves were created by the Change Plague—the result of ill-considered biotechnology. It was only their annual winter die-off that saved humanity. But every spring the Change Plague returned to create a new and more deadly crop of werewolves.

People adapted and managed to carry on despite the increasingly precarious situation.

One man, trapped on his farm north of Toronto, began to piece together hints of a deeper and more dangerous threat. With werewolves closing in, time was running out in a desperate race to uncover answers.

A novel of modern horrors, ancient prophesies, data analysis, and nerds who save the world.

The Final Doom

Felix Kurtsius discovered that the Change Plague was being dispersed as part of a deliberate attack. Toronto appeared to be the epicentre for the infection, which targeted Canada preferentially. He escaped to Toronto after werewolves began purging the rural areas of humans, only to discover insidious forces at work. In a race against the clock, Felix and his friends must use all their skills to unravel the forces behind the werewolves, and prevent the destruction of humanity.

A novel of modern horrors, ancient prophesies, data analysis, and nerds who save the world.